Minds Against Wicked Things

By

Jim Meaders

A-Argus Better Book Publishers, LLC

For information:
A-Argus Better Book Publishers, LLC
9001 Ridge Hill Street
Kernersville, North Carolina 27285
www.a-argusbooks.com

ISBN: 978-0-9158832-5-0
ISBN: 0-6158832-5-7

Book Cover designed by Jim Meaders

Printed in the United States of America

PROLOGUE

This is the next chapter in James' and Lilith's adventures. When we last visited with them in *Signals From Passionate Minds*, things were looking up as they had just found out that they would be returning to art school for their second year. In addition, the faculty and administration of the art school had asked them to become tutors beginning in their second year for the underachievers at the school, especially the first year students. That first year at art school had proven to be productive for them as artists as well as being very exciting and dangerous. Their Spring semester trip touring Italy with their instructors and new best friends the Cheltims was educational and fun, but James and Lilith were glad to be back in Sarasota and hopefully away from the likes of the greater evils lurking the earth that they had encountered in Italy. The couple was quite successful when dealing with humans, but the monsters, ghosts, and aliens they encountered in Italy had been new challenges for them.

That was back in 1968, nearly 32 earth years ago. Upon graduating from art school in 1971, our young couple settled down in Sarasota, Florida, and decided to have the one child that Voresha females can have. When their attempts to get Lilith pregnant failed over the next few years she was finally examined by several Voreshan doctors, only to discover that her reproductive organs had not developed properly. Lilith would never be able to have a child. Although Lilith felt as if she were letting her species and James down, the Elders, her parents, and especially James assured her the opposite was true. During this time that James and Lilith were trying to have a child the Elders were keeping the really bad evils of the world from crossing their paths, because they did not want James and Lilith to worry about such things during that time in their lives. The couple still had to occasionally deal with disgruntled, mean, sad, and depressed humans, but those were easy assignments even during this time.

James and Lilith had also opened an art studio and gallery after graduating from art school and it was located just off the circle in St. Armands and they were already having a good amount of success selling their art work. As charged by the Elders early on when they were back in high school, James and Lilith continued to create art work that brought pleasure to the people who saw it. Sad and lonely people who happened to venture into their gallery always left happy and feeling like they had just made two new friends, even if they didn't buy anything. Although our two lovers were sad over not being able to have a child, they were still very happy with each other and their purposes in life. Their love for one another over the past three decades grew stronger every day and their accomplishments as a Voresha team were unparalleled in Voreshan history.

The Cheltims, who had been in their forties when they took James and Lilith to Italy back in 1968, had both passed away during the last decade of the 20th century. They had been the only friends that the couple had known during this time who knew the truth about them being Voreshan aliens and that they aged much slower than humans. It was especially difficult for the Cheltims in their later years to be seen with James and Lilith, since the Voreshan couple didn't look like they had aged very much at all. All other humans who knew them had to have occasional memory adjustments so that they never realized that James and Lilith weren't aging the same as everyone else. If you will remember, the aging process for the Voreshan species is much slower than that for humans and James and Lilith only aged what appeared to be about seven or eight years, while the Cheltims actually aged about thirty years.

We now pick up James' and Lilith's story in 2001, when they were visited by Elder Thegh's replacement after he had died of old age, Elder Jiobalami Bitu Meiy. Elder Meiy was one of the younger Elders at around 200 years old, but his knowledge about James and Lilith was very thorough since Elder Thegh had tutored him well in their history and accomplishments. Elder Meiy had visited James and Lilith on several occasions since taking over from Elder Thegh, but most of those visits were simply to check in on the couple on a regular basis to see how they were getting along. However, this visit in 2001 was not a social one. Elder Meiy had come with an important request from the Elders. A request that would be long in term, arduous, and very dangerous in the end. This is where James' and Lilith's story continues.

CHAPTER ONE

Some say that when life gives you a lemon you should make lemonade, but I say that life is a lemon and you should be the "lemonaid."

It was just a few minutes before closing time on that Saturday afternoon late in March, 2001, when the front door buzzer sounded indicating that someone had just entered the gallery. Lilith emerged from the studio at the back of the gallery to see Elder Meiy standing on the other side of the counter. "Elder Meiy," she exclaimed. "What brings you to Sarasota so late on a Saturday afternoon?"

"I have been sent here by the Elder Council to discuss some things with you and James, my dear Lilith," Elder Meiy said.

Having overheard that the visitor was Elder Meiy, I put down my paint brush and emerged from the studio and greeted him with a big "Hello!"

"Good afternoon, James," replied Elder Meiy. "As I was just telling Lilith, I have been sent here by the Elder Council to discuss some things with the two of you. I am glad that you are both here together to hear this as I am somewhat pressed for time."

"Well, as you know, we are usually inseparable," I replied.

"A rare quality not often found among human couples," Elder Meiy informed us. "Many of the friends you had at art school have been married and divorced two or three times."

" That's very sad to hear," I said. "We were just getting ready to close up, sir. Do you have the time to join us down the street for some dinner? We called the restaurant about 30 minutes ago and they said they were preparing a new batch of clam chowder."

"Oh, my dear James," Elder Meiy replied, "I know the restaurant you are talking about and it is one of my favorites. They have absolutely the best clam chowder on the planet! For that matter, in the universe since clam chowder isn't found anywhere else in the universe except on Earth. However, what I have been sent here to talk with you and Lilith about needs to be said in private. Besides, I am afraid that I don't have that much time for a casual visit as I am expected back at the Elder Council as soon as I can get there with your answer. I do apologize."

"There is never any apology needed from you or any of the Elders," Lilith said. "You are always welcome here and we're always glad to see you, even if your visit has to be short."

While Lilith was saying this I had gone to the front door and locked up for the day. Turning back to Elder Meiy, I said, "This visit is starting to sound very serious, sir. Is something wrong that requires our attention?"

"I am very glad to know that I am always welcome here, my friends," Elder Meiy said, "but you may think differently after I tell you why I have been sent here."

"Well, let us at least go back in the studio and sit down where we can all be more comfortable," Lilith proposed. "We have a new coffee machine that makes the most delicious coffee if you would care for a cup."

As we were entering the studio, Elder Meiy said, "Yes, it is a good idea that you two are sitting while I tell you what this is all about, but I am afraid that I will pass on the coffee this time."

"Now I'm starting to get a little bit concerned," I said more to Lilith that Elder Meiy.

Lilith and I had not only set up a wonderful working space for us both to be able to paint in the studio at the back of the gallery, but we had also made a space with five or six comfortable chairs and a couple of tables where we could relax and drink our coffee and even eat our lunch. We often invited guests and friends back to the studio to see what we were working on or just to have pleasant conversation. After Lilith and I had settled into our chairs, Elder Meiy, who was nervously sitting on the edge of his chair, said, "My dear, dear friends, I do not know where to begin. This would not have been a problem for our late friend, Elder Thegh. He always seemed to know how to bridge the chasm of difficult subjects, especially with you two."

"Now, I'm getting scared, too, James," Lilith said. Turning to Elder Meiy, she asked, "Are we going to have to deal with some really bad evil that is heading our way, Elder Meiy?"

"If it were only that simple, Lilith," Elder Meiy answered. "The simple answer, Lilith, is that the evil isn't coming your way, the Elders are asking you to go to it."

"This doesn't sound good at all, Lilith," I said.

"James, I am afraid that you are correct," Elder Meiy said. "I will tell you as much as I can at this time and then try to get back to you before you have to leave."

"Leave?" I asked.

"Oh, James," Lilith put in, "it sounds like we are going to have to go away from Sarasota for a while."

"I would say that you are absolutely right, my love," I replied. "Just where do the Elders want to send us this time, Elder Meiy? Lilith and I are very happy here in Sarasota and had never planned to leave."

"All of the Elders are quite aware of that, James," Elder Meiy said, "and we are all very sorry to have to ask you and Lilith to make a journey that might mean you never returning to Sarasota."

"This doesn't sound like something that we would be interested in," I said.

"I am afraid that you and Lilith do not have a choice in this matter, James," Elder Meiy replied.

"I beg your pardon," Lilith interrupted.

"Please let me continue and explain everything to you before I have to leave," Elder Meiy said. Lilith and I looked at each other and decided to remain silent for a while and Elder Meiy continued with why he had been sent to us. "As Lilith has always known and as you, James, have learned over the years you and Lilith have been together, Voreshans are from a planet in the Monocerotis Constellation, as humans call it. We are known as Voreshans because that is the name given to our planet thousands of years ago, but Earth scientists will refer to it as COROT-7b, but it hasn't been discovered yet. Because Voreshan technology is much more advanced than human technology, it only took our ancestors about 100 earth years to travel the 489 light years from Voresha to this planet. Today, our scientists have perfected our space vehicles to travel twice as fast, thus reducing the travel time by 50 earth years."

"Whoa!" I exclaimed. "Are you suggesting that Lilith and I are going to give up 50 earth years of our lives and travel to Voresha?"

"Oh, James!" Lilith exclaimed.

"It is not a suggestion, James," Elder Meiy said. "The Elder Council has decided that you and Lilith are the best Voreshans on this planet to make this journey back to our home planet."

"But why would the Elder Council want to take us away from our home and send us on such a long journey?" Lilith asked. "Did we do something wrong and this is our punishment?"

"My dear, dear Lilith," Elder Meiy began, "you are not being punished and you and James are held in the highest regard by all of the Elders. You have been chosen because of this high regard for you both and because you are still young and far more developed in your powers than other Voreshans your age. There are not even any Voreshans twice your age who could better carry out the mission that the Elder Council wants you to take on."

"Whatever this mission may be," I said, "we are talking about 100 or more earth years and 25 or more Voreshan years to go on this journey before we could get back here to Sarasota, if returning will even be an option. Things would change drastically during that time, and we might not be able to pick up where we left off if we made this journey that you are saying we must make."

"And why do we have to make this journey back to Voresha?" Lilith asked.

"There is a little known species called the Exidihovads that live far from here and even far from Voresha and who invaded Voresha about 60 earth years ago. This knowledge has only recently arrived to us here on Earth, even at the warp speeds that Voreshan space vehicles can travel. I say invaded, because the Exidihovads are gradually and violently taking over Voresha."

"But I thought that with their superior telepathic powers that Voreshans could control anyone or anything," I interjected.

"Yes, Elder Meiy," Lilith added, "can't the Voreshans there control the minds of the Exidihovads and defeat them without our help?"

"That my dear young friend is the problem," answered Elder Meiy. "The Exidihovads have two brains. The brain located in the upper part of their oversized skull is much like our brain in that it is used for logical thinking. If this were the only brain they had, we would not have a problem dealing with them, much as we do not have a problem dealing with humans. However, their second brain, located in the lower part of their skull, only knows fighting and killing and this is the one they switch to when they go out on their raids. Because this lower brain in the Exidihovads knows only to fight and kill, Voreshans have not been able to use their telepathic powers against them during this attack on Voresha."

"So, if I understand you correctly," I started, "the Elder Council believes that Lilith and I have the telepathic power to use against the Exidihovads?"

"That is correct, James," Elder Meiy replied. "The way you handled the Érioneteb at the Coliseum in Rome and the tannînim in Naples has convinced the Elders that the two of you working together against the Exidihovads is our home planet's only hope."

"But this sounds like a far more formidable opponent than either of those were," Lilith put in.

"They are that, my dear Lilith," Elder Meiy replied. "And they are many in number."

"Do you happen to have an estimate of how many of these Exidihovads there are on Voresha?" I asked.

"There are only about 300 or so of them at last count, because that is all that still exist in the universe," answered Elder Meiy.

"Only about 300!" Lilith and I exclaimed in our customary two-part harmony.

"You are sending two young Voreshans, who have only fought a handful of seriously evil aliens, off on a long journey to face 300 savage aliens whose sole purpose is to kill the inhabitants of Voresha?" Lilith asked. "I don't mean any disrespect for the Elder Council, Elder Meiy, but that idea seems incredibly insane to me! Besides, how do you know the Exidihovads haven't already wiped out the remaining Voreshan race there?"

"The Elder Council takes no offense at your concern, Lilith," Elder Meiy replied. "Because the planet Voresha is three times the size of earth, we believe that it would take so few Exidihovads a very long time to conquer the entire planet. Besides that, the Voreshans who inhabit the planet are putting up a physical fight against the invaders although they are not a match for the brutality that those savages are able to inflict. However, the Voreshans have been able to slow down the progress of the Exidihovads according to the emissaries who were sent here to warn us. When we received word recently from the Voreshans who traveled here, some 10,000 Voreshans had been killed by the Exidihovads. That number has no doubt increased considerably since that was some 50 earth years ago."

"I was under the impression that there were not many Voreshans left on your home planet and that is why many traveled to earth so long ago," I said.

"Relatively speaking, James," Elder Meiy said, "the population of Voresha was only about one million several thousand years ago when many of our race left to find another inhabitable planet, which is when those who survived the journey arrived on earth. As of 50 earth years ago, the population on Voresha had diminished to less than 100,000, mainly because of the decreasing number of males, just as has happened here on earth. Voresha is a very beautiful planet and those who are still there do not want to leave and have it destroyed by the likes of the Exidihovads."

"I believe all that you have told us, Elder Meiy," I said, "but do you believe there will still be any Voreshans left after 100 years of battle against the Exidihovads has passed? I mean, mathematically speaking, if 10,000 Voreshans were killed in a ten year period and there were less than 100,000 at that time, it would only make sense to assume that the rest of the Voreshan population has been decimated. That being the case, mine and Lilith's 100 year journey there, and hopefully back, would only be to save what would be left of a planet occupied by these savages. Quite frankly, Elder Meiy, I don't understand why the Elder Council wants to take 100 or more years of mine and Lilith's lives away from us."

"You do make a good point, James," Elder Meiy replied, "and I guess it is very selfish of us to sit back and hope that the two of you could make some kind of difference by traveling back to Voresha."

"I mean no disrespect for you or the other members of the Elder Council," I said, "but 100 earth years is probably going to be a third of our remaining lives. To ask us to give up our lives here in Sarasota and spend the next 100 years traveling through space, provided we weren't killed after arriving on Voresha, just isn't fair."

"Do you feel the same way, Lilith?" Elder Meiy asked her.

"Because I was born a Voreshan, I do have feelings for my nearly extinct species," Lilith began, "but my love for James comes before that and I really do not want to leave our life together here in Sarasota, especially for such a long period of time."

"I appreciate and understand the love you have for each other and your concerns about losing 100 earth years of your life together traveling through space," Elder Meiy said. "And, yes, there is a possibility that you might not return to Earth. I must leave soon, so I will take your concerns back to the Elder Council, although I do not think they are going to be very happy about it. I promised Elder Thegh on his death bed that I would always look out for you and be on your side, but because of my age, my voice on the Elder Council is a small one and they may not listen to me. I just want you to know that because of my promise to Elder Thegh and my high regard for both of you, that I will do my best to convince the Elder Council to reconsider their request of you."

"Thank you so much, Elder Meiy," Lilith said. "It means a lot to James and me that you care that much for our well-being."

"I second that, Elder Meiy," I said. "I would give up my life as a Voreshan and go back to pumping gas for a living to continue my life here with Lilith."

"Oh, James!" Lilith exclaimed. "I love you so much!" and Lilith gave me a big hug. When we turned back to say goodbye to Elder Meiy, he had already unlocked the front door and disappeared into the late afternoon sun. "Do you think the Elders will make us go on this journey anyway, James?"

"If they insist on it, Lilith," I replied, "I will give up my Voreshan abilities and go back to just being human, even though it would mean living a much shorter life. We have worked hard for what we have together, Lilith, and I don't want that to be "lost in space."

"I do love you so much, James!" Lilith said and smiled at my attempt at old TV humor.

CHAPTER TWO

To say that the next couple of days were somewhat nerve racking would be a huge understatement! We stayed up later than usual that Saturday evening talking about our possibilities, including revisiting the idea of doing as the Elders had requested and journeying to Voresha. Neither of us were too keen on the idea of such a long space voyage, but conceded that we would at least not be separated for the journey. We didn't get much sleep that night and it wasn't because we spent the night having our usual dessert. We closed the gallery on Sundays and Mondays and called that our weekend, when we would usually do those things that we enjoyed doing together so much, such as going to the beach and going to the beach and going to the beach. Every few months we would also make a trip back to the carillon park where we first met and just hang out there and then have dinner with Lilith's parents, who you will remember lived near the park, before heading back home.

Since Elder Meiy left so quickly on Saturday, we didn't get a chance to ask him what the time line was for the Elders making a decision about us traveling to Voresha. Since he had seemingly been in such a hurry to leave we also thought that we shouldn't bother him telepathically and that we would just bide our time and try not to worry too much. This was certainly a case where no news was good news. By the following Saturday we still had not heard anything from Elder Meiy, so we decided to go up to St. Petersburg on Sunday afternoon to visit the Salvador

Dali Museum. We were roaming around from one gallery to the next when we were approached by an older man who looked amazingly like Dali.

"Good afternoon, James and Lilith," he said as he approached us.

"Ok, Lilith," I communicated telepathically, *"do you know this guy?"*

"No, James, I don't," she answered.

"If you would rather communicate telepathically, my friends, that is fine with me," the stranger said. *"It might be best since there are a lot of people around."*

"How do you know us and who are you?" Lilith asked.

"I was an old friend of Elder Thegh and Elder Meiy," the stranger replied.

"Was a friend of Elder Meiy?" I asked.

"I apologize," he said. *"Allow me to introduce myself. I am Elder Relvio Rumanth Saredem, and I come to you in Elder Meiy's stead."*

"Why isn't Elder Meiy here?" Lilith asked.

"I am afraid that I have been chosen to bring you some very bad news regarding your friend, Elder Meiy," Elder Saredem said. *"Shortly after Elder Meiy had brought your concerns back to the Elder Council, which had gathered in Toronto for his report, Elder Meiy was assassinated at the airport."*

"Oh, dear God!" Lilith exclaimed. *"You mean someone killed him? Why would anyone want to kill such a wonderful man?"*

"That's unbelievable!" I said. *"Who did this to him? Wasn't he aware that such a thing was going to happen?"*

"I don't mean to scare you two, but the assassin was an Exidihovad," Elder Saredem answered.

"That is not a word that we wanted to hear, sir," I said. *"Are there Exidihovads on Earth? If so, have they been here all along?"*

"Please slow down my young friend and I will tell you what has happened," he told me. *"It seems that several Exidihovads followed the Voreshan messenger ship that recently arrived on Earth to tell us about the invasion of Voresha. The Exidihovads stayed at far enough of a distance that the Voreshan ship did not know that it was being followed. Witnesses at the scene where Elder Meiy was killed report seeing six large figures cloaked in black, so as to probably hide their hideous appearance, attack Elder Meiy and brutally chop him to pieces with strange, long swords. We know that they have weaponry far to superior to what we have on Earth, but we believe they used swords so as not to reveal their alien identity."*

"Ok, Elder Saredem," I interrupted, *"you've got my attention. Large and hideous, you say?"*

"The Exidihovads average seven to eight feet tall and are an ominous red color with deep black wrinkles and oversized heads to accommodate their two brains," Elder Saredem answered. *"They are one of the most hideous creatures in the universe."*

"They don't sound like they would be that hard to defeat," Lilith put in, *"especially if they don't have some kind of superior weapons to use."*

"What you do not understand, my young friends, is that this particular group of Exidihovads seem to be acting strictly with their lower brains," Elder Saredem replied. *"This group attack on Elder Meiy is how they usually operate, not giving their opponents any chance to defend themselves. Some of the Elders also believe that these Exidihovads may be a specially conceived military group*

who have had their upper brain neutralized, thus making it impossible for us to use our telepathic powers against them."

"So even Lilith and I together probably don't have any chance of changing their minds about killing off Voreshans?" I said more than asked.

"That is correct," Elder Saredem replied.

"Then I still don't really understand why the Elders seem to want to sacrifice James and me to these creatures if we can't control their minds," Lilith said with a tinge of anger in her voice.

"My dear Lilith," Elder Saredem began, "yours' and James' exploits as related to the Elders by Elder Thegh have almost become legendary during your short lives. Your ability to defeat the evil that lurks around this planet both here and in Italy, against insuperable odds, makes the Elders believe that you are our only hope against the Exidihovads. This is why you were asked to travel to Voresha and face them there, however it now seems that your place is here on Earth where you may have some advantage over them."

"I'm almost afraid to ask," I said, "but are there more than six of these creatures on Earth? Elder Meiy had indicated that there were only about 300 left that attacked Voresha."

"The number that attacked Voresha was around 300 at the time of the initial attack, Elder Saredem answered. "The report brought to the Elders here on Earth was that only about ten of those had been killed on Voresha. However, I am nervous to report to you and Lilith that at least one-third of the original number traveled here to Earth with the sole purpose of eliminating all Voreshans from this planet as well, and thus the universe."

"Oh my God!" Lilith exclaimed. *"You mean that the Elders are asking James and me to confront around 100 Exidihovads alone?"*

"Yes, Lilith," Elder Saredem answered matter-of-factly. *"However, let me explain further."*

"Please do," I said matter-of-factly.

"The Elders understand your concern in this matter, my friends," Elder Saredem began, *"but as you both well know, Voreshans are essentially a peaceable species whose sole purpose here on Earth is to help humans be better people. Voreshans have never been a warrior species and have tried to maintain their simple lifestyle and to go about the business they came here to perform. You two are the only Voreshans in the universe who have ever had to confront and battle the extreme evils that exist on this planet. Not only have evil humans increased in population as this planet has grown, but it has become a haven for many other evils from across the universe, and as the two of you found out in Italy, there are evils on this planet that have always been here."*

"But those battles were all done telepathically or telekinetically," Lilith stated. *"You are asking us to do battle against a foe who is not only larger than us and outnumbers us, but whose lower brains can't seem to be telepathically penetrated. How are we supposed to fight that kind of battle without becoming weapon-carrying warriors ourselves?"*

"The Elders realize that over the past century you have only had to kill another species once, but you two and Elder Thegh are the only Voreshans who have ever done that," Elder Saredem answered. *"That is why you have been chosen by the Elders to fight this battle for the preservation of*

our species. We believe that together you are our only hope for survival."

"That kind of makes us sound like hired guns, except that our only payment is the knowledge that we might be able to save the Voreshan species," I said.

"I agree with, James," Lilith said.

"I promise you the Elders do not like this any more than you do," Elder Saredem said, *"but, as I just said, we are afraid you are our only hope,"* and his eyes began to get watery.

Now, over the past 30 or so years I have learned one thing about Voreshans, they can't fake their true emotions. Elder Saredem beginning to tear up was a sincere emotional response on his part. The few really bad Voreshans, such as the likes of Harmony Beckham and her parents, like most humans, could easily lie about things, but they just couldn't control their true emotions. Lilth and I looked at each other and, seeing the look of dismay and concern in her expression, I could tell that Elder Saredem's statement had had a real impact on her as well.

"Well, since you put it that way," I said, *"I guess Lilith and I are at your disposal,"* and I was literally thinking "disposal." *"Are we going to have to go out and hunt these creatures down or do we sit and wait for them to find us?"*

"If you wait for them to find you, you will probably end up like Elder Meiy!" Elder Saredem said emphatically. *"And their plan may be to eradicate the rest of us before approaching you two. They would not be too hard to find, however, because of their size and appearance. Their best disguise is the black cloak that they wear when they are out in public."*

"But how will we know where they are at any given time, Elder Saredem?" Lilith asked. *"And what is to keep*

them from splitting up into 15 or 20 groups and attacking Voresha in many different places?"

"The Elders have a plan that we hope will bring them all together in one place, that being here in Sarasota," answered Elder Saredem. *"The Elders are going to let it be widely known that the Voreshan Elders are planning to congregate here in Sarasota for a special meeting to plan what to do about the Exidihovads. We feel that because there are so many Elders that the Exidihovads will concentrate on us first and that they will all come here to do that. The other Elders are already beginning to arrive in Sarasota and we will all take up residence not far from here in an old abandoned mansion that is situated on 200 acres of land. So far, it seems they only attack us when we venture outside of our dwellings. The plan is for no more than two or three Elders to venture outside at a time and not to go beyond the boundaries of the property where we will be staying. The two of you will be our body guards and hopefully be able to deal with small numbers of Exidihovads at a time. It seems that these creatures are a very prideful species and take great pleasure in boasting about their kills. Because of that the Elders do not believe more than a handful will attack any given small group of us. Most of the 200 acres surrounding the mansion are wooded and we suspect the Exidihovads will conceal themselves in those woods except when they are on the attack."*

"Well, Elder Saredem," I said, *"that sounds like as good of a plan as any provided the Exidihovads take the bait. Are Lilith and I to stay with the Elders at this mansion while we are trying to deal with the Exidihovads?"*

"That is what we were hoping that you and Lilith would agree to in order for this plan to have any chance of succeeding," Elder Saredem answered. *"The old mansion*

has already been fixed up and you will have a fully furnished suite of rooms that were once used as guest quarters at the opposite end of the building from the Elders, so as to give you your privacy."

"That will be greatly appreciated, Elder Saredem," Lilith said. "When do you want us to move into the mansion?"

"The Elders were hoping that you would move in tomorrow since you close your gallery on Mondays."

"Wow!" I said. "That is kind of short notice, but I guess all we need are the essentials for our everyday life. Will we be able to carry on as normal and have our gallery open during the week and on Saturdays?"

"That was a difficult part of this entire plan," Elder Saredem answered. "However, we have arranged for a young human couple that we trust implicitly to operate your gallery during this time. You have nothing to worry about as they are experienced in such matters and are totally worthy of your trust. If anyone inquires about where the two of you are, they will simply reply that you have taken a long overdue vacation."

"Will this couple be safe from the Exidihovads?" Lilith inquired.

"As far as we know, Elder Saredem replied, the Exidihovads have absolutely no interest in humans and are only here to exterminate all Voreshans. If they accomplish that goal, we believe that they will go back to Voresha and help finish the job there. I hate to end our conversation on this terrifying thought, but I must get back to the mansion in Sarasota and stay with my fellow Elders until the two of you arrive tomorrow."

"Will you be safe going back to Sarasota alone," Lilith asked.

"The Exidihovads are not the brightest creatures in the universe, especially this warrior breed," Elder Saredem replied, *"who are only able to use their lower brains. Although they are usually able to somehow recognize Voreshans, they don't seem to be able to recognize us when we are in disguise. Thus, the Dali-like disguise I am wearing today. I think I will be fine getting back to Sarasota. Besides, I rented a brand new Bentley to make this trip to St. Petersburg and everyone knows that Voreshnsa are not that extravagant."*

That gave all three of us a good laugh that we needed at that time, and then Elder Saredem departed our company to head back to Sarasota. Lilith and I sat down on a bench in the gallery, held hands, looked at each other and sighed, wondering if our lives were going to be cut short in the very near future or if we could deal with this problem as quickly as possible and get back to our normal lives.

CHAPTER THREE

Lilith and I left the Dali Museum shortly after Elder Saredem had departed and headed back to our home in Sarasota. On the way back we discussed what our options might be in fighting the Exidihovads as well as what we would take with us to the mansion where the Elders were holed up. As far as we understood the plan, the presumption was that the Exidihovads had planned to kill off the Voreshan Elders first with the hope that that would discourage all other Voreshans from fighting and make their elimination that much easier. If this plan that the Elders had devised worked, Lilith and I might only have to take on a handful of Exidihovads at a time. If the plan didn't go as the Elders hoped it would, then there probably wasn't much hope for Voreshans, either here on Earth or back on Voresha.

We drove along in silence after that for a while, but we each knew what the other was thinking. I broke the silence by asking Lilith, "Are you as worried about this whole scheme as I am?"

"I am, James," Lilith answered. "Sorry that I haven't been more talkative, but I am really worried about both our future and that of the Voreshan species. Have you been thinking about our personal plan of action, James?"

"Not very much, Lilith," I replied. "I guess that I am being very selfish in that I am mostly concerned about us and if we are facing our last days together."

"I've been thinking about that, too, James," Lilith said. "I know that we have had a wonderful 34 earth years together, but in terms of Voreshan years, we are still quite young and I just knew that we would grow old together."

A note here: although Lilith and I had lived nearly 52 earth years, we were only 26 ½ years old in Voreshan years. If you remember, Voresha age the same as humans until they are 18, and then the aging process slows down to one Voreshan year for every four earth years.

"My sentiments exactly, Lilith," I said. "However, since we don't seem to have much choice in this matter, maybe we should start thinking about our personal plan of action."

"I agree, James," Lilith said.

"A couple of things I picked up on that Elder Saredem told us was that the Exidihovads seem both quite vain and not too bright when using their lower brains. And since these Exidihovads supposedly only have a lower brain to use, they might just be stupid enough for us to fool some way. In addition, Elder Saredem also indicated that they were quite emotional. I'm thinking that these are three areas that you and I might possibly break through to and possibly be able to fight them successfully. If so, we need to get our heads together and maybe test out my theory on one if we can find one."

"That's a marvelous idea, James," Lilith replied. "Maybe we can use their vanity, stupidity, and emotions against one another and turn them on each other like we did with the Snaanads in Florence. If they are as stupid as Elder Saredem indicated, this might not be as hard a task as we first thought."

"Provided, of course, all 100 or so don't come at us at the same time," I said with a little bit of a tremor in my voice. "However, even if they only attack a few at a time, if their lower warrior-like brain can't be altered in any way, we are probably doomed."

"I would rather not think about that, James," Lilith said. "All we can do in this matter is to apply all of our telepathic and telekinetic powers together and hope for the best."

"Lilith!" I exclaimed.

"What, James," she said. "Did you think of something else?"

"You are the genius in this family, my love!" I said.

"Why, James?" Lilith asked. "What did I say just now that sparked your imagination?"

"You mentioned our telekinetic powers and I hadn't even given that a thought!" I replied. "Whether or not they respond to our telepathic orders or not, we can pick them up telekinetically and slam them against trees if need be!"

"Now that's thinking like a warrior, James," Lilith said. "It has certainly worked for us in a number of situations so far. I think that your human side is starting to come out and I think that the Elders know that you still have that fighting urge that male humans seem to always exhibit."

"As long as it means defending you and our life together, Lilith," I said, "I will fight to the death and that is no idle threat!"

"Well, my dear," Lilith said, "if we don't ultimately win this battle, then the Exidihovads will at least suffer some casualties and know that they have been in the battle of their lives!"

"Charge!" I exclaimed, and we both had to laugh a little.

Lilith and I were just arriving back at our home about this time and everything seemed unusually quiet around our neighborhood. Although our home was in an older neighborhood where mostly retired people lived, there were usually several of them out walking around or working in their yards. We didn't even hear any birds singing and the wind was nonexistent.

I got close to Lilith and whispered, "This is really strange. I do not like the way this feels, Lilith."

Communicating back with me telepathically, Lilith said, "*I think we should communicate this way, James. If somebody or something is lurking about it's unlikely that they or it can read minds.*"

"*Good idea, Lilith,*" I replied. "*I'm not sure that we are ready to start doing battle yet, but I feel like something is watching us.*"

"*I agree, James,*" Lilith said. "*I have been searching around telepathically and I can't discover any mental activity going on, not even old man Niedal dreaming about the widow Kanzer,*" and that brought a chuckle from both of us. Of course, what we didn't take into consideration was that it was probably nap time for most of these folks.

"*Let's stay close together, Lilith,*" I said, "*so that we can at least use our powers collectively if need be.*"

As we were pulling into our driveway a large figure suddenly emerged from behind our garage and started walking toward us. He, or it, was dressed from head to foot in a hooded black cloak and was mumbling something to himself.

"*According to Elder Saredem's description of the Exidihovads that killed Elder Meiy, this is one of them,*" I said.

"*I think you are absolutely right, James,*" Lilith replied as we were getting out of the car.

The Exidihovad then reached beneath his cloak with both hands and withdrew what appeared to be two ancient

Egyptian Khopesh swords, vicious looking weapons to say the least. We recognized them from some of our art history studies.

"I come to kill Voreshans," he said in a deep throaty voice.

"We are not whatever it was you said," I replied. "We are humans."

"You smell like Voreshans," He replied.

"The people we were with about an hour ago must have been what you said," I told him. "Their smell must have rubbed off on us."

"Where are these Voreshans that you were with?" he asked.

Now, knowing that I was probably dealing with a creature whose intelligence was probably less than that of a stuffed alligator, I thought I would try to trick him. "They rode back with us and they are asleep in the trunk of the car," I told the Exidihovad warrior pointing at the rear of our car. "Maybe you should call your friends out and check the trunk." I was hoping to find out if he was alone or not.

"I here alone," he informed me. "Show me where these Voreshans are and you will not die." Saying this he began swinging the two swords back and forth like he knew what he was doing.

"Lilith," I said telepathically, *"play along. I am going to try and trick him into leaning into the trunk when I open it and maybe we can slam the trunk lid down on his head."*

"It's a plan, James," Lilith said.

"Follow me to the back of the car and I will open the trunk for you," I told our new friend.

I slowly walked backwards to the rear of our car so as not to take my eyes off this hulk of a creature and unlocked the trunk for him. I indicated to the Exidihovad that he should be quiet and whispered to him that he would have to look far back in the trunk to find them because that was where they were sleeping.

"That good," he tried to whisper in his throaty voice.

I opened the trunk quickly and shouted, "Back there they are! Quick, look deeply in the trunk!"

The Exidihovad leaned way over and stuck his head far back into the trunk and jabbed at the space with his swords, but he did not find the Voreshans that were supposed to be there. He was far too tall to fit in the trunk, but I slammed the trunk lid down on his back repeatedly. He began screaming and started trying to back out of the trunk and kept saying that he was going to slice us up into little pieces and feed us to the sewer rats that he had captured for his lunch. When he was nearly out of the trunk except for his head, I slammed the lid down hard on his neck and Lilith and I both jumped up on the trunk hoping that our combined weight might disable him long enough for us to try some sort of mind control over him. Much to our surprise the edge of the trunk lid and our combined weight was enough to cut right through his neck and sever his head from his body. The rest of his seven foot height fell backwards onto our driveway and the trunk lid shut tight with his head lying on the floor of the trunk. The amazing thing was that there wasn't any blood as we know it, but only a small seepage of clear liquid coming from the Exidihovad's neck.

Lilith and I were still sitting on the trunk lid and stared at each other in wonder. "I can't believe that this Exidihovad was that easy to defeat," I said.

"I'm as dumbfounded as you, James," Lilith replied. "Now, if only we could get them one at a time and trick them to look in the trunk so we could chop off their heads we could accomplish this task without much effort."

"If only, my warrior princess" I replied. "I think we had better get this mess cleaned up before the neighbors start wandering around and asking questions."

"Thanks, James, I think," Lilith said. "I am beginning to think that maybe Voreshans do have that killer instinct hiding deep down in their soul or spirit and that I am maybe the first who has shown signs of it."

"Well, if you are, my love," I said, "I'm glad you are with me! Ninety-nine Exidihovads to fight, cut off one's head, 98 Exidihovads left to fight!"

"Real funny, James," Lilith said sarcastically, but she made a little giggle anyway.

I won't go into the details of how we disposed of the Exidihovad's body and head, but Voreshans have their ways of disposing of things they don't really want to keep around for humans to find. After Lilith and I had taken care of the mess that we had created in the driveway, we gave the nearby neighborhood a thorough scan with our telepathic powers to make sure that no one had been watching or was aware that anything had happened. When we were sure that the coast was clear, I pulled our car into the garage and closed the garage door so that none of the neighbors would see us packing up to leave for awhile. We felt bad about not telling our next door neighbors, but if we had told them we would have had to spend about an hour making up some ridiculous story about where we were going on vacation and then would have had to listen to all of their vacation stories. When we had loaded up our car with everything that we thought we would need, we headed on over to the mansion where the Elders were staying. We were sure they would be interested in, if not frightened by, our little escapade with one of the Exidihovads.

CHAPTER FOUR

Lilith and I arrived at the old mansion without much fanfare. Elder Saredem met us at the front door and let us in after unlocking about a dozen locks. After Lilith and I had both seen and defeated an Exidihovad, we really didn't think that a big wooden door and a dozen locks would stop even one of these creatures, much less four or five. After we had been shown our suite of rooms on the third floor of the mansion and on the opposite side from where all of the Elders were camping out, Lilith and I went downstairs to attend a meeting of the Elders. There were currently some 150 Elders worldwide, but only the 100 living in the United States and Canada were here in Sarasota. We were informed by Elder Saredem that we were not to speak unless spoken to as we would not be seated with him and thus he couldn't advise us. I thought it was a strange way to treat so-called honored guests.

When we walked into the large room where the Elders were holding their meeting we were ushered to two chairs at the front of the group, but behind a podium where the Head Elder would be speaking. The room we were in must have been the dining hall of the mansion at one time. The walls were covered in mirrors, some now broken, and five huge crystal chandeliers, which all seemed to be intact, hung in a row down the middle of the long room. The Elder who showed Lilith and me to our seats repeated what Elder Saredem had told us about not speaking. He also indicated that we would be asked to give a report concerning how we thought we would deal with the Exidihovads after the Head Elder had finished speaking to the group. Lilith and I had never met a Head Elder before, but when he entered the room through a doorway behind us he immediately walked over and introduced himself.

"Welcome my dear young Voreshans," he said as he walked up to us and extended his hand first to me and then to Lilith. "My name is Kish Tenhenk Sermeda and I am very pleased that you two have agreed to help our species deal with the Exidihovads."

Standing up, Lilith and I said in two-part harmony, "We are very pleased to meet you, sir."

"Ah, yes, Elder Thegh warned me about that little quirk of yours," he replied. "In a few minutes I am going to address the other Elders who have gathered here and bring them up to date about what has been happening and who you two are and why you are here. Now, just sit quietly until I introduce you."

"Yes, sir," Lilith and I said together and Elder Sermeda smiled.

After talking to the group of Elders for about 30 minutes and explaining to them what he and a few others had in mind about how to deal with the Exidihovads and briefly mentioning Lilith and I and some of our exploits, Elder Sermeda then turned and asked Lilith and me to come up to the podium. "Here, my fellow Elders," Elder Sermeda began, "is the young Voreshan couple I have just told you about. Their names are Lilith and James and they were the best of friends with the late Elder Thegh. I am sure that Elder Thegh spoke with many of you about them and their remarkable exploits both here in this country and in Italy. Lilith and James have been called on, as I have just indicated in my speech, to help us to deal with the Exidihovad invasion. You have been brought up to date as to why they are here and not on their way to Voresha as originally planned. I have asked them to our meeting today to hopefully explain to all of us what their plan of attack might be against this enemy. I give you Lilith and James."

Every Elder in the room immediately rose from their chairs and began to applaud us and did so for a couple of minutes. When they had finally settled down Lilith and I both said in unison, "Thank you so much!"

Lilith and I had planned while we were unpacking that she would speak to the Elders first and then turn the floor over to me to explain my ideas about how we might fight the Exidihovads. Lilith began by saying, "Your welcome of James and me has been far more than we either expected or deserve, but we sincerely thank you for that and for putting so much trust in us. James and I only hope that we can live up to your expectations in this serious business with the Exidihovads. What we have not had a chance to tell any of you yet is that we have already had an encounter with one of these creatures at our home just before leaving to come here." At this statement there were numerous gasps and some mumbling among the group of Elders. When they had settled back down, Lilith continued, "When James and I returned home yesterday from St. Petersburg, where we met Elder Saredem, aka Salvador Dali, and that brought a few chuckles from those who knew what Lilith was talking about, we sensed that something was wrong in our neighborhood and then an Exidihovad came out from behind our garage just as we got out of our car. He initially threatened to kill us, but James told him that we were not Voreshans. He then let us know how they can distinguish Voreshans from humans by telling us that we smelled like Voreshans." More gasps from the audience. "We tricked him by telling him that we had recently been with two Voreshans and that their scent must have rubbed off on us. We also told him that the other two Voreshans were asleep in the trunk of our car. When he looked inside the trunk to find the Voreshans, we slammed the trunk lid down on his neck and jumped on the trunk lid, thus severing his head from his body." The entire room began to whisper and mumble back and forth and Elder Sermeda had to get up and quiet them down. "James and I properly disposed of the Exidihovad's head and body before coming here to the mansion last night. I will now let James tell you his idea about how the two of us might deal with the Exidihovads."

The room once again erupted in applause for a couple minutes and once again Elder Sermeda had to calm them down. I had never spoken to a large group before and to say that I was a little nervous is an understatement. I actually managed somehow to get all the way through school without having to give an oral report. Trying to lighten things up a little and to help me overcome my nervousness, I said, "Lilith always gets to tell the best parts," and the room erupted in laughter. When the Elders had settled down, I continued, "It occurred to me when Lilith and I were driving back from St. Petersburg yesterday that even though our telepathic powers might not be that effective against these Exidihovads, that our combined telekinetic powers might give us an advantage over them. From our encounter yesterday, I can tell you that they are seven to eight feet tall and probably weigh around 300 pounds." My audience at this point looked both spellbound and frightened. "The amazing part about yesterday's encounter with one of the creatures was that Lilith and I didn't use either of these powers against him. Our trickery was very simple yesterday, but then the Exidihovad's intelligence level was somewhat less than that of a stuffed alligator," and the room once again erupted in laughter. Feeling much more confident, I returned to my explanation about how to deal with the Exidihovads. "Using only their lower brains, these creatures seem to only know how to fight and kill and their weapon of choice here on Earth seems to be swords. The one yesterday was carrying what appeared to be two ancient Egyptian Khopesh swords, at least swords that resembled those. Lilith and I have proven that our combined powers have developed to a higher level than most our age and we feel confident that if we only have to deal with a few Exidihovads at a time that we can defeat and kill them. We know that may sound somewhat shocking to you since Voreshans are traditionally a peaceful species, but killing the Exidihovads before they slaughter the Voreshan species is the only solution we have at this time. Thank you."

The entire room once again rose to their feet and applauded. Elder Sermeda then stepped forward and said to the group, "Although we have never had to deal this violently with an adversary, it now seems that we must do so in order to survive. Many thousands have already perished back on Voresha, and I am sad to say that our home planet may well be lost forever. However, even if that becomes the case, Lilith and James are here on Earth to try and make sure that the Voreshan species does not become extinct. You also know that Voreshan Elders are not permitted to kill anyone or anything, but I believe that time has now past and that we should make a new rule that allows us to take part in the defense of our kind, even if it means killing off another species." Once again all of the Elders rose from their chairs and this time cheered. When they had settled back down, Elder Sermeda said, "Then it is confirmed! The Voreshan Elders will help in this fight against the

Exidihovads when and where they can, but we will be at the command of Lilith and James in this matter. Is there any opposition to this?" The room was silent. "Good!" Elder Sermeda said, "I would hate to have to excommunicate any of you!" and this time he evoked some laughter with his response. Turning to Lilith and me, Elder Sermeda asked, "When do you want to try out your plan? We believe that all of the Exidihovads have gathered in the surrounding woods and plan to attack the Elders when small groups of us go outside."

Getting up and addressing the entire room of Elders, I said, "The danger to you is great if you venture outside the walls of the mansion. However, not to do so a few at a time would no doubt invite an attack by all of the Exidihovads that you believe to be surrounding us. If there are as many as 100 of them, then they would have no trouble crashing through the doors and windows of this old building and probably killing all of us." More concerned mumbling among the group of Elders. "Lilith and I are convinced that these creatures are not intelligent enough to figure out our little plan, even after using it several times. We believe that the Exidihovads would continue to attack small groups of Elders with small groups themselves. So, we can begin our little experiment at any time. It is really up to all of you when you want to start and who will go outside with Lilith and me, especially the first time. As you make these decisions please keep in mind that you might not return to the group. Dealing with one Exidihovad is no doubt a lot different than dealing with several at the same time."

Elder Saredem stood up and addressed the group, saying, "The youngest Elders here, including myself, are in the early third century of their lives, but that only makes us about 60 earth years old. If we were humans, that age would not usually be very effective against such a formidable enemy, but we are Voreshan and even at 400 years old I believe that we can bring the battle to the Exidihovads and defeat them, with the help of Lilith and James, of course." A huge cheer went up from the crowd and then when they had quieted down, Elder Saredem said, "I volunteer to be among the first group of Elders to venture outside to face our enemy. How many of us do you want to accompany you and Lilith, James?"

"Lilith and I," I began, "think that we might be able to handle eight to ten Exidihovads at a time and that they wouldn't attack with more than a two to one advantage. That said, we were thinking that three of you would accompany us on the trial run to test our theory."

Two of the younger Elders immediately stood up and volunteered to go with Elder Saredem, Lilith, and me on our trial run. "Thank you for volunteering to go on this dangerous first excursion against the Exidihovads," I said. "I think the five of us should get together this afternoon and make our plans for tomorrow, if that meets with your approval."

"As Elder Sermeda told us earlier, James," Elder Saredem said, "we are at your command. Whatever Lilith and you tell us to do we will do to the best of our abilities. Every Elder in this room, as well as those across the planet who could not be here, have placed our confidence in you, but we do not expect you to carry out this battle against this terrible enemy alone."

"James and I thank you for that sentiment, Elder Saredem," Lilith said. "James and I will see you this afternoon to make our plans for tomorrow." Lilith and I then went back to our room to await our afternoon meeting with

Elder Saredem and the other two Elders who had volunteered for tomorrow's excursion outside.

CHAPTER FIVE

Around 2:00 that afternoon Lilith and I went back downstairs to a small room at the back of the mansion where we made ourselves comfortable in some very plush, oversized, soft, burgundy leather chairs. The three Elders were already there waiting for us and seemed to be pacing around nervously and mumbling to no one in particular. The two who had volunteered from the audience that morning approached us and one of them said, "We apologize for not introducing ourselves this morning, but I am Elder Cescasing and this is Elder Retcarshac. We were so nervous about volunteering that we forgot to tell you who we are."

Lilith said, "James and I are very pleased to meet you and are glad that you have volunteered for our first mission outside. We know this has to be scary for you, but if all goes according to plan we should come out on top."

"Well, Elder Cescasing and I," Elder Retcarshac began, "like Elder Saredem, are among the youngest of the Elders here and we had already discussed last evening that we would try to be the first to volunteer. It just did not seem right for the much older Elders to have to be put through this ordeal. To be perfectly honest with you, we are quite nervous about this little adventure."

"I certainly tend to agree with you regarding the older Elders," I said. "If our little plan works, there may not be any reason for the older Elders to participate outside of the mansion against the Exidihovads. If Lilith and I were to tell you that we weren't nervous, too, we would be lying, but someone has to do something about this threat to the Voreshan species."

"So the two of you already have a plan for us to follow?" asked Elder Saredem.

"Would you like to take this one, Lilith?" I asked her.

"Well, the idea," Lilith began, "is that the three of you, or whoever happens to be with us when we venture outside, won't have to do very much at all. This is a terrible way to put it, but you will essentially be the bait to draw out a few of the Exidihovads, hopefully no more than ten at a time."

"I am not too crazy about being 'bait', as you say," replied Elder Cescasing, "but if that is what it takes to defeat these awful creatures, then so be it. Elder Saredem, Elder Retcarshac, are you both ok with this idea?"

"Absolutely!" said Elder Retcarshac. "I am willing to do whatever it takes to win this battle! Although I have lived a long time by Earth standards, I am not ready to call it quits!"

"I feel the same way, too," said Elder Saredem a little less enthusiastically. "So, do we all five just saunter out into the woods and hope that the entire horde of Exidihovads doesn't attack us at once?"

"No," I said, "mine and Lilith's plan is not to venture any further than about fifty yards away from the mansion. That way, if we fail in eliminating the Exidihovads that come out of the woods after us, the run back to the mansion wouldn't be quite so far. However, if our first attempt to extirpate this noxious bunch of creatures works, then we might have found our solution to eliminating all of them one small batch at a time. Until we have that first confrontation, we won't know whether or not our idea will work."

"I don't think I have ever heard of such a nefarious species before in my time on this planet," said Elder Saredem and the other two Elders nodded in agreement. "It seems especially odd in this day and age that a species from the far reaches of the universe still fight with swords."

"Lilith and I have given that some thought as well," I said. "We only hope that the swords aren't a ruse to mislead us from expecting more advanced weaponry. We believe that they are using swords so as not to draw too much attention to their plan of annihilating Voreshans."

"What if the Exidihovads do have a more advanced weaponry?" asked Elder Saredem. "Are you prepared to deal with that as well?"

"We will just have to wait and see what happens, but in the meantime is everyone ready to give this plan a try?" Lilith asked.

The three Elders all nodded, but without much enthusiasm. "Well then," I said, "Let's get this party under way. The other Elders will be watching us from various windows throughout the mansion to see how we handle this situation, providing of course that we are attacked."

We had decided that we would use one of the rear entrances to the mansion and cautiously and slowly make our way into the backyard area, strolling along as if we were simply going for a walk. Lilith and I thought that if we were nonchalant enough about it that the Exidihovads would think they had the upper hand. We had only gone about 20 yards when I signaled for the others to stop. Communicating telepathically, I said to all, *"It feels like we are being watched, but I haven't noticed any movement at the edges of the woods. I hope the Exidihovads can't make themselves invisible, too!"*

"You're right, James," Lilith said. *"Something doesn't feel quite right, but I do feel like something is about to happen. Everyone stay alert."*

The three Elders were playing their part quite well, too well as a matter-of-fact. They were all three just standing there shivering, although it was at least 80 degrees that afternoon in Sarasota, and nervously glancing about. What we hadn't thought about was that the Exidihovads had an extraordinary sense of smell and could probably smell fear on any species, from rats to humans to Voreshans. Lilith and I should have thought about this since the one we defeated at our house had indicated that we smelled like Voreshans, although I have never thought that Voreshans smelled bad. Lilith always smells nice!

"It has suddenly occurred to me," I said, *"that the Exidihovads may have a pretty good sense of smell."*

"That's right, James," Lilith said. *"The one we killed at our house said we smelled like Voreshans. And thank you, by the way. That probably means they can smell fear as well."* Turning to the Elders, she said, *"We know that you are scared to death by the way you are acting, but if at all possible, please try not to show so much fear. If the Exidihovads can smell your fear, it might make them more vicious than ever and even harder to stop. We believe that they do have a superior sense of smell."*

"We are very sorry about that, Lilith," Elder Cescasing said, *"but we are not the fighting type and have never faced such evil before. I think that our nervousness is only natural under the circumstances. If the Exidihovads can smell fear, then they must not be any better than wild animals!"*

"However," Elder Retcarshac put in, *"we will try to be brave for you, but it is difficult when none of us has ever*

been in a physical fight or has a weapon to defend our-selves."

"Your efforts are appreciated," I said. *"Lilith and I are depending on our combined telekinetic powers as a weapon against these creatures. If that doesn't work, we will retreat to the mansion and then we will have to try and find some kind of weapons for our next try."*

Lilith and I had been standing back-to-back and surveying our surroundings carefully during this conversation, so as not to get too distracted by the Elders' nervousness. Suddenly I felt Lilith go tense and when I turned to face in her direction and ask what was wrong I could see that her eyes had widened in fright and she was pointing to one area of the woods with a slightly trembling finger.

Looking in the direction Lilith was pointing, she whispered, "Look! There! They have come for us!"

We had now all turned to see how many Exidihovads were emerging from the woods where Lilith had pointed. Going back to telepathic communication, I said, *"I only see five so far. Lilith, do you sense more than that right now?"*

"I don't, James," Lilith replied. *"I wonder if these five have been sent out to see how a few of them would handle us?"*

"That would be a possibility," I said, *"except that they aren't supposed to be that intelligent when they are using their lower brain."*

The five who had emerged from the woods had stopped and looked as if they were sizing us up and mumbling among themselves, probably about their plan of attack. Then the central figure among them began to move forward and the others followed in a V-shape behind him. We continued to hold our position about 20 yards from the mansion as the Exidihovads slowly approached us with their swords drawn, one in each hand, and raised high above their heads. Their swords were of the same kind as the one Lilith and I had killed at our house had used. They probably thought this display of weaponry would make us fall down on our knees and cower before them as they chopped us to pieces, but they were in for a big surprise.

"Lilith, I said telepathically, *"Notice how they have their swords raised so high."*

"I see that, James," Lilith said. *"Are you thinking what I'm thinking?"*

"You know I am," I replied. *Let's wait until they get a little closer before we try it."*

"What is your plan?" asked Elder Saredem, who seemed to have gotten his fear under control.

"I'm afraid you will just have to watch and hope for the best," I briefly answered, because the Exidihovads were now only about 20 yards away from us and still approaching in the V formation. Lilith and I noticed that the other two Elders were frozen solid and would be easy pickings if we couldn't defeat these five creatures.

When the Exidihovads were about ten yards away from us Lilith and I went to work combining our telekinetic powers on the swords of our attackers. If we could overpower their arm strength we might succeed in turning their weapons against them like we had done in Italy against the Snaanads. My first thought was to work on the last two in the formation, thinking that if we succeeded with them the others might stop their advancement to see what was going on.

"Are you ready, Lilith?, I asked.

Ready, James! Let's do this!" Lilith answered as the Exhidihovads slowly inched closer.

Together we began to concentrate our telekinetic powers on the four swords being carried by the last two Exidihovads in the V formation. As it turned out, it was amazingly easy to rip the swords from their grasps and use two of the swords to decapitate those two and then we used the other two swords to decapitate the two in front of them. The leader of the group had now turned around and saw that his four comrades were lying on the ground dead and headless. When he turned back to face us, the Exidihovad leader of the group was only about five yards away and he let out the most blood-curdling scream I have ever heard and then charged toward Lilith and me with both swords slashing back and forth through the air. We had to think fast and Lilith made his feet fly backwards, thus making the eight foot tall creature slam face first onto the ground. His two swords went flying when he hit the ground and I rushed forward kicking one away from him and grabbing up the second one. I hadn't noticed, but Elder Saredem had followed me and grabbed the second sword and ran back to the other Elders. In the meantime, the Exidihovad lying on the ground had jumped up and before I could act he backhanded me and I went flying for about ten feet hitting the ground with a thud and losing my grip on the sword. He then rushed at me and started to grab up the sword I had dropped when Lilith brought the sword up from the ground with her telekinetic powers and ran it through his chest. The Exidihovad screamed in agony and then collapsed next to me jerking spasmodically until he gasped his final breath.

"Lilith, we did it!" I yelled while I was trying to get up.

"Yes, we did, James!" Lilith exclaimed while the three Elders were just standing there dumbfounded by the whole experience.

Lilith and I walked back over to where the three Elders were standing and I said, "Our little plan seems to have worked, at least on these five."

Elder Saredem was the first to speak and said, "That was a very frightening experience my young friends. I don't remember ever having witnessed such violence before."

"Yes, indeed," said Elder Retcarshac and Elder Cescasing in unison.

"I never thought that Voreshans would have to turn to such violence one day to protect our species," said Elder Saredem, "and I am sure that the older Elders feel the same way, but I am also sure that the other Elders are glad that you two are here to help us."

"My human nature," I said, "still comes out sometimes, especially when it comes to protecting those I care deeply about. Humans have always been a fairly violent species who seem to like the idea of fighting and war, but I only do it when necessary."

"If James, Elder Thegh, and I had not had to fight the Snaanads with such force back in Italy," Lilith interjected, "I don't think I would have been able to kill our enemies either. However, like James said, I will do whatever I have to do to protect those I care about."

"You two are remarkable creatures," said Elder Saredem. "I know from my conversations with Elder Thegh that he thought Voreshans would have to defend themselves one day in such a manner as this. Most of the Elders were skeptical about his prognostications, but if they were watching from the mansion what has just transpired, then I am sure they will have changed their minds."

"Well," I said, "I'm not sensing any more activity nearby from the Exidihovads, so maybe we should get back to the mansion and further refine our plans for the next encounter with them. We can deal with their disposal later."

"Good idea," Lilith said and we headed back to meet with the other Elders.

CHAPTER SIX

When the five of us entered the mansion through the back door we encountered a boisterous and cheering group of Elders who hoisted Lilith and me onto their shoulders and paraded us around the large dining room for several minutes. Fortunately, the ceilings were about fifteen feet high. When we were returned to our feet Elder Sermeda quieted the group and said, "That was an extraordinary exhibition of swordsmanship!" and he actually chuckled which was followed by a few laughs from the other Elders. "Forgive me for finding humor in the slaying of other beings, but I now know that Elder Thegh was right when he warned us that we would have to defend ourselves to the death against evils that were looming on the horizon. However my young friends, I am not sure that other Voreshans have it in them to either physically fight or especially kill other beings."

"Elder Sermeda," I interrupted, "Lilith and I don't expect the Elders, and especially not other Voreshans, to change what they believe and feel overnight, but I agree with what Elder Thegh predicted. Lilith and I are willing to fight to defend ourselves and the Voreshan species, but we have no intention of fighting all of the battles. After all, we do have a quiet peaceful life to live for the most part."

"Yes," Lilith continued, "I think that James and I can handle the current situation here in Sarasota and protect the Elders from any more harm, but it is going to take a combined effort on the part of all Voreshans to defeat the enemies that may come in the future. James and I believe that these Exidihovad warriors have somehow been programmed or had their upper brains neutralized, if you will, to carry out this attack against Voreshans until the last one of us is dead."

"If Lilith and I can battle the Exidihovads here in Sarasota a few at a time," I continued, "I am sure that we can defeat them, even though we may at some point have to actually pick up weapons to use against them in hand to hand combat, which, by the way, I do not look forward to. But there may come a day when all Voreshans will have to become warriors."

"Of course," Lilith put in, "James and I don't want to have to do that and hope that our telekinetic powers are sufficient in dealing with the Exidihovads. These creatures are accomplished swordsmen and I'm not sure that James and I could win in a face to face sword fight."

"When Lilith and I were fighting the Snaanads in Italy, we were able to make them turn their guns on each other," I said, "but we can't use guns here because of the attention gunfire would attract. So, that may mean doing hand-to-hand combat at some point."

"Maybe we could lure the creatures to a remote area of the desert," Elder Saredem suggested.

"I think that would be far too risky," I said. "For all of you to pack up and leave would make you easy targets along the way, even if the Exidihovads had to kill you one at a time. For now, I think you should all stay here until the battle here has been won."

"That is a very good point, James," Elder Sermeda added. "The loss of just one Elder has sent a shockwave through the Voreshan community here on Earth, not to mention what it would do on our home planet of Voresha.

We certainly don't want panic running through the Voreshan communities."

Elder Sermeda hesitated for a few seconds to see if there was any reaction from either Lilith or me when he mentioned the planet Voresha. Elder Saredem jerked his head toward us immediately to see if we were going to say something about this, but seemed relieved when we acted like we hadn't even heard what Elder Sermeda said.

Not pursuing the topic of sending Lilith and me off to the planet Voresha to fight the battle there, Elder Sermeda continued with the current plan here in Sarasota. "I think it would be wise for all of the Elders to remain here in this facility as well and not venture out until this enemy has been defeated by James and Lilith," he said to the group of Elders.

"Does that mean none of us can go out with James and Lilith to help them?" Elder Cescasing asked. "No disrespect, Elder Sermeda, but some of us are ready to fight this battle alongside Lilith and James."

"I am open to the idea of a few of the younger Elders helping out our young friends as is needed," answered Elder Sermeda, "and I admire your bravery. However, I am not too thrilled with the idea of being blamed for sending you to your deaths if that were to happen. But, if you must, you must."

"Elder Sermeda," Lilith said, "James and I don't expect any of you to risk your lives for this cause, but if a few of the younger Elders are willing to go out with us to help draw out the Exidihovads it should make our task much easier. And, if that means helping in the actual fighting, then we will take all the help we can get."

"Yes," I said, "if Lilith and I have to search out the Exidihovads it might take much longer and they might divide into smaller groups or even as individuals to seek out Voreshans wherever they find them and kill them. Even though we believe that all of those who came to Earth are here in Sarasota to kill off the Voreshan Elders as a plot to dishearten the rest of the Voreshan species, their primary purpose is simply to kill Voreshans. Any Voreshan! Anywhere!"

"You and Lilith are wise far beyond your years," said Elder Sermeda. "All of the Elders are at your command and we will do our best to help you as we can, but please be patient with those of us who are not yet sure about all of this killing. Please don't think less of those of us who can't bring ourselves to fight like you do."

"You will also have to be patient with us," I said and Lilith gave me a nudge with her elbow to indicate that I had no right to tell Elders what to do.

Chuckling a little, Elder Sermeda responded, "Lilith, your young man is not only brave and dedicated to you like I have never seen in a former human, but his sassiness is somewhat unprecedented as a Voreshan."

"I apologize for him," Lilith said.

"No apology necessary, Lilith," Elder Sermeda replied. "If the two of you can save our species from extinction, then I am comfortable with all of James' quirks."

"He does have a few quirks," Lilith said while trying not to giggle.

"Not to ruin this little party at my expense," I said, "but we really need to make some more plans where the Exidihovads are concerned."

"You are absolutely right, James," Elder Sermeda said. "Where do you think we should go from here?"

"Well, sir," I began, "Lilith and I believe that what we just did in drawing out the five Exidihovads will not work for long, even if they aren't supposed to be the brightest bulbs in the pack. We are also concerned as to whether or not the other Exidihovads witnessed what just happened out in the back of the mansion. If they did, then they may try to eliminate us before trying to kill off more Elders. They might even try to sneak into the mansion at night and kill as many of you as possible."

"What would you propose then instead of your first plan of attack?" asked Elder Saredem.

"Lilith has a good idea as to how we might both find out if we are now specific targets or if the remaining Exidihovads think that the Elders killed off their comrades," I said. "Lilith, why don't you explain your idea to the Elders?"

"Ok, James," Lilith said. "Elder Sermeda, everyone else, here's what I was thinking. If James and I go out tomorrow alone and the Exidihovads don't attack us, it may mean that they aren't yet interested in regular Voreshans, but only want to concentrate on Elders for now. That might provide James and me the opportunity to go into the surrounding woods and do some exploring. If we do that, then maybe we could weed out a few more."

"That presents several questions for me," said Elder Sermeda. "What if a small group of Exidihovads ambush you and James in the woods and while they have you occupied the rest attack the mansion and kill all of us.?"

"Want to tackle that one, James?" Lilith asked me.

"Well, Elder Sermeda," I started as I was trying to quickly think of a good answer. "You indicated at one point that you believed there were only about 100 Exidihovads who had been sent here to destroy the Voreshan population on Earth. Is that correct?"

"That is as accurate an estimate as we have, James," Elder Sermeda replied. "I have not heard anything to the contrary."

"Then, let's just say that it was exactly 100 Exidihovads that came to Earth," I continued. "That being the case, and if the other Exidihovads saw what happened today to their five friends, then I would guess that they would think they needed at least ten or twelve to do battle with Lilith and me. That would leave 80 to 85 to attack the mansion, so they would be outnumbered by Elders."

"My dear young friend," Elder Sermeda said, "do not forget that most of us are not inclined to physical confrontation, nor do we want to be."

"Well, sir," I said, "forgive me if I am being disrespectful, but if the Exidihovads are to be defeated it is probably going to take more Voreshans than just Lilith and me to do the job. You and the other Elders are going to have to rethink your priorities if Lilith and I don't survive our battle with the Exidihovads at some point." Turning to face the entire group of Elders I continued saying, "Even if Lilith and I do manage to stay alive and uninjured, there may come a point where all of you will have to defend yourselves against this enemy. All of you have superior telekinetic powers and you should be able to successfully do battle on a one-to-one basis. You witnessed a little while ago how to do that. If you don't have an attitude adjustment about killing these creatures that have come to kill you, then many of you will probably die. This enemy doesn't take prisoners! They are solely programmed to kill Voreshans at all costs and seem intent on killing off Elders first!"

Communicating with me telepathically, Lilith said, *"Wow, James! That was some speech!"*

"Well, well, well, my young friend," Elder Sermeda said with a very serious and somewhat frightening tone to his voice, "if I did not respect you so highly, as I did Elder Thegh whom I had the highest respect for, I would have you banished to an unknown and remote cave in the Byrranga Mountains in Russia for your insolence!" At that statement all of the other Elders gasped. "But because I do respect you and Lilith so much, and because I would not do that to Lilith who loves you so much, I am going to overlook your insolence, at least for now. I am calling a meeting of all of the Elders this evening and we will decide as a group how we will go about this situation and if your insolence deserves some kind of punishment. If there is a majority vote to support your idea, then we will begin tomorrow to train both our minds and our bodies for self defense and any among us who refuses will be removed from the ranks of Voreshan Elders forever!"

"No offense, Elder Sermeda," Lilith said, "but that seems a little drastic to me."

"It is the way it will be," replied Elder Sermeda. "However, you and James have been charged with fighting this foe to the death and you will continue to do so, because you are not afraid to kill your enemies when it is necessary. Also, unless you want to join your husband with being charged with insolence, you will learn to watch how you address the Elders!"

"Yes, sir," Lilith and I responded in our familiar two-part harmony.

"That did not sound too convincing. You are now to go to your quarters and get some rest from your trying activities today," Elder Sermeda instructed us. "You will not eavesdrop on our conversation tonight either. Is that clear?"

"Yes, sir," Lilith and I once again responded together and we left the Elders side of the mansion and went back to our side.

When we were back in our bedroom, Lilith said, "James, I don't know whether to kiss you or kick your ass for standing up to Elder Sermeda like that!"

"Quite frankly, Lilith," I replied, "I would prefer the kiss, but probably deserve the kick more. However, I refuse to continue this battle for the Voreshan race or any other race if it means our imminent death. I'm not afraid to do battle for a good cause, but when it comes to you and me, I'll pack up and head off in the opposite direction!"

"Well, my dear," Lilith said, "you have more balls than a mongoose attacking a cobra!"

"Really?" I said. "How many balls does a mongoose have?"

Grinning from ear to ear, Lilith pushed me down on the bed and climbed on top. Sitting on my chest, she brought her face close to mine and with as serious a look as she could muster said, "I don't know about a mongoose, but you've got all I need."

Laughing, I rolled Lilith over and began kissing her passionately and you can guess the rest. You know, dessert before dinner.

CHAPTER SEVEN

Lilith and I had our own kitchen at our end of the mansion and had fixed our own meals so far, which was fine by us. We knew that the Elders were somewhat of an elitist group and only when being visited by one or two at a time did we ever dine with them. We didn't hear anymore from the Elders that evening, but Elder Saredem informed us that they met into the early morning hours when he came to collect us around 9:00 the next morning. He literally marched us over to the Elders side of the mansion and said that he was forbidden, for fear of being banished, from telling us what had taken place the night before when the Elders were meeting. All he would say was that Elder Sermeda wanted to meet with us privately to discuss what the next step was going to be in dealing with the Exidihovads. Lilith and I just held hands and followed Elder Saredem like obedient little soldiers and giving each other concerned glances. We had discussed during the night the sudden change in Elder Sermeda's attitude and wondered what he was up to. He was certainly not being as compassionate as Elder Thegh would have been with us. When we arrived at Elder Sermedas' door, Elder Saredem knocked and announced our arrival. A few minutes passed, which seemed like a few hours, and then a rough sounding voice from within the room told Lilith and me to enter and close the door behind us. That should have been our first clue that something was awry, but we were both so anxious about this private meeting with Elder Sermeda that we didn't give it a second thought at that particular moment. After we had entered the room and closed the door, we heard Elder Saredem moving quickly down the hall away from the room and that made us doubly suspicious about what plans were in store for us. Had he been instructed by Elder Sermeda to immediately leave the area or was something else afoot? Hopefully, he and some of the other Elders were on our side.

Elder Sermeda's quarters were more spacious than the other Elders' and Lilith and I found ourselves standing in what appeared to be a large sitting room, but we didn't see Elder Sermeda anywhere. "Elder Sermeda," I said rather loudly, "Lilith and I are here for our meeting. Come out, come out wherever you are," I said trying to lighten up the situation.

Giving me a little punch in the arm, Lilith communicated silently, *"This is not the time to be funny, James!"*

"Sorry," I replied.

At that moment the odd sounding voice we had heard before entering the room spoke up again from the adjoining room saying in a somewhat angry voice, "There are chairs out there, so sit down now! I communicate from here!"

Trading glances, Lilith and I were now starting to get more than a little suspicious. Lilith spoke up and asked, "Are you feeling well, Elder Sermeda? You don't sound like yourself."

Making what sounded like a few fake coughs, the voice in the other room said, "No, I am not well at all. That is why I am not coming out there to talk with you. I do not want you to become sick."

"Are we here to find out what the Elders decided last night about how to go about fighting the Exidihovads or what to do with me?" I asked. "Again, I apologize for being so disrespectful."

"Yes, that is exactly why you are here," the voice replied. "Your Elders and me have decided to make peace with your kind and want you two to leave Sarasota as soon as possible."

Quickly communicating telepathically with Lilith, I said *"I find several things wrong with that sentence, Lilith."*

"Me, too, James," Lilith said. *"He should have said 'The Elders and I' and I know we aren't making peace with the Exidihovads and he referred to us as 'your kind', besides telling us to leave Sarasota!"*

"Bingo, my love!" I replied. *"I'm going to try to communicate telepathically with whoever is in the other room."*

"Great idea, James!" Lilith said.

"Elder Sermeda," I began, *"What kind of illness do you have? Should we try to call in a doctor to check you out?"*

There was no response from the other room initially and then after a couple of minutes the voice said, "Are you still there? I have not received a reply from you yet. You must leave Sarasota now!"

"That is not Elder Semeda!" I said to Lilith.

"You've got that right, James!" Lilith said. *"What do you think we should do now?"*

"I think we should try to contact Elder Sermeda," I answered.

"Good idea," Lilith replied. *"I'll give it a try. Elder Sermeda, if you can hear me please respond."*

The only response we got was a very impatient sounding voice from the other room. "You must answer me now!" the voice exclaimed loudly. "My patience wears thin!"

"Oh, we're here whoever or whatever you are and we're coming in there to face you," I said.

"You must not enter this room!" boomed the voice. "It is forbidden!"

"Are you ready, Lilith?" I asked.

"Ready as I will ever be," she replied.

'Well then, let's get in there and take care of business!" I said.

"You cannot enter!" the voice said even louder.

"Too late," I yelled back, "we're coming in!" and Lilith and I cautiously approached the doorway leading into the other room. As we got to the door, however, it slammed in our faces and we heard heavy footsteps pounding across the room and then we heard what sounded like a crash and glass breaking. Using our telekinetic powers we unlocked the door and rushed into the room slamming the door against the wall, nearly tearing it from its hinges. We immediately saw that the window and part of the wall had been broken through and a tall, lanky figure was running across the yard toward the woods. Looking around quickly, I saw two feet sticking out from behind the bed and yelled for Lilith to try and stop the escaping Exidihovad. While I ran over to see if the feet belonged to Elder Sermeda, Lilith concentrated her telekinetic powers on the Exidihovad running away from the mansion and caused him to put one big foot in front of the other and trip himself up. He went sprawling on the ground face first and then jumped up roaring loud enough to be heard in Miami. He then pulled out both of his swords and started running back toward the mansion, but Lilith immediately went to work on him and made him commit double seppuku in mid-stride. The Exidihovad went crashing face first to the ground with the blades of both swords sticking out of his back.

Lilith then turned to where I was standing and looked at me with that question on her face about the body lying behind the bed. "It's Elder Sermeda," I said.

"Is he dead?" Lilith asked.

"I'm afraid so, Lilith," I answered. "He has been cut in half and decapitated.

"Oh my God!" Lilith exclaimed. "These creatures are so barbaric!"

About that time we heard numerous footsteps approaching down the hallway and we hurried over to see if it was more Exidihovads, but were relieved to see several Elders headed our way led by Elder Saredem. As they got to Elder Sermeda's room, Elder Saredem said, "I knew something was wrong, so I rushed to get help. We hurried as fast as we could. The other Elders are not far behind us. What has happened here James?"

"I'm afraid that Elder Sermeda has been killed by one of the Exidihovads," I said, "but Lilith has disposed of the creature out in the yard as he was running away."

"Elder Sermeda is dead?" Elder Saredem said more than asked. "Oh my God! Whatever shall we do now? Who is to lead us now? Oh my God! Oh dear, what are we to do?"

"He must have already been dead when you brought us to his room a few minutes ago," Lilith responded trying to calm down Elder Saredem. "The Exidihovad crashed through the window and wall trying to escape when he realized that we had figured out that he wasn't Elder Sermeda. James found Elder Sermeda behind the bed, but he had been cut in half and decapitated."

"Oh my God!" said Elder Saredem again.

Elder Cescasing stepped forward and addressed the group of Elders who were gathering in the hallway, "The killing of our highest Elder was probably meant to discourage us from fighting these awful creatures, but we need to learn to fight back, and if necessary kill these beasts, more so now than ever! With the leadership of James and Lilith I believe that we can come together and defeat this enemy that is trying to eliminate our species! Are you with James and Lilith against the Exidihovads?"

A cheer arose from the entire group, except for Elder Saredem, who stepped up and tried to calm the group down, but who was also still acting very disturbed about the murder of Elder Sermeda. After about two minutes of excited cheering and talking among themselves, the other Elders quieted down to hear what Elder Saredem had to say. "You were all . . . uh, at our very long meeting . . . uh, last night and most of us, uh, voted with Elder Sermeda not to get physically involved in this battle. If Elder Sermeda were still alive he would . . . uh, be telling James and Lilith that their orders were to take the battle to the Exidihovads alone and, uh, when they had defeated those on Earth they would . . . uh, then travel to Voresha to fight the battle there."

"That was before one of the Exidihovads crept into our presence and killed Elder Sermeda!" exclaimed Elder Cescasing. "If I read your cheering correctly my fellow Elders for our cause to help James and Lilith in this battle, then cheer again!" and the roar went up once more.

"I demand that Elder Sermeda's orders be carried out!" yelled Elder Saredem, now seeming to be composed. "We struck a deal with the Exidihovads that the Elders would not fight them, but that we would send these two out as our warriors against them!"

"You did what?" Exclaimed Elder Retcarshac. "You had no right to do that without consulting all of the Elders!"

"For your information," Elder Saredem replied, "Elder Sermeda and I came to this conclusion after the rest of you refused to see things our way. We will do as Elder Sermeda has ordered!" and he stomped his foot down to emphasize this point. "He put me in charge in the event of his death and Lilith and James will do as I say!"

The hallway was silent for a few seconds and then Elder Retcarshac said, "It is obvious that Elder Saredem, like Elder Sermeda, is a coward and wishes to be enslaved by the Exidihovads and to serve them while letting his species be killed off one at a time. These two are traitors to our species! In addition, it seems a little too suspicious to me that Elder Sermeda would put Elder Saredem in charge without consulting the rest of us. If any of you are with Elder Saredem, then let him step forward and stand next to this traitor to our people."

No one moved and Elder Saredem took a couple of steps back into the room that had served as Elder Sermeda's quarters glancing around quickly to determine where the Exidihovad had escaped. Elder Saredem then sprinted for the opening in the wall and jumped through it and out into the yard at a full gallop. He immediately turned toward the woods running as fast as he could.

"After him!" yelled Elder Cescasing to the other Elders and half of the Elders headed for the back entrance to the mansion and the other half scurried past Lilith and me and went through the wall opening left by the Exidihovad.

"Should we follow them, James?" Lilith asked as we stood there rather dumbfounded by what had just occurred.

"Well, Lilith," I said, "I think we should at least watch and see what happens out there," and we moved to the opening in the wall to witness the spectacle of the Elders chasing another Elder. This event certainly had to be unprecedented in Voreshan history.

The Elders were closing in on Elder Saredem from several sides as he was getting closer to the woods when a sword came flying out of the woods end over end and slashed into Elder Saredem's chest, pinning him to the ground like a bug in a display case. All of the other Elders came to an abrupt halt and looked toward the woods where the sword seemingly flew out on its own. They stood there for a few seconds, no doubt waiting for the onrush of dozens of Exidihovads to emerge from the woods with their swords waving. However, everything was suddenly and eerily quiet. The Elders stood there for a few more minutes, prepared to do battle barehanded if necessary, but nothing happened and the Elders started slowly backing away from the scene of Elder Saredem's demise.

"This looks a little suspicious to me, Lilith," I said.

"It does, James," she replied. "I wonder if the Exidihovads are planning a new strategy to deal with this many Elders at once or if they are so confused by all of this that they don't know what to do?"

"I'd go with number two," I said. "I don't think they are smart enough to come up with a new plan so quickly and I would bet that they are almost as dumbfounded as us." I then yelled out to the Elders to come on back in for now and we would figure out a new plan of attack. I didn't want the Exidihovads to think that we were backing down, but that we had other ideas as to how to deal with them. "We'll deal with the rest of our enemy later," I yelled as loud as I could hoping some of the Exidihovads heard me.

When the Elders had all returned we assembled quickly in the large dining room where Elder Retcarshac spoke first, "James, Why do you think the Exidihovads killed Elder Sermeda and Elder Saredem if they were siding with the Exidihovads?"

"Lilith and I can only speculate on that," I answered, "but my guess is that it was only a ploy to get close enough to kill Elder Sermeda and then get Elder Saredem to convince the rest of you to essentially surrender to the Exidihovads. As disappointing as it is, I suppose that Elder Sermeda and Elder Saredem both thought their lives would be spared if they turned against their own kind."

"And then they would have killed all of us, too," Elder Cescasing said.

"I'm sure that was their plan," Lilith said. "Their next step after that, no doubt, would be to hunt for other Voreshans on Earth as well and eliminate them a few at a time."

"Well, I believe that the rest of the Elders are ready to follow the two of you into battle if that is what it takes," said Elder Cescasing and a cheer once again went up from the group of Elders. "First, however, I think that the Elders need to have a discussion about who becomes the next Head Elder. It is important to all of the Elders, as well as all Voreshans, that we have a leader."

"I second that," Elder Retcarshac said. "Maybe we should have some nominations from the group and then vote."

Another older Elder stepped forward then and addressed Lilith and me, "I know that you cannot remember all of our names, my young friends, but my name is Elder Murthan Nomrah Volier."

"We do remember you Elder Volier," Lilith said. "James and I are pretty good at remembering names."

"Well," I interjected, "at least Lilith is good at remembering names, but I do remember you Elder Volier."

"You are both very kind and I might add, very brave," Elder Volier said. "First, I want you to know that even the older more conservative Elders are now with you two in this matter. It is what we all decided last night. Secondly, and I am not trying to inject myself into the Head Elder position, but Elder law has always been for the next oldest Elder to become the Head Elder at the demise of the current leader. That would in this case be me."

"Elder Volier is correct in what he says," Elder Retcarshac said. "I think some of the younger Elders sometimes forget that there are long established laws that we abide by. I do not have a problem with Elder Volier taking over. Does anyone of you oppose this idea?"

Elder Volier spoke up quickly saying, "I did not bring this law up to put myself in that position, quite the contrary. I brought it up for discussion among the current Elders. Quite frankly, I do not believe that I am the right Voreshan Elder to take this important position. I believe that old men like myself have ruled our species for too long with outdated ideas and that we need some younger Voreshan blood to lead us forward both into the future and, for now at least, into this battle against the Exidihovads."

"Do any of you who stand closely in line to be the Head Elder oppose this idea?" Elder Cescasing asked. "It is not that I disagree with Elder Volier, but it does seem out of character for the Elders to take such a position."

For a few moments there was silence in the room except for the low mumblings between a few of the older Elders. Then another older Elder stepped forward and said, "I am Elder Jamor Siebes Semnag, my young friends, and I would indeed be in line for this position. However, like Elder Volier, I am not too anxious to make this move either and I think that Elder Volier's idea has been a long time coming. Being one of the older Elders, I would like to move that Elder Volier's idea be adopted and that we then decide on a new and younger leader."

There were several seconds from the group of Elders and then Elder Cescasing said, "How would the Elders like to go about making this unprecedented selection of a younger Elder to lead all Voreshans? Should there be nominations and voting or should the older Elders make the decision?"

"Well," said Elder Volier, "it seems that two obvious choices would be either you, Elder Cescasing, or Elder Ratcarshac since you both have been brave enough to volunteer to help James and Lilith do battle against our current enemy. In addition, you have the knowledge about the ways of Elders and their mission to lead our species."

"I am very honored to be mentioned for this important duty," said Elder Retcarshac, "but showing a little pseudo bravery is by no means the only qualification for someone to lead the Voreshan species into the future and most Voreshans, Elders and others alike, know the mission of the Elders. I would be lying if I said that becoming a future leader of the Elders hasn't crossed my mind, but I do not believe that I am anywhere near moving into that position. I think I would be more afraid of doing that than facing an army of Exidihovads!"

"I am sure that we all appreciate your honesty, Elder Retcarshac," said Elder Volier. "Elder Cescasing, would you be willing to accept this position?"

"As tempting as it is, Elder Volier, I am afraid that I am in the same boat with my close friend Elder Retcarshac," Elder Cescasing replied. "It takes far more than a little bravery to be the Head Elder. I believe that one needs much more knowledge of the human world and more common sense than most of us combined to move into this important position, something that Elder Thegh had and demonstrated often. After all, we are talking about someone who is a real leader and who would defend our species to the bitter end if necessary, not only to keep order among our kind, but to defend us against all enemies who might try to harm us. We also need someone who will inspire and lead us to continue our ancient purpose of doing good here on Earth. I also think that there are maybe too many Elders and that most of us who are Elders have found ourselves in a somewhat elitist position. Elder Thegh was a great Elder leader, but he was also brave and the friend to all Voreshans."

"This is becoming a more difficult decision than I had imagined," said Elder Volier. "I am not sure that there is anyone among us who could meet all of these things that you speak of, Elder Cescasing. There certainly is no one among us who can live up to the legacy of Elder Thegh. At the same time, however, it is very important to our species that we have one great leader to inspire and defend us as you say."

Elder Semnag spoke up then saying, "I was great friends with Elder Thegh and even in his advanced years I would have gladly accepted him as our new leader. Neither do I know of any one among us who meets the qualifications you have put before us, Elder Cescasing, but Elder Thegh would have met those qualifications."

"That certainly goes without saying," agreed Elder Volier and many other Elders voiced their agreement. "But, my dear friend, Elder Thegh is no longer with us and thus we still have the same dilemma."

"Well," Elder Semnag began, "I would agree with you except for a couple of things."

"What would those be?" asked Elder Volier.

"First," replied Elder Semnag, " we have all agreed on an unprecedented idea that we need younger blood to lead us and, secondly, there is someone among us right now who could take on this tremendous job."

Knowing our place in such an important meeting of the Elders, Lilith and I were honored that we had not been asked to leave, so we continued to stay to one side and as unnoticed as possible, but listening intently. During all of this conversation among the Elders, Lilith and I had been communicating telepathically as to how much unprecedented change was taking place right there in the dining room of this mansion in Sarasota, Florida, all because of the invasion of Earth by Exidihovads. We agreed that the death of Elder Sermeda and Elder Saredem was tragic, but that Voreshans didn't need leaders who would sell them out at the drop of a hat. At this point of the conversation among the Elders we were wondering which one was going to be asked to take over Elder Sermeda's position as the Head Elder and hoped that there were no more traitors among the Elders.

"Please," Elder Volier began, "who do you think is among us who would meet all of these qualifications that have been presented by Elder Cescasing? No one has come forward to claim this position."

"Are we agreed about moving forward in an unprecedented way where we will not only become fighters to protect our species, but that we will appoint a younger individual to be Head Elder?" replied Elder Semnag.

Elder Volier turned to the group of Elders and said, "Are we all in agreement with this statement?"

A unanimous "aye" went up from the group of Elders.

"Then, who do you say can lead the Voreshan people forward from here, Elder Semnag?" asked Elder Volier again.

Turning toward Lilith and me, Elder Semnag said, "Because of my trust in Elder Thegh and the fact that he believed we would someday be led by a female and because of the trust and respect he placed in the couple standing before you, I look to Lilith Lhuv Morgan as our new leader and with her mate, James Russell Morgan, by her side no one can stand against them!"

CHAPTER EIGHT

To say that the events of the day had been shocking thus far would have been the understatement of the past 50 plus years that Lilith and I had been alive, but this announcement by Elder Semnag shocked Lilith and me so much that for a few moments we were both speechless. After the roar of cheers from the Elders had subsided, they all stood there staring at Lilith and me and waiting for some sort of response. Lilith looking over at me only produced a shrug of my shoulders, because for once I was totally speechless!

When she could finally utter something after a few more minutes had passed and while the Elders all waited very patiently, Lilith said, "Oh my God! I don't know what to say. I have only lived about one eighth of my life expectancy as a Voreshan and feel that I am far too young to even be an Elder, much less the Head Elder and leader of my species. James, help me out here and say something. How do you feel about this revelation?"

"I honestly don't know where to begin or what to feel," I said. "I thought that becoming a Voreshan and marrying the most beautiful woman in the universe would be the highlights of my life. Especially the latter. The Elders have been so supportive of Lilith and me by letting us attend art school and continue our lives together here in the place we love so much. You made it possible for us to travel to Italy and see so much of the art that we love, even though you sent some interesting challenges our way while we were there. The events of this day have been unbelievably shocking and now you present this great honor, not to mention tremendous challenge, to Lilith. I'm simply dumbfounded, surprised, and at the same time honored to be married to such a beautiful and highly respected woman! If Lilith decides to accept this position as Head Elder, I will promise all of you to be her obedient servant and guardian for the rest of our lives together. But, if Lilith declines your offer, I will stand by her in that decision as well."

"It is because of the hard challenges that the two of you have faced together and won," began Elder Semnag, "the tremendous trust and respect shown to you by Elder Thegh, and the things that we have witnessed you doing to protect both the Elders and the Voreshan people here on Earth that we make this request. As much as all of the Elders standing before you believe in our ancient charge to help humans to be better people and as much as we love all Voreshans and would do what we could to protect all of our species, none of us could have fought and shown the courage and determination to defend us like you two have done. I would be willing to guess that there is not one among all of the Elders who would have done any more than cower with fear in the face of the things the two of you faced in Italy many years ago. We cannot force Lilith to become the Head Elder, and it is an unprecedented move on our part, but I am sure that Lilith will be well received by all Voreshans, both here and back on our home planet. I think I speak for all the Elders, especially those of us gathered here today, when I say that we would not make this request if we were not quite serious about doing so. We hope, at the very least, that Lilith will accept our invitation to become an Elder, if not our great leader."

"James and I both have the highest respect and trust in all of the Elders," Lilith said, "and you cannot know how honored and privileged I feel right now. I would be a liar if I told you that the thought of being an Elder someday hadn't crossed my mind on occasion, probably because one time Elder Thegh mentioned it as a possibility someday. To be chosen for this honor by the wisest men in the universe and to be placed above all of you is so mindboggling. I do not feel that I deserve such an honor. James and I have only done what we have been charged with doing and have only defended our friends and species because of our love and respect for them."

"I would beg to differ with you about deserving such an honor, my dearest Lilith," I put in. "I have always known, from the first time we met, that you were very, very special and when Elder Thegh indicated that you might be the first female Elder someday I totally agreed. You know how much I care for you, Lilith, and I will now say before all of the Elders here that I will stand by your side and serve you and all Voreshans until my death separates us!"

"Once again, James," Lilith said, "you always say the right things. Elder Semnag, Elder Volier, and all Elders who stand before me now, I have never doubted that James is the truest, most loyal mate that any woman in the world, Voreshan or human, could ever imagine being with, and with the hope that I can live up to your expectations and with your promise that James can always be by my side and that we may continue to reside in Sarasota, I will accept your request."

The cheers from the Elders up to that point in time had been loud, but now those cheers were at least three times louder and went on for several minutes. When they finally calmed down, Elder Semnag and Elder Volier stepped forward and addressed the group. Elder Semnag spoke first saying, "A new day has arrived in Voreshan history! With your approval and as representatives of all Elders world-wide, Elder Volier and I now pronounce Lilith Lhuv Morgan as the new Head Elder of all Voreshans and accept her conditions to serve in this important position!" And the cheers started again.

When the room was once again more quiet, Elder Volier said, "Lilith Lhuv Morgan, there is not a formal installation for this position, such as is done with presidents and the like, so being the oldest Elder here, I pronounce you Elder Lilith Lhuv Morgan, Head Elder of all Voreshans." and once again the cheers went up from the group of Elders.

I stood there in silence listening to all of this and being so very, very proud of Lilith. If only my parents could have known that our family name had become so important to this great species of people they might have been proud, too. Of course, they never knew that I had become a Voreshan back in 1967, or that I had married a woman whose ancestors were from another planet. Nevertheless, I think that they would still have been proud of both of us. I knew that Lilith's parents were going to be so proud of their daughter and how highly respected she was among the Elders.

"I guess that my first duty as Head Elder would be to discuss with all of you what you think we should do next against the Exidihovads," Lilith said when calm had been restored. "Whether as Head Elder or not, James and I were asked to help you fight this horrible enemy and that is still our first concern right now."

"We are all ears, to use a human expression," said Elder Cescasing. "We will do whatever you decide and whatever you charge us with doing to help you."

"Things happened so fast today that James and I have not had a chance to discuss what the next step might be," Lilith said, "however, we do believe that the Exidihovads are somewhat confused right now. Their plan to infiltrate our ranks and get one or two Elders to try and get all of you to surrender to them has failed and now they are probably doing the same thing as us and trying to figure out what to do next. I don't believe that they will attack us anymore today, but their simple lower brains aren't designed to spend too much time making plans, so I think they will probably attack in one way or another tomorrow."

"Do you think they will all come out tomorrow and attack us here in the mansion?" asked Elder Retcarshac. "Without weapons, this old structure might not be a very good defense against these creatures."

"James, what are your thoughts on that?" Lilith asked me.

"So far, they have either attacked us on an individual basis or at most five at a time," I said. "Lilith and I haven't seen any evidence that they would attack en masse. I think, however, that we might be able to surprise them if we were to attack them en masse."

"That plan would sound like a good one if the Elders were more experienced in fighting," Elder Volier said.

"That is why all of you need to start honing up on your telekinetic powers," I said, "and, if necessary, convince yourselves that you might have to actually pick up a sword and chop off the head of your enemies. You have witnessed how Lilith and I used our telekinetic powers to take their weapons away from them and use their own swords to kill them. As much as you have always been against such horrible violence against other beings, it will always be necessary to defend yourselves against your enemies, even if it means having to kill others to survive. Creatures like the Exidihovads can't be reasoned with or have their minds changed to be better."

"I may be an old man," said Elder Semnag, "but I will follow you and Lilith into this battle to guarantee that our species continues to survive here on Earth even if it means my death!" That statement was followed by assurances from the rest of the group that they would do the same.

"James is right," Lilith said. "I know that all of you have superior telepathic powers, but I don't know when you last practiced your telekinetic powers and I know from my own experience that it takes some practice to get back up to speed. It often takes both James and me together to perform our telekinetic activities, even if we aren't trying to kill our opponent."

"It might be a good idea for all of the Elders to pair up and learn to work together telekinetically," I put in. "All you have to do is agree on what you will do and then both work at the same thing."

"That is an excellent idea, James," Lilith said. "why don't all of you pair up and go off together somewhere in the mansion and practice your telekinetic powers while James and I continue to come up with our plan of attack. We will check back with you later."

After the rest of the Elders had left our presence, Lilith and I began to talk about our plan of action against the remaining Exidihovads. "James," Lilith began, "I think that you and I should do a little reconnaissance out in the woods to see how the Exidihovads are organized. We need to know if they are planning to attack en masse, as you put it, or if their plan is to continue to approach us a few at a time."

"I totally agree, Lilith," I responded. "I really don't think that all of the other Elders are going to be that much help when it comes right down to killing the Exidihovads. I am going to guess that the Exidihovads, having seen what has happened so far, will probably plan to attack en masse and may do so after dark."

"And I agree with that, James," Lilith said. "Maybe we can sneak out the front and then approach the woods from the street side or maybe even from the other side of the woods away from the mansion. If we can determine how they are organized, then maybe we can develop a good plan for ambushing them before they know what is happening. I do believe that the Elders will follow us and even if they don't participate in the battle it might scare the Exidihovads away."

About that time we heard the first of several vases crash to the floor in one of the other rooms. "You know, Lilith," I said, "it may be that we will end up having to deal with all of the Exidihovads by ourselves." Then there was another crash in another room.

"If that keeps up, James," Lilith said, "I think you may be right. Shall we get going on our reconnaissance?"

"You bet," I said and we slipped quietly out the front door of the mansion and walked nonchalantly down the street until we were just past the mansion's property line.

Along the way we did not sense any Exidihovad activity anywhere near us and when we got far enough along we approached the woods from the back corner closest to the street. When we got to the edge of the woods we noticed that the ground in the woods was covered with dried leaves. We realized that our footsteps would make a lot of noise when we entered the forest and Lilith communicated telepathically with me, *"We can't continue on foot like this, James, because they are bound to hear us walking on all of these dried up leaves."*

"I just realized that, Lilith," I said. *"Besides having a keen sense of smell, I'm sure their hearing is just as good. Do you have any ideas how we might be able to approach them so that they don't hear us?"*

"I do, James," Lilith answered, *"but I haven't tried this for a very long time. The last time I tried it was before we met back in high school."*

"What is it, Lilith?" I asked.

"I'm not sure that all Voreshans even realize that they can do it," Lilith said, *"but our telekinetic powers can be used to levitate ourselves and move us along without touching the ground."*

"No way!" I exclaimed. *"You've kept a secret like that from me for all of these years!"*

"Quite frankly, James," Lilith said, *"I haven't thought about the idea of personal levitation all of these years. I really don't think that the Elders could master the technique without a lot of trying and we probably don't have that much time before the Exidihovads attack. However, I do believe that our telekinetic powers are stronger than most Voreshans and that together we can do this."*

"You forget, my love," I said, *"that I'm not a true Voreshan. I don't know if my powers are that well developed."*

"From what I have seen over the years, James," Lilith said, *"your powers are far more developed than most Voreshnsa, including the Elders. We can do this, James. Just concentrate with me and let's see if we can levitate or not."*

Over the next few seconds we combined our mental powers and concentrated on levitating ourselves. After about 30 seconds I began to rise from the ground and move around about one foot above the ground. "Holy crap!" I exclaimed out loud and immediately fell back to the ground.

"James!" Lilith exclaimed silently. *"You must remain quiet and keep concentrating! If that happens in the woods the Exidihovads are bound to hear us!"*

"Yes, dear," I meekly responded.

Once again Lilith and I began to concentrate on levitating ourselves and learning how to successfully move about in any direction at will. We did this for about ten minutes and then thought that we could successfully move through the forest without being heard and hopefully not seen or smelled by the Exidihovads. As it turned out, it seemed to be exceptionally easy for us to maneuver around the trees and stay relatively out of sight. I led the way, not because I'm a chauvinist, but because in this situation I was in the position of protecting the Head Elder and would die doing just that if necessary. When we had gone about 100 yards into the forest, Lilith communicated silently with me to stop.

"I'm sure I just heard some voices somewhere nearby, James," Lilith said.

"I didn't hear them, Lilith," I responded. *"which direction do you think the voices were coming from?"*

"I think they sounded like they were off to our right," Lilith said. *"Let's move slowly in that direction."*

It hadn't occurred to me while Lilith and I were stopped that we were still levitating and that realization almost caused me to fall back to the ground. However, with Lilith's help I was able to regain the height above the ground at which we had been traveling through the woods and we headed off in the direction of the voices. After about another 25 yards, I also began to hear the voices that Lilith had heard and we moved even more slowly in their direction. We had gone about another 15 yards when the entire group of remaining Exidihovads came into view.

"There they are, James, Lilith said silently. *"Let's get just a little closer and see if we can hear what they are saying."*

"Follow me," I said and we moved a little closer. We came to a stop behind a large growth of bushes, but continued to float above the ground.

The large group of Exidihovads were gathered in a circle around one figure that we assumed to be the current leader of the group. He was a little hard to understand, but was speaking English as we caught the end of a statement, ". . . kill those evil, ugly Voreshans!"

"Kill them now!" shouted someone from the group.

"Not wait! Must kill before they come after us!" another one shouted.

"No!" the figure in the center of the circle shouted back. "We need plan! These beings are smart and have defeated our efforts so far!"

"Plan for weak warriors!" someone else shouted. "I say we attack big house now!"

"You are not leader!" the leader shouted back. "I am leader and you do as I say!"

"I wonder why they haven't smelled us," I said silently to Lilith as we hovered there behind the bushes.

"I bet that the one back at our house couldn't really smell us, James," Lilith said. *"I bet it was just a trick to get us to reveal ourselves as Voreshans to him."*

"Then their hearing might not be very good either," I suggested.

"That or they just always shout at each other," Lilith said.

About that time the Exidihovad who had last spoken to the leader stepped in the inner circle and said, "It time for new leader! I challenge you for that position!" and then he drew both of his swords and rushed at the Exidihovad leader.

Shouts arose from the entire group, but Lilith and I couldn't discern who was cheering for whom. The leader of the group stood his ground and within a split second as the challenger got to him, the leader drew one sword and ran it through the challenger's chest and he fell to the ground dead. "Does anyone else challenge the great Cleathmarb?" he shouted. All of the other Exidihovads took a step backwards indicating that they were satisfied with their current leader.

"Good!" said the great Cleathmarb. "Now we make plan for attack on horrible Voreshans in big house!

"Lilith," I began, *"what if we could pull all of their swords out of their scabbards at the same time and turn them against the Exidihovads?"*

"I don't think that even you and I together have that much telekinetic power, James," Lilith said. *"However, we might be able to do a few at a time making it look like they were turning on each other."*

"That just might work, Lilith," I said. *"If they are as stupid as we think they are, they probably wouldn't catch on to what was happening to them."*

"Let's try it on a few of them and see what happens, James," Lilith replied.

Lilith and I then began to concentrate our efforts on removing several of the Exidihovads' swords from their scabbards and then used them to kill the Exidihovad closest to them. Angry shouts went up from the group when they saw what had happened and then most of the Exidihovads starting pulling out their swords and started slashing away at each other. The Exidihovads were excellent swordsmen and thus this battle went on for about 30 minutes while Lilith and I watch in amazement at how easily they turned on one another. The leader of the group, the great Cleathmarb, however, had backed away from the melee and hid behind a tree to protect himself from all the slaughter taking place there in the woods. When the battle finally settled down some and the remaining Exidihovads looked around at all of their kind lying dead all around them and they all screamed and howled out loud enough to be heard by the Elders back at the mansion. Lilith and I counted only about 20 of the creatures still standing and some of them had received some pretty bad wounds. When they had quieted down, the great Cleathmarb stepped out from behind the tree where he was hiding and addressed the remaining Exidihovads. "My fellow warriors, we have obviously been tricked into killing each other and now we are only a few. Our great leader back on Voresha will not be happy when he hears about this!"

One of the remaining Exidihovads stepped toward the great Cleathmarb and said, "You are no warrior! You hid behind tree and did nothing to stop this horrible thing that we have just done! I believe you should die!"

Just as the great Cleathmarb was about to speak, another Exidihovad threw one of his swords at the leader splitting his skull in half down the middle and the great Cleathmarb fell dead to the ground. A great cheer went up from the remaining Exidihovads and when they had settled down they all sat down in a circle and began to discuss their strategy for dealing with the Voreshan Elders that were still alive in the "big house."

Lilith and I were still hiding behind the bushes, but we couldn't hear what the Exidihovads were saying because they were now communicating in lower voices. They all kept looking around suspiciously as if they now knew that someone was watching them and listening to their conversation. Lilith and I were still somewhat stunned by what we had instigated among the Exidihovads and hadn't communicated for some time now. I broke our silence saying telepathically, *"Lilith, that was unbelievable! I never imagined that they would all start fighting each other."*

"I know, James," Lilith replied. *"I was simply hoping that eight or ten of them might fight each other to the death, but what we just witnessed was way beyond my expectations of these creatures."*

"I think we should probably get back to the Elders as soon as possible and report on what has happened here," I suggested.

"You're right, James," Lilith said. *"If the Elders heard any of the Exidihovads commotion they might have decided to come out to see if we were ok."*

Lilith and I then floated away from the battle scene between the Exidihovads and headed back to the street near where we had entered the woods. As soon as we had exited the woods we set our feet back on the ground and began to walk back to the mansion double time and we weren't a minute too late.

CHAPTER NINE

The mansion was very quiet and seemed to be deserted when we walked through the front door, but then we heard some voices out in the back yard. Being cautious, we first went to a window and peeked out to make sure the voices weren't those of any of the Exidihovads. Although Lilith and I were pretty sure that we had seen all of the remaining Exidihovads in the woods, there wasn't any guarantee that there weren't more of them in the area than what we had originally thought. What we saw in the back yard of the mansion was all of the Elders gathering into a formation of lines that looked somewhat like a small Civil War regiment of soldiers preparing to march to their death. They started to march slowly toward the woods and Lilith and I quickly ran out to the back yard yelling for them to stop.

"Elder Morgan and James!" exclaimed Elder Cescasing. "We were sure that you were in terrible trouble from all the yelling and shouting that we heard coming from the woods! We tried to find you, but you weren't anywhere in the mansion and figured that you had gone out into the woods on your own. We were heading out to see what we could do to help you."

"There is no need for any of you to go into the woods to do battle with the Exidihovads," Lilith informed them. "James and I did sneak out and went out into the woods from the back side to do some reconnaissance. We have just come from there and we managed to actually cause the Exidihovads to turn on each other and begin fighting, thus the noises that you heard coming from the woods. When they finally stopped their fighting, there were only about 20 Exidihovads left alive and some of those were seriously wounded."

"Are you saying that you and James killed the other Exidihovads?" asked Elder Retcarshac.

"Not exactly," Lilith said. "All James and I did was to make a few of their swords come out of their scabbards and kill a few other Exidihovads. When that happened a melee began and all of the other Exidihovads began fighting and killing each other. When they finally realized what had happened and stopped, there were only about 20 of them left. When we left the forest the remaining Exidihovads were gathering close together to make plans for what they would do next."

"Elder Thegh had told us the stories of you two fighting together and how remarkable you were," said Elder Retcarshac. "What you have just told us reinforces all that Elder Thegh ever said about you."

"Yes," said Elder Cescasing, "but any doubts we had have certainly been changed. Elder Morgan, you are no doubt the right Voreshan to lead all Voreshans for the next three centuries!"

"Here, here!" arose from many of the Elders.

"The other Elders and I had a little discussion after we discovered that you and James had gone off on your own, Elder Morgan," Elder Volier said. "As I am sure that you know, when a Voreshan becomes an Elder, their common human name that they have adopted for living on Earth is changed to a more appropriate Voreshan name to indicate that one is an Elder."

Interrupting Elder Volier, Lilith said, "I do not want to change my name from what it is now. I would rather not be an Elder if I have to do that. Even though James crossed over to become Voreshan, I still married a former earth man and took his name as mine. I didn't make that as a condition of accepting my role as Head Elder, but that is how I feel about it."

"That will not be a problem, Elder Morgan," Elder Semnag said. "The Elders all know how you two feel about each other. We have also already agreed to several unprecedented changes in how we think and how we will operate into the future, so we decided to tell you that we are fine with you being known as Elder Morgan. Besides, that rule has always been applied to men because there has never been a female Elder, so the new rule for female Elders is that they can keep their human married names."

"Thank you for that support," Lilith said. "I think that we now need to meet and decide what our next move will be. I also request that James always be in on any meeting that takes place between myself and the Elders."

"That is certainly not a problem, Elder Morgan," Elder Volier said. "You are now our leader and we will do as you say. What did you have in mind for dealing with the remaining Exidihovads.?"

"I believe that the remaining Exidihovads are going to decide to operate either individually or maybe in pairs," Lilith said. "They may not be too bright, but they probably don't want to suffer such a great loss again like they have just experienced out in the woods. I believe that they are quite aware of having been duped. I think that all of the Elders should remain in the mansion and stay vigilant, because it seems they are quite sneaky and able to get into the mansion unnoticed, regardless of their enormous size. James and I will patrol the grounds during the daytime and ask that you all takes turns keeping a night watch. If the

Exidihovads decide to try a night attack, whoever is on watch can awaken James an me and we will do battle as is needed. What do you think, James?"

"I think that is a very good plan, Elder Morgan," I said, knowing that the other Elders expected the same title of respect to be used by all Voreshans, including me. "Even if the Exidihovads attack the mansion en masse, I believe that Elder Morgan and I can defend the rest of you against them and maybe even eliminate them completely."

"Then it shall be as you say, Elder Morgan," said Elder Semnag.

Lilith and I were expecting an attack by at least two or three of the Exidihovads at a time over the next couple of days, but much to our surprise, and the Elders surprise as well, there was no visible activity by the Exidihovads. Lilith and I had been keeping our daily patrol around the grounds of the mansion and several of the Elders were taking turns keeping watch all around the perimeter by night. On the third day after the battle in the woods, Lilith and I were walking near the woods and I communicated telepathically to her, *"Do you think we should go into the woods and see what the Exidihovads are up to, Lilith?"*

"I am a little reluctant to that, James," She replied, *"because they may have decided to wait us out and then ambush us when we enter the woods because we got tired of waiting for them to come out into the open.*

"That's a very good point, love," I said, *"but this waiting for something to happen is almost as bad as dealing with it when it does happen."*

"I actually feel the same way, James," Lilith said, *"but I would hate to have to put the Elders through the excruciating ordeal of having to select a new leader if I got killed in the process,"* and I noticed her grinning.

"You're right, as usual," I said. *"The Elders trying to figure out who was going to be the new Head Elder seemed almost worse than if they were being attacked by the Exidihovads!"* and we both chuckled a little at our private joke. *"I hope they aren't eavesdropping on our conversation."*

"That will never happen, James," Lilith said, *"or at least it shouldn't happen. Eavesdropping on either the telepathic or out loud private conversations of the Head Elder is almost as bad as trying to assassinate the Head Elder."*

"No way!" I exclaimed.

"Way, James," Lilith said. *"It is second of the three High Rules surrounding the Head Elders where all other Voreshans, including Elders, are concerned."*

"You would think that after being a Voreshan for the past 34 years I would have learned most of the Voreshan secrets," I said. *"Am I allowed to know about these three High Rules?"*

"Well, James," Lilith said, *"since I am the Head Elder, I think that it is perfectly ok for me to tell you about the three High Rules. Most Voreshans who have not been humans and made the crossover, learn these things at a very young age. Human crossovers are generally not told about these rules concerning the Head Elder, because in most cases they never meet or get close enough to the Head Elder to break the three High Rules. That has obviously changed with the election of a female Elder who is married to a former human."*

"Lilith, you know that I can be impatient sometimes and this is one of those times," I said.

"I know, James, Lilith said, *"but if you can be quiet for a few minutes and listen, I'll tell you about these three rules.* Lilith waited for a few seconds for me to say some-

thing else, but I kept my big trap shut for once. *"The first High Rule is that if anyone, Voreshan or human or other alien species, makes an attempt on the life of the Head Elder, even if it is an unsuccessful attempt, he or she will be hunted down, if not captured immediately, and beheaded without further ado. That is what should have happened to the Exidihovad who killed Elder Sermeda, but I guess a double seppuku was sufficient. The second High Rule says that it is forbidden for any Voreshan to eavesdrop, as you put it, on any private conversation of the Head Elder. If a Voreshan does this, he or she will be exiled to the remotest part of the planet for the rest of their life. That may sound a little bit drastic, but eavesdropping is a sign of disrespect and must be dealt with severely. The third High Rule says that no female or human crossover shall ever become an Elder."*

"Whoa, wait a minute," I said. *"Number one, I'm 99.99 percent sure that you are a female. Either that or I have a more vivid imagination that I thought I had. Number two, you have been unanimously selected to be the Head Elder by all of these Elders who are here in Sarasota right now!"*

"James, your sense of humor is one of the many things I love about you!" Lilith said. *"I am 100 percent female, as you well know, and this third High Rule has obviously been changed by the Elders gathered here."*

"Do they have the right to make such a drastic change to this edict that has no doubt been in place for thousands of years?" I asked my 100 percent female Head Elder.

"To my knowledge, James," Lilith answered, *"the murder of Elder Sermeda is the first time in our history that the other Elders have been put in this position. When an Elder is reaching the end of his life, he always picks the*

next Elder who will follow in his footsteps, so breaking the third High Rule, though unprecedented, was something that the current Elders believed had to be done. Even if the other Elders had decided to not make a female an Elder, much less the Head Elder, they would have had to break the rule to select a new Head Elder, since it has never been done this way before."

Lilith and I stopped close to the woods to listen intently for any sounds coming from the woods, besides those of nature. There seemed to be an unusual silence even from the birds and other creatures normally found scurrying around the woods. Continuing our telepathic communication, I said, *"Lilith, do you think we are being watched right now by the remaining Exidihovads? This is a very eerie silence."*

"I'm not sure, James," Lilith replied. *"If we are being watched, then I don't think we should get any closer until we have some idea as to what the Exidihovads are up to."*

"I don't mean to tell the Head Elder what to do," I said, *"but I think we should venture into the woods and if necessary confront the Exidihovads. It has been several days now without them trying anything and I'm getting a little nervous about that."*

"As always, James, your input is very valuable in this relationship," Lilith said. *"I wouldn't have it any other way, my love. Maybe we should go into the woods and get this business over with, maybe then the Elders will leave and we can get back to our relatively normal lives."*

"Should we do the levitating thing again, Lilith?" I asked.

"I think that would be a good idea, James," Lilith said and we began to slowly venture into the woods floating

about a foot off the ground to search for the remaining Exidihovads.

Lilith and I were being extra careful this time using the trees and bushes for cover as we carefully moved deeper into the woods. We hadn't gone very far when Lilith stopped and communicated silently to me, *"I think I should probably let the Elders know that we have left our patrol of the perimeter and for them to keep a close watch for any Exidihovads."*

"Good idea, Lilith," I said. *"That's why you're the leader."*

We continued to hover there for a few minutes while Lilith contacted Elder Cescasing about what we were up to and that the Elders should be on alert. When Lilith had finished her communication with Elder Cescasing, we continued our reconnaissance through the woods. Lilith and I had decided that we would move around the edges of the woods first in a circular pattern and gradually close the gap toward the center of the woods. This was simply a precautionary approach to ensure that none of the Exidihovads were on the fringes of the woods where they could sneak up on us from behind if we went straight into the woods. After about 45 minutes we had made our first pass around the perimeter of the woods and hadn't run into any of the enemy or heard anything from the Elders. Thinking now that the Exidihovads must be in the center of the woods trying to figure out a way to deal with Lilith and me, we made our way deeper and deeper in and still didn't see any Exidihovads.

Lilith and I had searched nearly every square inch of the woods and finally we found ourselves in the spot where the battle that killed so many of the enemy had taken place. There was plenty of evidence that a big battle had taken place in this spot, but there was no sign of any Exidihovads. The creatures had obviously cleaned up after the battle and disposed of their dead somewhere, hopefully not in our backyard. Lilith didn't think that was very funny at all. We stopped levitating and settled down on the ground for the first time since we ventured into the woods. However, I kept my communication silent and said, *"Lilith, do you think the Exidihovads have given up and gone away?"*

"That would be way too simple, James," Lilith said. *"You and I have never quite had it that easy. I don't know why there aren't any Exidihovads here in the woods, but the Elders haven't contacted us so I'm guessing that everything is ok back at the mansion."*

"Well, Lilith, we know that there aren't any Exidihovads in the woods," I said, *"so should we head on back to the mansion and report our findings?"*

"That and to make sure that all is ok there, too" replied Lilith and we headed back to the mansion, this time walking on solid ground with the crunching sound of dried leaves echoing around us.

As we approached the mansion Lilith and I were rather amused to see about half of the Elders surrounding the house and wielding big sticks that had obviously been cut from some of the trees on the grounds. When we walked up to Elder Cescasing, Lilith asked, :What's going on here, Elder Cescasing?"

"We all took your message to me very seriously, Elder Morgan," said Elder Cescasing, "and decided that the youngest Elders should take up positions surrounding the mansion and since we didn't have any other weapons we fashioned these out of branches from the trees."

"That was very brave of you to do," Lilith said, "but James and I are back to report that we did not find any

Exidihovads in the woods. Quite frankly, I am quite baffled by their disappearance."

"Do you think the Exidihovads have left Earth or just Sarasota?" Elder Retcarshac asked, who happened to be standing nearby and listening to the conversation.

"I am hoping that they have left Earth," Lilith replied, "but there is always the possibility that they have split up and are out searching for individual Voreshans to kill."

"Oh, my!" exclaimed Elder Cescasing. "What are you and James going to do now?"

"Well," Lilith said, "James and I discussed this matter on the way back from the woods and I have decided that you and the rest of the younger Elders will divide up into teams of two and search for the remaining Exidihovads."

"No disrespect, Elder Morgan," Elder Retcarshac said, "but do you think we are ready for such a dangerous mission?"

"You are going to have to be ready for this mission," Lilith answered, "and maybe even more similar missions if our species continues to be attacked by other species, either by those here on Earth or from other places in the universe. We now know that there are species that are hell bent on destroying us and as your Head Elder I have to make hard decisions like this. It is now up to the younger Elders to take over many of these battles for the sake of the species."

"You are right, of course, Elder Morgan," said Elder Cescasing. "Should we meet as soon as possible and decide who will go with whom and then begin our search?"

"I think that is a very good idea, Elder Cescasing," Lilith answered, and I don't think you should waste any more time. You have been sort of a leader for the other Elders and I am putting you in charge of this search for remaining

Exidihovads. I want you to report on your progress at least every three days, or more often if necessary."

"Thank you, Elder Morgan," Elder Cescasing replied. "I will get on it immediately," and he left our presence and started gathering the younger Elders together.

Lilith and I then went into the mansion and gathered all of the other Edlers together to make our report and to tell them what Lilith had decided about hunting down the remaining Exidihovads. Elder Volier spoke up and said, "This my young friend is why the Elders are glad that you are in charge. You and James are so much more experienced and even more advanced in your powers than any other Voreshan and we have placed our complete trust in your decisions. I think this is a very good plan, but I don't think that I would have been able to make such a difficult decision."

"You are far too kind, Elder Volier," Lilith said, "but James and I are thankful for your confidence in us and always promise to do what we think is in the best interest of our species."

"What would you like for all of the other Elders to do in this matter, Elder Morgan?" asked Elder Volier.

"I think that you should all divide up and go to all the places on Earth where other Voreshans reside," Lilith said, "and start spreading the word about the Exidihovads and that you have a new Head Elder. All Voreshans should be on guard and know that there new Head Elder is working to protect them as much as is possible."

"We will meet and decide who goes where and be on our way no later than tomorrow morning," said Elder Volier.

"Good," said Lilith. "In the meantime, James and I are going to get back to our home and business and will wait for updates from all of you. If any of you come across any Exidihovads, then you should be prepared to deal severely with them and let me know as soon as possible about that as well."

"It will be done, Elder Morgan," Elder Volier said and then he gathered the other Elders together to discuss their plans.

Lilith and I went back to our quarters and gathered our belongings together and headed back to our home feeling good about what we had accomplished where the Exidihovads were concerned. As we were packing, I asked Lilith, "Why do you think none of the Elders have brought up the idea about us traveling to Voresha to fight the Exidihovads there?"

"I don't know, James," Lilith said, "other than they have made me Head Elder and don't think it appropriate to bring up the subject anymore. I'm actually glad that it hasn't come up for now, because if it had I would have had to dismiss the idea or select a group of Elders to make the long journey back. I really don't think that any of us traveling to Voresha is going to do any good, James."

"Do you think that the Exidihovads have conquered Voresha by now, Lilith?" I asked.

"I hope that is not the case, James," Lilith said, "but the odds of peace loving Voreshans defeating such warriors is unlikely. Sending more Voreshans back to a planet that has probably already been conquered just doesn't make any sense to me."

"Me either, Lilith," I said. "If you're ready, let's get on back to our home and shop. It will be good to get back to some normalcy."

"You've got that right, James," Lilith said and we left the mansion.

CHAPTER TEN

Lilith and I didn't talk much on the drive back to our home. Neither did we intrude in each other's thoughts, but I'm sure Lilith was also thinking about all that had happened recently and if our troubles with the Exidihovads were over. When we turned down our street I pulled over to the curb and asked, "Do you think we should approach our house cautiously, Lilith? I don't think the Exidihovads are smart enough to realize that it was us that caused all their problems, but I'm still a little nervous about not knowing where the rest of them got off to."

"That would be my suggestion, James," Lilith replied. "It is quite possible that the Exidihovads did figure out that we were responsible for their problems and where we live. It is also quite possible that they are waiting to ambush us when we get back. I'm not sure that we could survive an ambush by 20 Exidihovads or not."

"Well dear," I said, "I guess there is only one way to find out if they are waiting for us."

I pulled away from the curb and slowly drove down to our house and pulled into the driveway. Lilith had been looking around carefully to try and get a glimpse of any Exidihovads that might be in the area, but she didn't see any. Neither did we get any feelings that we were being watched or that there were any strange creatures near our house. We sat in the car for a couple of minutes after I turned it off, waiting to see if we were approached by anyone or anything. When all seemed ok, Lilith and I got out of the car and, still being very cautious, headed for our front door. Before entering the house we listened intently at the front door for any noise that might be coming from inside, but hearing nothing we unlocked the door and entered our house for the first time since having relocated at the old mansion.

We carefully checked out the entire house room by room and the garage and even peeked in the attic and then Lilith and I decided that we would head on over to our gallery and relieve the couple who had been taking care of our business while we were confined to the mansion and its surroundings. We left our house feeling that all was now fine and headed on to our gallery. When we pulled up out front and parked the car everything seemed to be ok, except that there was a closed sign on the door and it wasn't even lunch time yet. We got out of the car wondering if the couple who was supposed to be running the gallery for us had ever even been there at all, even though the Elders had assured us that they were dependable and trustworthy. The front door was locked and the lights were turned off, but everything seemed to be in place when we entered. After entering the front gallery area, I called out to the couple before entering the back area where we kept our studio, "Charles, Anna, anybody home?" There wasn't any answer and Lilith and I looked at each other with the fear that they were never there or that something was terribly wrong. "Lilith, you stay here while I take a look in the back," I said.

"Oh no, James," Lilith said. "You are not going through that door alone! We either go down together or we get the heck out of here now!"

"Yes, your highness," I said teasingly, but she gave me a cold stare that would have frozen an attacking polar bear in its tracks. If only that stare worked against Exidihovads!

I approached the back room door from the right and Lilith was on the left. We jumped into the room quickly with the hopes that we could surprise anyone or anything that might be lurking in our studio waiting to ambush us. At first everything looked fine, but upon closer inspection we found Charles and Anna curled up on the floor in a back corner of the studio that was hidden by an oriental screen. The dried pool of blood surrounding their bodies told us that we were too late to help them. Approaching the bodies of the couple we discovered that they had been decapitated, but their heads were nowhere in the studio or gallery.

"This is so terrible, Lilith," I said. "This couple was only trying to be helpful and this is how they get rewarded. We should have realized that someone should have been here with them to help in case they were attacked."

"I know, James," Lilith replied. "Either us or the Elders should have had someone here to watch over them in case of trouble. I can only hope that they didn't suffer too much."

"This has to be the work of the Exidihovads, Lilith," I said.

"No doubt, James," Lilith replied. "I hate to say this, but the Exidihovads must have found out that this was our gallery and came here after the fight in the woods to kill us. Either that or this happened prior to the event in the woods."

"Oh my God!" I exclaimed. "Charles and Anna were killed because the Exidihovads thought they were us!"

"That's my guess, James," Lilith said. "That has to be why the Exidihovads are no longer in Sarasota. I hope that Elder Cescasing and the other Elders can find them and destroy them quickly before they hurt anyone else."

"To fight and kill Voreshans is one thing," I said, "but to kill unsuspecting humans for no good reason is unacceptable! They all must die before they cause any more harm to either humans or Voreshans!"

Lilith and I stood there for a few moments trying to decide whether we should contact the police or not, knowing that the police would never figure out who killed Charles and Anna. "Lilith, if we contact the police about this," I began, "they are going to want to know where we have been and what we have been up to. They are also going to want to know why Charles and Anna were here in the first place. I don't think the police are going to buy into the story about us being on vacation, especially since we don't have any proof."

"You're right, James," Lilith said. "I think that we clean up here and not let this incident get out to the police or anyone else for that matter. I'll contact Elder Cescasing and let him know what has happened here and ask him to contact Charles' and Anna's next of kin about their deaths. I am also going to reiterate the sense of urgency that hunting down the Exidihovads needs to take on. They must be stopped and stopped sooner than later."

Using the secret Voreshan method of disposing of bodies, Lilith and I spent the next hour returning everything in the gallery and studio back to normal. When we were finished, Lilith contacted Elder Cescasing telepathically and conveyed to him what had transpired and what we believed the Exidihovads were going to do now. He assured us that he and the other younger Elders were already searching for the Exidihovads and would spare them no mercy. We then opened the gallery and spent the rest of the afternoon trying to decide if we should stay put or go on the prowl for Exidohovads as well. Quite frankly, I was ready to take them all on single-handedly.

"I guess we should have guessed that the Exidihovads wouldn't just give up and leave," I said, "but I would never have guessed that Charles and Anna would be hurt."

"You're right again, James," Lilith said. "Our lesson learned here is to never let our guard down and to never think that any situation we confront is going to end so easily. This may well be the hardest thing to get over that I have ever experienced."

Trying to change the subject, I said, "Ah, for the good old days, Lilith, when all we had to do was help people to become better individuals and live happier lives. I wonder what ever happened to all those kids from art school that we helped. I know that for a short time some of them stayed around Sarasota, but then we seemed to have lost all contact with them."

"When I was growing up, James," Lilith said, "it just never sank in that after living over fifty years that I would still look so young in human terms of age. Neither did I ever think that I would be put in the position that I am in now."

"What I didn't realize when I first crossed over to become a Voreshan," I said, "was that my metamorphosis for the first fifty years or so would be even slower than it is from here on out. Of course, beautiful alien women and fighting their battles was only something out of Edgar Rice Burroughs *Mars Series* of books."

"That was part of the equation that passed right over my head, too, James," Lilith said. "I know that my parents explained all of that to me, but my strong suit was never math."

"Well, love," I said, "I liked math and I still didn't have it figured out."

"Not to change the subject, James," Lilith said, "but I hope that Elder Cescasing and the other Elders can find the remaining Exidihovads and eliminate them soon. I may be the Head Elder now, but I really only want to get back to our normal life here in Sarasota."

"There isn't anything I want more either, Lilith," I said. "I'm glad that we have enough artwork in our inventory to keep the gallery full for a while, because I'm really not up to being very creative right now."

"Me either, James," Lilith said. "By the way, and I know this sounds terrible on my part, but did you happen to check the receipts to see if Charles and Anna sold anything while we were gone?"

"Nothing terrible about keeping up with our income," I said. "I didn't check the receipts yet, but I will do that right now." Lilith was feeling pretty tired and depressed about what had happened to Charles and Anna and decided to stay in the studio and relax while I checked the receipts. Surprisingly enough, in the short time that we were away from the gallery Charles and Anna sold several of our paintings and took in more than $10,000. "Holy crap!" I nearly shouted when I came up with this figure.

Lilith jumped up from her chair in the studio and ran out front to the gallery and asked, "What's wrong, James? Did you see some Exidihovads? Do we need to prepare for battle?"

"Slow down, Lilith!" I said. "I'm sorry to have alarmed you like that, but Charles and Anna sold over $10,000 worth of our work while we were gone!"

"Holy crap!" Lilith now shouted. "That's more than we sold during the entire previous two months! If they were still with us I would suggest they keep running the gallery."

"That's for sure," I said. "I guess that we are just too humble about our work to push it like that."

"Well, James, " Lilith said, "you're right when it comes to us trying to sell our work. I mean, we do ok, but I have never been able to go on about how wonderful my work is to a potential buyer."

Just then the front door opened and a tall, cloaked and hooded figure, who had to duck as he entered, stepped into the gallery. Lilith and I immediately recognized the figure as an Exidihovad and took a defensive posture to protect ourselves. My first impulse was to use my telekinetic powers to throw him back through the glass of the front door and then grab his swords and slay him, but before I could do this he spoke.

"Please do not be afraid," he said. "I have not come to harm you. My name is Treyfarnkom and I come to you in peace."

"What do you want with us?" I asked. "And how can you say you come in peace when you have murdered our friends right here in our gallery?"

"My species set out to conquer your kind on Voresha," Treyfarnkom began, "and many of us were sent here to this planet you call Earth to make sure none of you left Earth to go back to your home planet. We were not told about your marvelous powers and how you can defeat your enemies without raising a sword. We know not how you communicate so quickly with your kind, but many of those who had gathered at that big house are now destroying the rest of my kind that came here. I have come to beg you to stop this slaughter and to allow the rest of us to leave your planet peacefully."

"What makes you think that we can stop the others of our kind?" asked Lilith. "And what about our friends that you murdered here in our gallery? What's to keep us from killing you right here and now?"

"We now know that the two creatures we killed here earlier were not of your species," Treyfarnkom replied. "We also know that you two control all the rest of your kind and that is why I am asking you to stop the slaughter of my species."

"To repeat what she just said, what's to keep us from killing you right now like you killed our friends?" I asked the Exidihovad.

"My species does not know the emotions that your kind feels about such things," Treyfarnkom said. "All I can say is that we made a mistake in killing your friends and in coming to this planet to eliminate your kind. We are warriors and we do as we are told. I know not what else to say."

"I guess that will have to serve as an apology," I said, "but just so you know, I would just as soon kill you here and now for what you have done. What you are saying sounds more like a surrender because you have been defeated than regret over having murdered our friends."

"I understand that you wish revenge on me for the death of your friends, but beg that you not kill me," said Treyfarnkom. "Maybe it is the atmosphere of this planet or the strange gasses emitted by the vegetation here, but those of us who remain no longer want to fight."

"If we stop killing those of you who remain on Earth," Lilith said, "what guarantee do we have that you will keep your word and leave Earth?"

"By the time we have ended this conversation," said Treyfarnkom, "more of my species will have died at the hands of your kind. The few of us who remain only want to leave and live our lives where no one can harm us."

"Or where no one can defend themselves against you," I said.

Treyfarnkom then removed his two swords from their scabbards and Lilith and I both stepped back a few paces and took defensive postures against this Exidihovad. However, Treyfarnkom laid his swords on the floor of the gallery and stepped back a couple of paces himself.

"I lay my swords down and leave them with you," he said. "I can only say with words that the remaining members of my group here on Earth will leave our swords behind and leave Earth to find a place where we can live out our lives in peace. We know that you can defeat us and do so in the most terrible of ways by turning our own weapons against us."

Telekinetically, I lifted the swords off the floor and pointed them at Treyfarnkom and even moved them a little in his direction. His eyes grew as big as oranges and were almost the same color, but I floated the swords back to Lilith and me and we each took one in our hands.

"We will not kill you, Treyfarnkom," Lilith said, "but if we ever hear of your kind seeking out other species to conquer, my kind will find you and finish the job of destroying your species. Your kind has turned my kind from a peaceful species into a killing species. Maybe it was time for us to fight the bad in the universe, but we would have much rather kept our peaceful ways!"

Treyfarnkom bowed deeply and said, "I thank you for all of the few of my kind that remain and I promise that we will leave your planet as soon as we can assemble at our space craft. My species has never known how to live peacefully, but we will now try. Please contact the others of your kind and tell them to stop the slaughter of the remaining members of my war party."

"Why don't you go in the back, my love," I said, "and make the contact with the others to stop their pursuit of

Treyfarnkom and the remaining members of his species here on Earth while I keep an eye on this character?"

"I will," Lilith replied, catching on to not use our names in front of the Exidihovad and she went into the studio to contact the other Elders.

"As for you, Treyfarnkom," I said, "you will stay where you are until we have confirmation that your kind is retreating to your space craft. Then we will contact the others of our kind to make sure your kind are preparing to leave Earth and then I will let you return to your space craft as well."

"That is fair," replied Treyfarnkom and he actually hung his head as if in shame.

I stood there eyeing this Exidihovad up and down and having my suspicions about if he were telling the truth and should be trusted. Quite frankly, I did not trust this Exidihovad any more than any of the ones Lilith and I had confronted so far. However, since I still had one of his swords in my possession, Treyfarnkom stood still without moving a muscle for the next several minutes while we waited for some indication from Lilith that would allow us to let him leave.

"James," Lilith communicated telepathically, *"all of the Elder groups have now contacted me and assured me that only a handful of Exidihovads are still alive, maybe no more than five or six. The Elders have stopped their assault on the Exidihovads as I commanded and the Exidihovads have lain down their swords and are retreating. It almost seems too good to be true."*

"That does seem a little strange, unless these creatures can communicate telepathically," I said, *"which I think is highly unlikely."*

"Maybe they were under orders from this one in our gallery to retreat if the Elders stopped attacking them," Lilith said. *"I have just been contacted by the Elders watching the retreat of the remaining Exidihovads. They have returned to their space craft and entered it. Maybe this Treyfarnkom is telling the truth after all"*

"Ok, Treyfarnkom," I said, "you are now free to go, but know that you and the others of your kind that remain are being watched closely and we will know immediately if you don't keep your word, in which case my kind will finish their job of eliminating you and the remaining members of your war party."

"Thank you," Treyfarnkom said. "We will be on our way within one of your Earth hours," and he left the gallery and disappeared down the street very quickly.

Lilith came back into the gallery and asked me, "Do you really trust him, James?"

"I only trust you my dear," I said. "All others have proven themselves untrustworthy at one time or another. We can only wait to hear from the Elders if the Exidihovads have left Earth or not."

"I feel the same way about you, too, James," Lilith said. "I just hope that this Exidihovad that was here was telling the truth and that Voreshans are forever rid of them."

"Me, too, Lilith," I replied. "Do you think we will ever know if the planet Voresha was conquered by the Exidihovads who were left there?"

"We can't know that for at least another 50 earth years, James," Lilith said, "and then only if another Voreshan or group of Voreshans travel to Earth with that news. If I were to send a few of the Elders to Voresha, we would have to wait for 100 earth years before knowing. Even though you and I should only be about half way through our life span, that is still a very long time to worry about it."

"So, your plan, Lilith, is not to send anyone to Voresha to either do battle against the Exidihovads or report back about the situation there?" I asked.

"That is my plan, James, since I am now in charge," Lilith answered. "It would be such a waste of any Voreshan's time to make such a trip, one way or the other. It is why I would have given up being a Voreshan, just as you said you would do, before I would have traveled there for any reason. It isn't because I don't love my species, because I do, but my life with you, James, is far more important to me than anything else."

"I think it is my turn, Lilith, to say I do love you so much!" I said.

CHAPTER ELEVEN

After all that had happened recently, it seemed strange for Lilith and me to get back to our usual routine of going to the gallery everyday and going home every night after spending our days painting and occasionally selling our artwork. Now being the Head Elder, Lilith's contact with the other Elders was far more frequent, but for the most part it didn't really interfere with our everyday lives. The main controversy was about sending some Elders or other Voreshans back to the planet Voresha to either fight the Exidihovads that had invaded the planet or at least find out what was going on there. When Lilith had communicated her thoughts on this not to send anyone to Voresha to the other Elders, most agreed that her plan made more sense. However, there were four or five who really wanted to go to Voresha with the understanding that they would either fight and die there or, if the Exidihovads had been expelled from Voresha, finish out their lives in peace on the planet where their ancestors had once lived. These few Elders said that traveling to Voresha was something that they had thought about most of their lives. It wasn't that they didn't love their life and purpose on Earth, but it was just a desire to go back to where it all began for Voreshans. Lilith gave them the permission to make the journey and to spend the next several weeks preparing for their long journey to the planet Voresha.

For the next several weeks everything was going well and Lilith and I hadn't even encountered the usual sad, angry, disgruntled humans that we were charged with helping to become better people. To be honest, this type of activity really wasn't within her purview as the Head Elder, but rather was something normally left up to those Voreshans who were not members of the Elder group. The seven Exidihovads who had survived the Voreshan onslaught had left Earth to hopefully never be heard from again and the Elders had a nice collection of unusual swords to add to an otherwise empty arsenal. The five Voreshan Elders who wanted to travel to the planet Voresha were close to being prepared for their long journey and were anxious to get under way. All of this simply meat that Lilith and I could get back to what we hoped would be a more normal existence.

Because we were alumni of the local art school, we were occasionally asked to come to the school and talk with the students about our success as artists and even on occasion give a painting workshop. Of course, because of our aging so much slower than humans, we were periodically having to change the dates of our attendance at the school. We also had to change the minds of the staff and teachers who remembered us on a regular basis. People would certainly begin to ask questions if our degrees still read that we graduated in 1971, about forty years ago, especially since we were only supposed to be about 26 years old. It was during a weeklong painting workshop at the art school about this time that Lilith and I had our next encounter with a very disgruntled female human, or what we initially thought was a female human.

We were both demonstrating our painting technique on the third day of the workshop when a dark-haired female participant about our age and who wasn't a student at the school walked up to my easel and said in front of the entire class, "That sure is a pile of crap you are painting! You certainly have not improved very much since I first knew you!" The entire class stopped what they were doing and listened intently.

"And just who are you," Lilith asked, "besides being probably the rudest person I've ever met?"

"Why don't you ask your little hubby here?" the woman replied. "He and I used to be a really hot item before you came along."

"I don't have a clue who you are and I would never have had an interest in a woman like you!" I said with what must have been a noticeable degree of irritation in my voice. "Why don't you enlighten us?"

"Oh, you remember all right!" the woman nearly yelled. Turning to address the entire class she said, "I'm the one you jilted for this bitch you're married to!"

"I didn't jilt, as you put it, anyone for my wife," I replied. "Any girlfriends I had before marrying Lilith dumped me."

"Well, it has been quite a few years and I'm sure you thought you would never see me again, but here I am anyway," the woman said. "Maybe you should take a closer look, James, and imagine me with blond hair."

After staring at her for a couple of minutes I suddenly recognized the person standing before me. "Holy crap!" I exclaimed. "Lilith, I don't know how she escaped, but this is the dreaded Harmony!"

The students in the workshop were now all gathered around us and very interested in what was being said. One of the male students in the group asked, "Hey, Mr. Morgan, should we call security and have this woman removed?"

"That won't be necessary," I said. "Lilith and I will take care of this matter."

Lilith then stepped between Harmony and me and said, "If you know what's good for you, my dear, you will leave here immediately and go back to the hell you were exiled to!"

"And what do you plan to do if I don't leave?" Harmony asked Lilith.

"I will have you sent to an even worse place than you have been for the past fifty years," Lilith told Harmony.

The rest of the students in the class were now really getting interested and were starting to whisper among themselves. The more they listened to this little confrontation between Harmony and Lilith and me, the more concerned they seemed to be. They certainly had puzzled looks on their faces when Lilith said this to Harmony. I immediately went to work on their minds and put them into a mild standing slumber that would make them forget anything they had seen or heard up to that point when they awoke.

"And what makes you think you can do that?" Harmony asked Lilith as she sneered at me and moved closer to Lilith. "I'm going to get rid of you and take what's mine before I leave here!"

"As the Head Elder," Lilith said, "I can do whatever I want with you, Harmony. And right now I am inclined to ship you off to the far reaches of outer space!"

"Ha!" Harmony said. "You? Head Elder? What makes you think I would ever believe that a female was Head Elder of the Voreshan species? You certainly must think very highly of yourself, bitch!"

"You obviously haven't been informed of anything that has been going on since you were exiled so long ago," Lilith said. "Maybe I should put you in contact with an Elder so you can ask him yourself."

"Quit stalling, bitch, and let's get it on!" Harmony yelled at Lilith, getting right up to her face with her fists. I immediately stepped between them, but Harmony was ready for me and shoved me out of the way and I fell backwards over a nearby drawing bench hitting my head against the wall which temporarily dazed me.

"You don't touch my man in any way!" Lilith told Harmony and then Lilith set to work on Harmony with her telekinetic powers, something that Harmony had obviously not practiced for a very long time, if ever. As I watched dazed, Lilith made Harmony rise into the air about four or five feet off the ground.

"What the hell?" Harmony yelled. "You let me down now!"

Then Lilith started spinning Harmony in the air like a child's top, slowly at first and then faster and faster. "We'll let you keep doing that for a few minutes, Harmony, and then I'm sending you off as a prisoner to Voresha with five Elders who are traveling there very soon. When you get there in about 50 years, you will be placed in a Voreshan prison where you will spend the rest of your miserable life!"

"Well, Lilith," I said as I was picking myself up off the floor and shaking my aching head, "that should keep her out of our lives for at least another 100 years."

Lilith let Harmony spin in the air for a couple of more minutes before setting her back on the floor. Harmony was so dizzy that she stumbled around bumping into things and finally fell down on the floor with her butt resting on a wooden palette with several bright colors on it.

"Get that duct tape over there, James, and bind her up good with it," Lilith instructed me.

Before Harmony could clear her head enough to resist, I had her hands and feet bound with the duct tape and a big piece wrapped around her head that went across her mouth. "That should hold her until the Elders get back to Voresha," I said.

"Well, James," Lilith said, "the Elders won't keep her bound up, but she will be kept in a very secure cell on the space craft for the entire journey to Voresha. She does have to eat, you know."

"Quite frankly, Lilith," I replied, "if I were going on that trip I would probably shove her out into space after about two years into the journey. That way, she wouldn't be able to bother anyone ever again!"

"You do have a mean streak sometimes, James," Lilith said, "but in this case I'm with you. However, even if I gave that kind of order to the Elders making the journey, there is no guarantee that they would carry it out."

"I hate to think that you would ever be disobeyed, Lilith," I said, "but as I indicated before, I only trust you 100 percent, my love. I just hope that Harmony hasn't brought any henchmen with her thinking that they could really help her out."

"You know that you and I can handle any Voreshans or humans that might come along, James," Lilith reassured me.

"I know, Lilith," I said, "but I would rather not be fighting our own kind.

"Agreed, James," Lilith said. "I am going to contact the Elders now who are making the journey to Voresha and let them know they have an extra passenger."

"I just hope they obey your orders and keep her locked up," I said. "She is one viciously seductive little vixen!"

"I'm sure that you are being polite when you say "vixen," James. I will be sure to pass that message along to the Elders, Lilith said with a sexy, evil little smile on her face.

"Now, James, I think we should hide Harmony somewhere, wake up the students in our workshop that you put to sleep, and get back to our demonstrations. Two of the Elders who are going on the journey to Voresha will be here waiting to pick up Harmony right after we finish the workshop."

I put Harmony in a closet at the rear of the large studio where Lilith and I were conducting our workshop and then woke up the students I had put to sleep when Harmony first interrupted the workshop. Although they were all a little drowsy, Lilith and I picked up where we left off and none of the students were any the wiser. When Lilith and I had concluded the painting workshop at the art school and the students had left the studio, the two Elders who had been patiently waiting outside came in and hauled Harmony off for her journey to Voresha with them. They weren't very happy about having a prisoner aboard for their trip, especially a female Voreshan prisoner, but at the same time they were anxious to please their new Head Elder.

On the way back to our gallery and studio Lilith and I talked some about my old flame, Harmony, showing up in Sarasota and wondered how she had managed to escape from her exile. We had only heard of someone escaping exile the one time when Harmony's parents, the Beckhams, sent an escapee to try and kill me as revenge for me denouncing Harmony and taking up with Lilith. Yes, you could say that I had jilted Harmony, but that was her plan for me as well after we were to be married, so I'm putting the blame on Harmony. Because the Beckhams had not done as instructed by the Elders back then, Harmony and her parents were sent away forever, supposedly never to be heard from again. It was definitely a shock when I realized who the woman was that had interrupted mine and Lilith's workshop at the art school. My guess was that Harmony had used her feminine wiles to get away from her exiled place.

"Well, Lilith," I said as we were heading back to our gallery, "I certainly hope that Harmony can't fool the Elders who are taking her away, hopefully for good, and escape again before they get under way back to Voresha."

"I want to tell you now, James," Lilith said, "that if she were to show up again tomorrow or in 200 years, she will have come to the end of her life!"

"Wow, Lilith!" I said. "That is pretty extreme, but I hope you keep that promise. I guess there are bad seeds in every species, no matter how good the general population of the species tries to be."

"I grew up believing that all Voreshans were good, James," Lilith said. "My parents, and probably all of the Elders, would never have believed that there could be any bad people among our kind. However, I would not kill her if she were to show up again. Maybe I would just turn her brain into the one she had when she was a dumb blond and treated you badly."

"Well, Lilith," I began, "I'm sure that after all this time on Earth, a few Voreshans had to be influenced by humans' innate capacity for evil. Hopefully, we won't have to worry about evil Voreshans ever again. Before I became a Voreshan, I knew there were probably as many evil humans as there were good humans. Crossing over to your side was exciting for me, because I always thought that I could do good in the world, but never really knew how that could happen while I was still human. I can't think of a better way to help people than being a Voreshan."

"That is what my parents and I saw in you, James," Lilith said, "when I was looking for a human mate. I know that it was a little disturbing for you when you found out that my parents had been checking you out, but I felt sure you were the one the first time we met, especially since I had actually selected you before Harmony selected you."

"I felt the same way, Lilith," I said. "When I looked into your eyes and you first touched my hand to help me out of the reflecting pool at the carillon park, I knew I had met the girl of my dreams. I had already decided when I got to the carillon park that I was going to try and get out of the situation with Harmony, even if it meant going back to being a lonely human."

CHAPTER TWELVE

A few days later the five Elders who wanted to make the journey to the planet Voresha were ready to take off on their long journey. Lilith and I were at the secret launch site late that night and made sure that Harmony was properly locked up in the space craft's prisoner accommodations. Although she would spend the next 50 years or so living in the prisoner's cell, it was large and comfortable enough to accommodate about a dozen individuals. Essentially, it had all the comforts of home and she got three meals a day. We saw the space craft off and wished the Elders a safe journey and reminded them to be very wary of Harmony Beckham.

After the Voreshan space craft had disappeared into the night sky, Lilith turned to me and said, "I never thought that one day some of our species would actually travel to Voresha from Earth. Growing up, I had never heard my parents or any other Voreshan ever talk about traveling to Voresha one day, because it would be such a long journey. Our species' history was taught privately to children by their parents, but we were always told that there wasn't any reason to ever return to our home planet and I would have never given it a thought before now. Some Voreshans, including my parents and I, have always believed it to be a deserted planet with no inhabitants. I guess that some stayed behind and were prolific when the others came to Earth."

"As a human growing up," I said, "it was always drummed into my head that the future was unpredictable.

My father always said that if you expect one thing to happen, the opposite is more likely to happen. Of course, he was never much of an optimist. In the 19th century, no one would have ever believed that we could fly around like the birds, but then airplanes were invented. We then didn't believe that space travel was possible, even though authors like Edgar Rice Burroughs wrote about it in the early 20th century. Then we sent men to the moon. Can you imagine what would have happened if people had known that Voreshans came to Earth thousands of years ago?"

"That is why Voreshans blended in, James," Lilith said. "Our charge was to not disturb or alter the progress of the planet, but to simply try and help humans to be better. Looking back on human history, I'm not sure that we did a very good job."

"I can't imagine, Lilith," I said, "how so few Voreshans who came to Earth could possibly have had much affect on the millions of humans whose instincts were to conquer and kill anyone and anything that got in their way. Humans have always been a greedy, selfish, destructive, hateful species by nature. You and I in our lifetime have experienced that on a fairly constant basis. I believe that for each person we change for the good, that person will then have a positive effect on another person and so on and so on. If that is the case, then you and I have helped hundreds more than we could ever have helped otherwise."

"You're right, James," Lilith said. "We can only deal with those that cross our path and hope that most are feeling pretty good on those days. I had never thought about how the good we do with one individual might actually affect more people. I like that idea, James. It makes me happy."

Looking up at the night sky, I said, "Lilith, it's a beautiful, romantic night with a nearly full moon and millions of stars shining brightly. What would you say to a late night stroll on the beach where we were married? We might even see a UFO."

"You are a hopeless romantic, James," Lilith said, "but I would love to take a walk on the beach tonight with you and I won't give you the chance to search the night sky for a UFO!. Who knows, there might even be some late night dessert in it for you!"

"That makes me want to skip the walk on the beach and go straight home!" I said.

"Oh no, mister," Lilith told me. "You are going to take that walk on the beach with me or there might not be any dessert for a week!"

Keep in mind that although Lilith and I had lived a little over 50 earth years, we were only about 26 years old in human terms. Dessert was still a regular feature of our life together as man and wife and would be so for a long time to come.

After being threatened with no dessert for a week if I didn't take Lilith for that walk on the beach, I ushered her into the car and we were off to Longboat Key. Although many of the things that Lilith and I had known through the years in Sarasota were almost the same as they were back in the 1960s and 1970s, many things had also changed over the past 30 to 40 years. When we were married on Longboat Key it was mainly a long stretch of undeveloped beach with the occasional beach house nestled back among the trees that were about 100 yards from the water's edge. Over the past 40 years, Longboat Key had over-developed in our minds and it was now almost completely wall-to-wall high rise condominiums and hotels, what Lilith and I called mansions, and numerous other attractions that brought people to the area from all over the world. Progress in Sarasota, like so many places in the world, had kept up with the demands of the growing population, but at the expense of much of the natural beauty that had once existed. Florida had changed nearly everywhere and little of the old Florida we knew growing up still existed. Even though many people had been concerned with the destruction of the planet Earth in the late 20th century, the pollution and development during that time continued to get worse and worse.

That aside, however, Lilith and I did occasionally manage to get out to Longboat Key and take a walk, mostly during the day on weekends, but it was just as safe at night with all the lights from the buildings illuminating the beach. The spot on the beach where we were married was now overtaken with an exclusive housing development that catered strictly to the very well-to-do. When we just couldn't stand the thought that this beautiful spot had been ruined by so much development, we would take off and go back to the carillon park where we first met and spend the day there. At least the State of Florida had kept this beautiful spot undisturbed for all of these years and we hoped that they would continue to do so forever, because for us it is still the most beautiful spot on the planet. It also gave us the occasional chance to visit with Lilith's parents who still lived in the same house nearby, saving them a trip down to Sarasota every two or three months.

On one of these spur of the moment excursions on a Monday when we were closed, Lilith and I were driving along the old back road 64 that we preferred over the faster more developed routes to the town where the carillon park was located. Not too far past Lake Manatee and the junction of 675, we saw a little boy about seven or eight years old standing at the end of a dirt road that led down to an old farmhouse and barn in the distance. He was holding a stick as long as he was tall with a sign attached which read "I have a secret – help!" scrawled on it in big, bright crayon colors. He waved at us as went passed by, but we realized that his wave was more like a gesture to stop. I wasn't driving that fast, so I slowed down and turned the car around and headed back to where the little boy was standing. He seemed to be excited as I pulled off onto the dirt road and over to one side where I parked and Lilith and I got out of the car. He came a little closer to us, but he still maintained his distance, no doubt having been told by his parents to beware of strangers.

"Hi there," Lilith said.

"Hi," was all he replied with both a scared and excited look in his eyes.

"Why did you want us to stop?" I asked.

"Did you see my sign?" the little boy asked back.

"Yes, we did," Lilith said. "Are you out here because you want to share your secret with someone else?"

"Yes," he replied.

"You know," I said, "you aren't supposed to share secrets. That is why they are called secrets."

"But I need to share this secret, because my parents aren't here," he said.

"You certainly made a pretty sign," Lilith said. "Hasn't anyone else stopped to ask you about your secret today?"

"No," is all he said.

"Well," I said, "most people are in a hurry and don't have time to stop and talk to strange boys on the side of the road."

"But I have a secret," he said again, "and I don't know where my parents are and I need help to find them."

"So your sign says," I replied. "What do you mean that you don't know where your parents are? Did they leave you all alone here?"

"No," is all he said.

Trying to make small talk and at the same time figure out what was up with this kid, Lilith asked, "Have you been out here all day?"

"I've been out here since Friday night," the little boy answered.

"Won't your parents be worried about you?" Lilith asked.

"My parents aren't here," he said. "I already told you that."

"So you did," I said. "Where are they?"

Pointing down the dirt road, the little boy said, "See that big old barn down there at the end of the road?"

"Yes," Lilith and I both said.

"That's where they went on Friday, but they didn't come out," he said.

Lilith and I looked at each other now with a lot of concern and then Lilith asked the little boy, "Did you go in there to look for them? Maybe they are in there waiting for you."

"No!" he exclaimed. "There's a big metal-looking monster in there and I'm afraid that it ate my momma and daddy! I'm afraid to go in the barn!"

"What is your name?" Lilith asked the little boy.

"Coky Warders," he replied. "What's your name?"

"My name is Lilith and this is my husband, James," Lilith answered.

"Lilith is a pretty name," Coky said.

"Why, thank you very much," Lilith replied. "I like Coky a lot, too."

"Would you like for Lilith and me to go down to the old barn and look around inside for your parents, Coky?" I asked.

"I don't want you to get eaten, too," Coky said.

"But, weren't you out here with your sign hoping someone would stop and help you find your parents?" I asked him.

"Yes," Coky said more shyly, bending his head down and kicking at the loose gravel in the roadway.

"Then I think James and I should go down there and have a look around," Lilith said.

"Ok," was all the little guy said.

"Now, Coky," I said, "you stay here and if we don't come back after a while, you try to stop someone else for help. Ok?"

"Ok," Coky said. "Don't get eaten by the metal monster!"

As Lilith and I started off down the dirt road toward the old barn and the nearby farm house, I communicated telepathically with Lilith, *"What do you think of Coky's story, if that's his real name?"*

"Sounds pretty strange to me, James," Lilith said, *"But did you see the fear in the little guy's eyes?"*

"I did see that fear in his eyes, Lilith," I said, *"and that same fear seemed like it was emanating from him to us."*

"I got that same feeling, James," Lilith said. *"I have been trying to pick up any thought waves from the barn, James, but I'm getting nothing."*

"If Coky's parents were alive, you would certainly be picking up something," I said. *"Do you think they ran off and left the little guy and he's making up this story to hide that?"*

"I don't know, James," Lilith said, *"but he didn't seem like a malicious little fellow. I can't imagine that his parents would abandon him out here in the middle of nowhere. We are almost to the old barn, so I think we should approach it with some care anyway."*

"Good idea," I said and Lilith and I crept up the side of the barn near the front where the barn's two large doors were closed.

The barn itself was constructed of sheets of tin and resembled half of a long, large tube. The sheets of metal overlapped, so it wasn't possible to peak through any cracks in the side. Lilith and I crept our way around to the front of the barn near to the two large doors keeping an ever vigilant eye open for possible trouble. All I could think about was that this was the Exidihovads' hideout.

"I wonder if this metal barn itself is the metal-looking monster in Coky's mind?" I asked Lilith.

"As we were approaching the barn that did occur to me, too, James," Lilith said as she peeked through the narrow slit of an opening between the two closed doors, *"but there is a large metallic-looking object inside the barn, James. From here it kind of looks like a giant cube of some sort."*

Peeking through the slit, I saw what did appear to be a large shiny cube about twenty feet in each direction, but which couldn't have fit through the front doors of the old barn. *"What do you think we should do now?"* I asked rather hesitantly, *"and how do you think that thing got in there in the first place?"*

"The doors don't seem to be locked or bolted from the inside, James," Lilith said, *"so I think we need to investigate this. How it got in there is a mystery. As much as I am not anxious to have another encounter with angry aliens, I*

have a sneaky suspicion that Coky's parents are inside that big shiny cube. If so, we should try and get them out."

"Ditto," was all I replied and we slowly opened one of the doors to the old barn hoping that it wouldn't squeak. Remember what my father used to say about hoping for one thing and the opposite happening? Well, that old barn door squeaked louder than a cat whose tail has just been stepped on!

Now, Lilith and I know that there are a lot of strange things in the universe, both as we know our universe and beyond. We know that there are more different species in the universe than the writers of *Star Trek* could have ever imagined. What we didn't know about, nor would have ever guessed possible outside of some old movies back in the 20th century, was what happened next! This big shiny metallic-looking cube that had had one flat side toward the doors, now rotated silently so that one edge was facing toward Lilith and me. Then that edge began to separate and a light burst forth from inside the cube equal to the sun's in intensity, yet it wasn't a blinding light. Lilith and I tried to communicate with each other both telepathically and out loud, but nothing came out of either our brains or our mouths. It was if we had been put in a state of suspension where the other didn't exist.

In the next instant we were involuntarily being gently pulled toward the opening in the cube. Although we tried very hard to resist this force that was pulling us along, we were pulled into the cube anyway and then we heard the cube close behind us and found ourselves inside a structure that appeared to be at least 20 stories tall. Once inside, we realized that we could now communicate with each other and I said *"How can this be, Lilith? Look at the size of this place we are in! It couldn't have been more than twenty feet tall when we were on the other side!"*

"I don't know how this is possible, James," Lilith replied, *"but at least we can communicate again. I was really worried there for a moment that we would be separated and not be able to communicate at all!"*

"This must be some kind of an illusion," I said, *"because there is no such thing as a Tardis, like in the old television series of* Dr. Who*!"*

"Well, James," Lilith said, *"at least not that we have ever heard about in our lifetime, but this thing seems to defy that assumption. There is one other theory that occasionally comes up in Voreshan conversations."*

"And that is what, my dear?" I asked.

"Remember the old science fiction movie, Fantastic Voyage, *where people were shrunk down and sent traveling through a human body?"* Lilith asked.

"No freaking way!" I exclaimed. *"Are you suggesting that as we were being pulled inside this cube that we were also being shrunk down to around six or seven inches tall in the process?"*

"Well, James," Lilith replied, *"it's either that or this structure grew 10 times larger as we were being dragged into it."*

"That's even harder to believe," I said. *"I'll stick with your first idea. Growing up, I had always thought it would be great to either be able to shrink or even become invisible, but this is crazy science fiction!"*

"We seem to be in what looks like a lobby area, James," Lilith said. *"The rest of this place looks like a maze of ramps continually moving upward. Almost reminds me of an M.C. Escher picture. They must lead to some room or rooms somewhere in this structure."*

"*Wherever that room is, Lilith,*" I said, "*it might be where Coky's parents are hiding out.*"

"*Or are being held against their will, James,*" Lilith said, "*if they are still alive.*"

"*Lilith, do you think this place is some kind of military experiment and the Warders are somehow involved with it?*" I asked. "*You can never tell what the government and military are up to these days.*"

"*That is always a possibility, James,*" Lilith said, "*but I would tend to believe this structure to be more alien than human.*"

"*Oh crap!*" I exclaimed.

"*Seconded!*" Lilith replied.

"*And you have never heard of anything like this existing in our known universe?*" I asked.

"*Never, James,*" Lilith answered. "*I know that humans have not discovered a way to shrink themselves down to one tenth of their original size, but alien technology, as you know, is far more advanced in some parts of the universe. Remember, my species traveled great distances by space craft to Earth thousands of years before humans put a man on the moon.*"

"*And humans still haven't gotten a manned space craft beyond the moon,*" I added.

"*Well, back to our problem here, James,*" Lilith said. "*I guess we either stand around here and wait for a welcoming party or we go looking around for Coky's parents. I only hope that they are still alive.*"

"*I'm perfectly comfortable hanging out right here,*" I said, "*especially since we don't have any weapons besides our telepathic and telekinetic skills for defense in case we are attacked by some new alien species we don't know about.*"

"It does seem odd that we haven't at least been approached by some sort of being by now," Lilith said. *"I guess there is always the possibility that this structure is some kind of intelligent machine placed here by another species. But, for what purpose?"*

"It seems odd to me, Lilith," I replied, *"that if it had been placed here by an alien species that they would pick such a remote area, unless this is just some sort of base of operations."*

"That does seem a little strange to me as well, James," Lilith said.

Just at that moment Lilith and I were startled out of our private conversation by a deep voice that seemed to emanate from all of the surrounding walls, "You seem to be of a higher intelligence than the first humans brought in here."

"Who are you and where are you and were you reading our minds?" Lilith demanded.

"This female specimen is much more bold than the last one," the voice replied "I detect her age to be twice what she appears."

"That didn't answer my questions," Lilith said with more concern in her voice as we both kept glancing around to try and discover who or what was talking to us.

"If you will take the ramp to your left," the voice instructed, "it will lead you to a door that will take you to an area where we can investigate you further."

"And just why would we want to subject ourselves to your scrutiny when you haven't even tried to answer our questions?" I asked the voice.

"You can either begin walking up the ramp as directed," said the voice in a more threatening tone, "or be dragged forcibly to the place where you will be further examined."

"Either way, it isn't going to happen," I said.

"Either you make yourself known and answer our questions or we will bring the wrath of all Voresha down upon you!" Lilith nearly screamed at the talking walls.

"So that is how you communicated telepathically," the voice said less threateningly, "you are something called Voreshans."

"So, you were reading our minds?" Lilith asked. "Are you an intelligent machine or are you an actual being?"

"Having been programmed to not be any more intrusive than necessary and to cooperate with the beings of this planet as much as is possible in order to study them," the voice said, "I have to inform you that I am a highly intelligent machine. I was placed here four of your planet's days ago to lure humans in and to examine them and then store the information in my data banks. The species that built me are known in our universe as Durabracca. Their plan is to retrieve me in 1,981.95 of your planet's days. Now, if you will proceed as directed you will come to no harm until your vivisection."

"Vivisection?" I exclaimed more than questioned. "You have another think coming if you think we will go willingly to our death for the purpose of your scientific research! And by the way, did you shrink us somehow?"

"The Durabracca are only about seven or eight of your earth inches tall," the machine replied, "so all creatures are shrunk or enlarged to Durabracca size when brought into the vivisection machine."

"Well, that's a technology that I'm sure the Elders don't know about," Lilith said.

"You are not going to get away with this!" I exclaimed. "We will get the other humans back if they are still alive and then destroy you!"

"I do not know how to deal with Voreshans," the machine answered. "I have only been programmed to attract and examine humans. You cannot destroy me. Only the Durabracca can do that."

"Well then," Lilith said, "I suggest that you release us and release the two humans you lured in here three days ago. There little boy is scared that something awful has happened to his parents. And you, my dear machine, will be destroyed!"

"I must obey you because I have only been programmed to deal with humans," the machine responded. "The humans you speak of have not yet been readied for examination. They are in suspension and will join you momentarily after I release them."

"Smart move," Lilith said. "I wonder what the machine meant by 'suspension'?"

"I don't know Lilith," I said, "but I hope that Coky's parents are ok."

Everything was quiet for several minutes before we heard footsteps coming in our direction. Not knowing whether to trust this machine or whether we had been talking to some alien species hiding somewhere inside this structure, Lilith and I prepared to fight if Coky's parents didn't appear before us. It took a couple of more minutes before the feet belonging to the footsteps emerged from behind a nearby wall and much to our relief those feet did belong to a man and a woman.

"Are you Coky's parents?" Lilith asked as they cautiously approached us.

"Yes, we are," answered the man. "I'm Robert Warders and this is my wife Mildred. Is Coky ok?"

"Coky is fine," I said. "He flagged us down a while back and told us that you had disappeared into this barn and didn't come back out. We decided to check out his story and here we are. By the way, I'm James and this is Lilith."

"Mildred and me was really worried that this thing had taken our boy and done something terrible with him," Robert said. "Are we going to be able to get out of this thing?"

"We will be leaving shortly," Lilith said. Speaking louder she continued, "Ok, whatever you are, we are ready to be released from this cube and returned to our normal size!"

Looking at me, Mildred said, "What's she talking about?"

"It's a long story, but the important thing is that we get out of this structure as soon as possible."

"You got that right, friend," Robert said. "This here thing gives me the creeps!"

A few seconds later one corner of the structure began to open and all four of us were literally blown along and back out into the barn in that intense white light that had sucked us into the cube. The cube, which was once again only about twenty feet in each direction, had shut behind us and once again sat quietly in the barn. We quickly got out of the barn and were standing in the barnyard with our backs to the barn doors when we heard them slam shut.

Dusting ourselves off, we all turned around to look at where we had just been and Robert said, "I'm gonna tear that damn barn down first chance I get and destroy whatever that thing is inside! I don't know what it is or why it's in our barn, but it's gotta go!"

"We don't advise that," Lilith said.

"And just why not?" Robert asked.

"You wouldn't believe me if I told you," Lilith answered, "but let's just say that the government has put it there and doesn't want it bothered for the next five to six years. You would be smart to build yourself a new barn and put up a high fence around this one with no trespassing signs all around. Otherwise, you two and your son may find yourself back inside that thing as the subjects of some terrible experiment."

"How come you know so much about all this?" Robert asked. "Are you two some kind of government spies or something?"

"We can't divulge that information," Lilith said, "but just be glad that James and I came along when we did to get you out instead of someone else stopping."

"Why's that?" asked Mildred. "You two are being kind of suspicious acting, if you ask me."

"Because of who we are and what we know is all that we can tell you," I said. "Anyone else would have ended up just like the two of you, and might have brought your boy with them."

"Or worse, someone else might have kidnapped your boy never to be seen again," I said.

"Speaking of Coky, where is the little tyke?" Robert asked.

"He's still waiting up by the road for us to return," I said. "I think he is going to be glad to see you."

"No more than we are gonna be glad to see him," Mildred said and we all walked back up to where I had parked the car to find Coky patiently waiting as he had been told.

To say that the reunion was moving would be an understatement as all three hugged and cried for several minutes. When they had calmed down a little, Robert turned to Lilith and me and said, "I don't know how we can ever repay you for saving us and stopping to check on our boy. If you need some lodging for the night and a couple of good home cooked meals, we can provide that."

"As tempting as that sounds, no thanks is needed," Lilith said. "Helping people when they need it is one of the things we do in this life. James and I are just glad that we could get you out of the barn and back to your son. Coky is one brave little man and he is the one who should be rewarded for saving you. If he hadn't been diligent and stayed out by the road for the past three days, you two might have been lost forever."

"We was in that thing for three days?" Mr. Warders asked. "My God, Mildred, I thought maybe it was just for a few hours at best."

"Me, too, Robert," Mrs. Warders said. Looking down at her son and hugging him closer to her side, Mrs. Warders said, "My poor, poor little boy. How brave you have been."

Being as grown up as he could, Coky said, "Aw gee, momma, it weren't nothing."

After a few more pleasantries, Lilith and I got back in the car and continued our trip to the carillon park, hoping that there would not be any more harrowing side adventures along the way. Most of the time when we went to the park on the weekend we ended up spending the night at the Lhuv's house and headed back the next day. We were sure that Lilith's parents would be very interested in hearing about our little side trip today, as would the Elder Council when we got settled in at the Lhuv's for the evening. Lilith would contact the Elder Council telepathically and discuss with them the happenings at the farm to see if any of the Elders had ever heard of the Durabracca before. With any luck, at least one of the Elders would know about this species and how to deal with their machine that sucked humans in for the purpose of vivisection. The message would spread around the planet quickly and hopefully we would

have more information about the Durabracca when we got
back to Sarasota.

CHAPTER THIRTEEN

Although Lilith kept in contact with the Elders for the next several days concerning our little adventure at the farm, none of the Elders anywhere on the planet had ever heard of the Durabracca species. The Elder Council came to the conclusion that the Durabracca and the machine they left in the old barn had come from an entirely different universe than the one with which we were familiar. Personally, I was having a hard time imagining any species traveling for so long just to come to Earth to study humans. Even knowing about Earth and its inhabitants seemed unlikely for most of the species in our own known universe, much less by a species from another unknown universe even farther away. Even if the Durabracca were far more advanced in space travel than Voreshans, it would have taken a very long time for them to get to Earth. I hypothesized that this species known as Durabracca must have been looking for an inhabited planet where the intelligent species wasn't intelligent enough to stop them from doing their experiments. Maybe their entire mission in life was to travel through space looking for beings to study. I wondered what they did with the remains after they performed their vivisections.

After Lilith had finished her last telepathic discussion with the Elder Council I shared with her what was running through my pea brain including my hypothesis. We were both in the back room of our gallery painting a few days later when I could no longer contain the suspicions running through my head.

"Lilith, dear," I began, "I have been thinking a lot about what happened back on that farm a few days ago and that strange machine that we encountered there."

"Me, too, James," Lilith replied, "but you go first."

"Well, first off, I don't think an alien species from another universe traveled all this way just to study Earth's inhabitants. My initial thought was that it had something to do with the government or even the military. They have been known over the past century for doing experiments on humans."

"That thought had crossed my mind, too, James," Lilith said, "especially since none of the Elders anywhere on Earth has ever heard of the Durabracca species."

"Exactly!" I exclaimed. "The other idea that has been running through my head is that if this machine isn't something our government, or some other government for that matter, has invented and placed at the old farm site for whatever purpose, then maybe it was put there by a species closer to home, disregarding my previous hypothesis of course. And then there's the question of why the isolated area instead of a more urban area?"

"Are you suggesting that whoever or whatever put that machine in that old barn resides on this planet?" Lilith asked.

"That's exactly what I'm suggesting, Lilith," I said.

"But none of the Elders have ever heard of this species before," Lilith said, "and if they have been on Earth for any length of time, then an Elder sometime in our history here would have known about it."

"Only if it had been written down or at least orally passed along," I said. "What if this species, let's call them the Durabracca for now, had been living underground ever since they have been on Earth? What if they are strictly an underground species and have been here even longer than Voreshans?"

"If that were true, James," Lilith said, "and they never came above ground, then that would explain why none of the Elders has ever heard of them. However, that brings up the question of how long have they been on Earth and how did they get that strange cube into the barn without the Warders noticing?"

"I have also put some thought into that, too, my dear," I said and thought back to something that I had noticed when Lilith and I first went into the old barn. The barn had a dirt floor and there was dirt piled up all around the cube. I actually didn't notice this fact until the cube moved so that the corner faced Lilith and me when we entered the barn.

"I'm waiting to hear this theory of yours about how these creatures got that cube into the barn," Lilith said with a little hint of impatience in her voice. "So far, it's all sounding a little farfetched."

"The cube was pushed up through the dirt floor of the barn and is somehow supported underneath," I offered.

"There was dirt piled up around the cube, James!" Lilith exclaimed with excitement.

"Yep!" was all I said being quite pleased with my theory.

"There was freaking dirt piled up around that cube in the old barn!" Lilith almost yelled at me.

"Yep!" was all I said.

"Is that the only word you know how to say, James?" Lilith asked me facetiously.

"Nope!" I replied and Lilith threw her paintbrush at me, but it missed me and hit my painting square in the middle with a huge splash of yellow.

I started laughing and then Lilith broke out laughing and we couldn't stop for a couple of minutes. I stepped back from my easel and looked at my painting with its new splash of yellow in the middle and said, "Nice touch, dear, how about some red now?" and we started up laughing once again.

When we had settled back down, Lilith asked, "James, do you think we should go back out to the old farm and further investigate that cube? Mind you, I'm not too thrilled with the idea of getting sucked into that thing again."

"I would love to satisfy my curiosity one way or the other," I said, "but we would have to come up with a better plan than we had the first time."

"Agreed, James," Lilith said. "I'm not sure how we could approach that machine without being noticed either. It seemed to be able to detect our presence almost as soon as we had entered the old barn."

"Wait a minute, Lilith," I said. "You may have just struck on the solution!"

"How do you mean, James?" Lilith asked.

"Remember how the machine seemed to be able to read our minds?" I asked.

"Yes," was all Lilith said.

"Maybe that's how it detected our presence," I offered. "We didn't seem to be noticed immediately, but we did continue to communicate telepathically once we were in the barn."

"That's right, James!" Lilith said. "If we come up with a plan that gets us into the old barn without being heard either out loud or telepathically, then we might be able to get close enough to investigate the exterior of the cube."

"Yep," I said again.

"I'm going to give you that splash of red you wanted in a minute, James," Lilith said, "but it's going to be coming from your nose!"

Lilith had moved over next to me now, so I thought I had better be on my best behavior and said rather pompously, "Why, yes, my dear. That is exactly the type of plan that we need to develop to further our investigation into this mysterious cube. Maybe we should call in Scotland Yard."

At that remark, Lilith punched me hard in the arm, something she hadn't done for some time. "You need to get serious young man, if we are going to try and investigate this situation," Lilith said.

"You are quite right, my dear," I said in my most pompous voice, while moving out of arms reach of Lilith. Standing there with both fists on her hips and giving me a very serious Head Elder look, I said as seriously as I could, "Right, let's get to work on our plan Elder Morgan."

"It's about time you showed some respect for your Head Elder," Lilith said.

Lilith and I then sat down at our little table in the studio and began to write down and discuss some strategies about how we might approach the cube in the old barn unnoticed. We talked about everything from digging our way in under the side of the barn to climbing into the loft from an opening in the back of the barn and then lowering ourselves near the cube by using a rope. We knew that we would not be able to communicate once inside the barn without being detected and were also concerned about making the slightest noise trying to get inside the barn. We weren't coming up with any plan that sounded good enough to us and were just about to give up on the idea when we were both contacted telepathically by Elder Semnag.

"Good afternoon, my young friends, Elder Semnag here" he said.

"Good afternoon, Elder Semnag," Lilith and I responded in our usual two-part harmony.

Elder Semnag continued, *"I am contacting you on behalf of all of the Elders, but especially on behalf of the Elder Council. Much discussion has been going on about this cube machine that you two encountered not far from Sarasota. The Elder Council has asked me to come to you with a proposal for your consideration."*

"James and I have been discussing this a lot today as well, Elder Semnag," Lilith said. *"We have been trying to come up with a plan as to how we could get close enough to the cube to further investigate it, but we don't have much yet I'm afraid."*

"Actually, it is somewhat of a relief that you and James have been talking about going back to the barn to further investigate this strange machine," Elder Semnag replied. *"The Elders thought that if you two would agree to further investigate this cube machine thing, that some of us could help by somehow distracting the machine while you got into the barn."*

"That would be great!," I said. *"Drawing the attention of the cube away from us was the part we were having the most difficulty with trying to figure out."*

"My only fear, Elder Semnag," Lilith said, *"is that the cube will suck the Elders inside it like it did with us and then we might not be able to get you out again."*

"Did you not tell us that the machine admitted to not knowing how to deal with Voreshans?" Elder Semnag asked. *"If that is the case, then it wouldn't matter as long as we identified ourselves as Voreshans and threatened to destroy it if it didn't let us go. In the meantime, maybe the*

two of you could figure out where the cube came from and how to get rid of it."

"That is true," Lilith replied. *"James has an idea that the so-called Durabracca have been on the planet for a very long time, but that they live underground. He thinks that the machine was simply pushed up through the dirt floor of the old barn, because there was dirt piled up around it."*

"Why, that is simply brilliant, James!" Elder Semnag said enthusiastically. *"If that is the case, then maybe we can figure out how to send it back underground and then confront these Durabracca about staying where they belong or leaving Earth all together."*

"If we can just get rid of the machine and make the Durabracca stay underground and away from humans, that would be a great accomplishment," I said. *"Of course, that all depends on the validity of my theory."*

"How many Elders do you think it will take to create a commotion big enough to allow the two of you to get inside the old barn and see what you can discover?" Elder Semnag asked.

"What do you think, James?" Lilith asked me.

"The more the merrier!" I replied. *"As a matter-of-fact, I think Lilith and I could enter the old barn among all of the Elders and then slip away while you continued to raise a ruckus. If you can keep the cube occupied long enough, maybe Lilith and I can figure out how to dispose of it or at least send it back to where it came from in the first place."*

"Well," Elder Semnag said, *"it sounds like there should be about a dozen Elders if you two are to temporarily blend in with us."*

"How soon do you think we can get under way?" Lilith asked Elder Semnag.

"The Elders thought that you would want to do this, so twelve of us are gathered at the old mansion," Elder Semnag replied. *"We will wait here until you arrive and then we can finalize our plan."*

"We will be out there as soon as we can close up the shop and drive out," I said.

CHAPTER FOURTEEN

Lilith and I closed up the gallery and stopped by our house briefly to get a couple of shovels in case we had to do some digging around the cube to see if it did come up out of the ground. After leaving our house we stopped by the old mansion, discussed the plan of attack with the assembled Elders, and then headed off to where we had discovered the cube in the old barn. The dozen Elders who were waiting at the old mansion piled into three cars and followed us to the farm about 30 minutes away from Sarasota. We pulled off onto the dirt road and stopped far enough away from the old barn hoping that we weren't detected. Lilith instructed the Elders to wait at their cars until we went to the farm house to check in with the Warders and to let them know what we were planning to do. They had been through enough trauma already without seeing 14 strange people show up and start prowling around their barn.

Lilith and I noticed that things seemed to be awfully quiet around the farm as we approached the house and barn and we both got an eerie feeling as we went up on the front porch and knocked on the door. Our worst fears was that the family had been murdered like the couple who had been watching our gallery for us. After a couple of minutes we knocked again, but there still wasn't any answer and we didn't detect any sounds coming from inside the house. The screen door wasn't fastened, so I opened it and tried the front door to see if it was open. The door knob turned and the front door opened and Lilith and I entered the house very slowly and cautiously hoping that the Warders were ok since their pickup truck was still parked next to the house. What we found when we entered the Warder's house was absolutely nothing! The entire house was empty of everything! There was no furniture, no draperies, not even a light bulb in the ceiling fixtures.

"Lilith," I said, "do you think the Warders packed up and got the heck out of here after their encounter with the machine in the old barn?"

"That would be my first guess, James," Lilith said. "Either that or they and everything they owned were vaporized."

"Except for their pickup truck," I said.

"There is that," Lilith said. "It seems odd that they would leave their pickup behind. I think we need to get the Elders down here and start our investigation into the thing in the barn."

Lilith made telepathic communication with the Elders and they were all standing on the front porch with Lilith and me in a matter of a couple of minutes, obviously forgetting that they needed to approach more cautiously. Lilith explained what we had discovered, or not discovered, inside the house and we discussed with the Elders if we should proceed with our original plan. It was agreed that we should move forward and see if the cube was still in the old barn or if it had disappeared as well. Our fear at this time was that the so-called Durabracca had taken all three of the Warders and their possessions and disappeared to wherever it was they came from in the first place.

Being married to the Head Elder also meant being assigned as her protector and so I led Lilith and the other Elders as quietly as possible to the front of the old barn. I moved forward to the two doors that led into the barn and peeked in through the opening between the two doors to see if the cube was still there. Communicating now telepathically to everyone at the same time, I said, *"The cube hasn't moved since we were last here. I don't see anyone or anything else in the barn, so I guess we should go ahead and move inside."*

"Do you think it can hear us communicating telepathically out here?" Elder Semnag asked.

"I don't think so," Lilith answered. *"Last time it didn't seem to hear James and me until we were inside, but it definitely picked up on our telepathic communication once we were inside."*

"So, when we enter we might as well make ourselves known to the cube by speaking out loud," Elder Semnag said.

"Create as much of a ruckus as you can," I said. *"Lilith and I will follow you in and then move off to the sides to investigate my theory."*

That said, several of the Elders moved forward, opened the doors wide and all 12 entered the barn making a raucous fuss that sounded like a herd of elephants arguing with each other. The Elders had obviously been planning this out and even seemed to be talking among themselves in several different languages in an effort to confuse the machine. Lilith and I had gone in behind the Elders and were now quickly and quietly moving away from the group and toward the sides of the cube. About that time the cube turned once again with its edge facing the group of Elders, which caught the Elders a little off guard and they became quiet and took a few steps backward. This time when the edge separated and the bright light came from inside the cube, the Elders were not sucked into the cube like Lilith and I were the first time that we were there.

The Elders remained quiet since Lilith and I were now on the opposite sides of the cube from them and then the familiar voice came from the cube saying, "You are all Voreshan and you have come to destroy me."

"We are Voreshan," Elder Semnag said, "but we have been sent here not to destroy you unless you fail to cooperate with us."

"I do not know how to deal with Voresha-shan," the voice from the cube said, "thus I do not know how to cooperate with you. I told the other Voresha-shan who were here the same thing, so why have you returned with more of your kind?"

"It is very simple actually," said Elder Semnag. "All you have to do is leave this building and never come back again or harm any humans ever again."

"I have not harmed any humans," the cube responded. "I released the two humans unharmed that the other two Voresha-shan who were here instructed me to do. My sensors do not detect them among you. Did they send you?"

"It is good to know that you have not harmed anyone," said Elder Semnag. "Now we are instructing you to leave Earth and never return."

"That is an order that must come from the Durabracca," replied the cube.

"Where can we find these Durabracca?" asked Elder Semang.

"I am not programmed to reveal that information," the cube responded.

"Can you contact the Durabracca and tell them what we have requested?" asked Elder Semnag.

"I cannot," replied the cube. "I was placed here to capture humans and carry out experiments on them. The Durabracca will return and remove me in approximately 5.3 earth years."

"Well then, I guess we are going to have to destroy you," said Elder Semnag.

"That is impossible," said the cube. "I cannot be destroyed except by the Durabracca."

"Why is that?" asked Elder Semnag.

While all of this conversation was going on, Lilith and I had been thoroughly examining around the base of the cube. However, even though we had carefully scraped away some of the dirt from around the cube, we had not discovered anything out of the ordinary. As best as we could determine, the cube was sitting on solid ground, thus debunking my theory about having come from underground. Lilith and I then started looking up at the top of the old barn to see if the roof had been messed with in any way which would have allowed the cube to be lowered into the barn. Everything seemed to be where it had been over the years, but an intelligent alien species could have easily put everything back the way it was. The only other possibility was that it had been constructed inside of the barn. Kind of like a ship in a bottle. Lilith and I now decided to rejoin the Elders and try to figure out what to do next and share our new theory.

As we walked back around to the front of the cube we heard it answer Elder Semnag's last question as to why it couldn't be destroyed. "Destruction is not in my programming," said the cube. "I now detect two more of your kind. Where did they come from?"

"We were waiting outside," Lilith said. "Because destruction isn't in your programming only means that you cannot self-destruct, not that you cannot be destroyed."

"I cannot be destroyed except by the Durabracca," replied the cube.

"What do you think we should do next, Elder Morgan?" asked one of the other Elders in the group. "Do you have a plan for trying to destroy this thing?"

"I'm thinking that this thing can't be destroyed by conventional means," Lilith answered. "James and I were inside the structure and it seems to be solidly built, which may be how it got here in the first place. Someone or something built it inside the barn. It even appeared from the inside that the exterior of this machine was made from one solid piece of some kind of metal that we have never seen before, but that still doesn't explain how it got here. I am pretty sure that it cannot move from this location on its own and if the Warders have moved away it probably won't get many visitors to harm."

"Are you suggesting that we just leave it alone and hope for the best, Elder Morgan?" asked another Elder.

"James," Lilith said, "do you want to tell the Elders the idea we had a little while ago when we were doing our exploring around the base of the cube?"

"Sure," I replied. "Lilith and I were thinking that we could collectively, in other words, all 14 of us, use our combined telekinetic powers to turn this thing upside down and then collapse the barn and wrap it up with the sheet metal that the barn is constructed with. Although we do not know what kind of metal was used to make this machine, it's walls seem to be quite thin and we are guessing that it isn't that heavy."

"I cannot be destroyed," said the cube. "I am constructed of a material not found on this planet and which is far stronger than anything on this planet."

"That would certainly discourage anyone from trying to get close enough to this thing for it to do any harm," said Elder Semnag. "I think this is a good idea. Shall we get started? I haven't had the opportunity to use my telekinetic powers for some time."

"Absolutely," said Lilith. "First, let's all concentrate on turning this thing upside down. When we have done that, if we can do that, we'll then wrap it up with the sheet metal from the barn and hope for the best for the next 5.3 earth years."

"Before we do that, Lilith," I said, "I would like to ask this machine one other question."

"Sure, James," Lilith replied. "what is it?"

"Tell us, machine," I began, "how is it that you can shrink or enlarge people or things when they are inside of you?"

"Having been programmed to not be any more intrusive than necessary and to cooperate with the beings of this planet as much as is possible in order to study them," the voice said, "I have to inform you that I am a highly intelligent machine."

"Yes, we know," I said. "we've heard that part before. Are you going to answer my question or not?"

"It is an illusion using an advanced form of what you call holography," the machine answered. "The light that you first see when the walls open is meant to temporarily blind you and after you are inside the dimensions of my interior appear to be larger than they are. You were not reduced in size."

"I don't know why we didn't think of that possibility, Lilith," I said. "I'm now beginning to wonder if this thing is really alien."

"I see what you mean, James," Lilith replied. "But if it was made by humans and the military or government built it, why here is this remote location? And what is its real purpose?"

"Can you enlighten us on that, Mr. machine?" I asked it.

"I have no controller, thus I must cooperate," the machine relied. "The people who were in here when you came into this structure were my programmers and they were finishing their programming when you interrupted them."

"You mean that couple just acted like they were ignorant about what was going on here?" I asked the machine.

"That is correct," it answered.

"So," Lilith began, "did they secretly develop you or were they working for someone else?"

"This is a secret project being funded by the government," the machine replied.

"What government?" Lilith asked it.

"I do not know," it replied. "I have not been programmed to know that."

"So, where are the couple and their son who were here?" I asked it.

"Since they were discovered by you, they have been relocated to another secret location to continue their work," the machine informed us.

"What is to become of you?" Elder Semnag put in.

"I cannot be destroyed," is all the machine said.

"Well," I said to the others, "we'll see about that. Shall we proceed as planned?"

"We shall," Lilith said and at her command, all 14 of us started concentrating on flipping the cube over. Amazingly enough, the cube closed up, turned back into its original position, and then began to slowly rise off the ground and began to rotate on an invisible axis. At first I thought that it might be getting ready to burst through the roof of the barn and take off into space. However, we all kept concentrating on the task at hand and about ten minutes later the cube was upside down. During the process, we kept hearing noises inside like things falling and sliding about. A couple of minutes after the cube was upside down, we heard a tremendous crashing taking place inside the cube and guessed that everything was falling apart. If that was the case, we all agreed that the cube probably wasn't programmed to fix itself and wouldn't be a problem for anyone ever again. However, we did tear the barn apart telekinetically and wrap the cube up in the sheet metal that had once been the barn. The structure that we had created looked rather strange, but because it was in a remote location we were hoping that it wouldn't attract any attention. And when the government came looking for it they were going to be in for a big surprise.

When we had finished our work, Lilith said to the group of Elders, "Well, that should take care of this problem and when the government or whoever comes to reclaim their cube they will have a little surprise waiting for them. When they see what happened here today, maybe they will reconsider leaving any more of these machines around for people to stumble into. It might be a good idea for all of the Elders to scan the planet to find any more of these contraptions. I want to thank all of you who came here today to help James and me with this task. I don't think we could have done this by ourselves, but with the combined effort of 14 Voreshan minds we succeeded in our task."

"This was a very mentally taxing activity, Elder Morgan," replied Elder Semnag. "However, it was quite exciting and we were all glad to be here to help you with this task. Now, if it is ok with you, Elder Morgan, we will be getting back to our other tasks in other places including your new charge for us to seek out more of these machines."

"Off you go," said Lilith, "and thanks again."

With that, the Elders all went back to their cars and disappeared off down the road back toward Sarasota where they would separate and get back to their normal lives. Lilith and I stood around for a little while longer wondering where the Warders had been relocated.

"I think we should check on this place periodically to make sure everything is ok," Lilith suggested.

"That's a great idea, Lilith," I said, "but I just hope we don't have a run in with the government."

"I agree, James," Lilith said and we headed back to our car to return home.

CHAPTER FIFTEEN

The rest of 2001 seemed relatively uneventful in the life of the Head Elder and her loving minion, except that I started having strange, if brief, dreams toward the end of the year. Lilith thought that my dreams were me just flashing back to the late 1960s when we first met, were married, and started art school together. The strange thing was that these recurring dreams were of individuals from the photograph on the cover of The Beatles' *Sgt. Peppers Lonely Hearts Club Band* album, which we still owned a copy of on vinyl from 1967. Lilith and I actually had quite a large collection of albums from the 1960s, 1970s, and 1980s and played them all the time on an old stereo system that we had set up in our studio. For lack of a better reason for having dreams of particular people pictured on this particular album cover, I initially went along with Lilith's diagnosis although I was sure that something else was going on in my converted human mind. I had looked at and studied the photograph on the album cover many times over the years out of curiosity, but had actually forgotten who some of the characters were that were pictured on it. The Beatles were still our favorite group of all time and if Voreshans had the ability to reincarnate people, Lilith and I would have brought The Beatles back as Voreshans who could then have entertained the world with their music for a very long time to come. John Lennon's untimely murder on December 8, 1980, lingers in my mind to this day. Music and the world would be a different place if at least one Voreshan had been around to protect John from his assassin.

For about a month from mid-October to mid-November, I dreamed almost every night about a different person from the 65 people shown on the cover, excluding the eight images of the Beatles. I have never come to a conclusion as to why my dreams didn't ever include any of the four members of the band, but I guess they just didn't need to wander into my dreams at that time. Maybe they were content with me being a huge fan and didn't think they needed to bother me. Lilith and I both believed that dreams probably meant something, and we spent a lot of time discussing and contemplating this issue. After the first few nights of having dreams about these characters, I decided to start writing down the names of each of the individuals that I had dreamed about the night before, starting with the first dream. My dreams about characters from the cover of the album finally stopped and I ended up with a list of 21 characters that were shown on the cover of the album and they went across from left to right and top to bottom beginning with Mae West. Because I am not the most organized or logical thinking person, Lilith wondered why the figures appeared to me this way. I don't know why some were skipped in my dreams, but my first guess would be that I wasn't as familiar with the rest of the group of figures as I was with these particular 21, or that I had never really shown any interest in them.

As I just mentioned, Mae West, third from the left at the top, was the person who visited my dreams on the first night, followed the next four nights by Lenny Bruce who is next to her, W.C. Fields two more over with the yellow hat, Carl Jung who is next to him, and Edgar Allen Poe who is next to Jung. After that the order went as follows: Fred

Astaire, Simon Rodia, and Bob Dylan on the back row, Aubrey Beardsley, Dylan Thomas, Dion, Marilyn Monroe, Stan Laurel, Oliver Hardy, and H.G. Wells on the next row down, Stuart Sutcliffe, Tom Mix, Oscar Wilde, and Lewis Carol on the next row down, Marlene Dietrich dressed in yellow on the far right next to George, and Shirley Temple as a young girl below her. These characters can all be explained as to their importance to me at the time or during the years immediately following the late sixties. Lilith and I were both interested in old movies and that would explain why I dreamed about eight or nine of the people on my list. The rest were writers, artists, or musicians and would explain the rest of the list because of my interests in their creative activities. It would have seemed more logical to me if I had dreamed about those individuals I knew less about, because, I surmised, they wanted me to know them as well as the ones I did dream about, but then no one ever told me that dreams had to be logical. Remember the summer of 1963?

However, for several weeks after the dreams stopped I couldn't quit thinking about them and I went over and over the list of names trying to make some sense of why I dreamed about those particular people. Each night that I dreamed about one of these individuals, she or he literally seemed to come to life, step out of the photograph and off the album cover and then beckon me to join them back in the photograph and, when I refused to follow them, that was the end of the dream. I never remembered going back into the photograph with any of these 21 individuals, or becoming a cardboard cutout, but each one had the same purpose each night that I had the dream. I actually worried for a while that these characters were beckoning me because I didn't have long for this world, but Lilith thought I was being silly, especially after all we had been through in our short lives as Voreshans and were still walking around on the planet in good health. I also thought about the idea that I was actually being contacted by the ghosts of these people and that they were visiting me because they were trying to tell me something. We know that ghosts exist from our experience in Italy. I do remember it being especially hard to resist Marilyn Monroe's and Marlene Dietrich's sexually intoxicating voices, but I remained true to Lilith even in my dreams.

Early the next year when I was once again talking about these dreams and having yet another discussion about them with Lilith, she came up with an interesting idea, probably to get me to shut up, but which I thought was intriguing. Lilith suggested that maybe these individuals came to me in my dreams because they wanted me to paint their portraits and maybe by doing so it would help me to get over my obsession with the dreams and their possible meaning. Lilith also suggested that maybe they liked my art work and wanted me to immortalize them in the same way that Andy Warhol did with celebrities back in the last century. These were things that I had not thought about and the ideas were intriguing to me and doing the portraits would be a change from painting the usual landscapes and seascapes of the surrounding area where we lived. Lilith and I both did the occasional portrait if the price was right and we were both as accomplished at that as we were at the rest of the things we painted. We had received our traditional training at the local art school after all and studied up close and first hand many of the portraits hanging in galleries when we were in Italy as well as the National Portrait Gallery in Washington, D.C. Finally, around the first of March, I decided to act on Lilith's suggestion and started doing small portraits of each of the people in my dreams, starting of course with Mae West. So, for the next several weeks I painted all 21 of the people from the *Sgt. Peppers Lonely Hearts Club Band* album cover who had appeared in my dreams a few months before and in the order that they had appeared to me.

Lilith and I had decided not to display any of the portraits of these individuals in the gallery until I had finished all of them and they were framed. When the time was right and I was ready to expose my dream inspired portraits, we sent out several notices about my new work and had an opening for the show on a Sunday afternoon in late May. The local newspaper even carried a short article about the portraits and the opening, mine and Lilith's other artistic efforts, and the gallery. When that Sunday afternoon had finally come to a close every one of the 21 portraits had sold for a good price and over 300 people had come to see them. Everyone who bought one of the portraits agreed to let me keep them in the gallery for a couple of weeks for others to see and it ended up bringing over 100 commissions that year for similar portraits for both Lilith and I to work on since we both worked in a similar style. Several people wanted a portrait of one of the remaining figures on the album cover and others just wanted a portrait of themselves or a loved one done in the same or similar style of the original 21 *Sgt. Peppers* album portraits. Although it disappointed a few people, I refused to paint more than one portrait of each of the individuals pictured on the cover of the album so it was first come, first served and Lilith respected my wishes. I also refused to paint portraits of any of the Beatles, more out of respect for their lives and music than the fact that none of them had appeared in my dreams. Lilith told me that the next time I had dreams like that to not waste any time contemplating them, but to get busy painting them. At the prices we charged, those 21 portraits and the commissions that followed kept us in soup and crackers for a long time.

Amazingly enough, the more portraits we painted for people the more portraits they wanted and when first-timers to the gallery saw the portraits many of them wanted one as well. There were several articles about us and especially about the portraits in the local newspaper and in several art magazines. Lilith and I had about two dozen patrons who each ended up with from 12 to 20 different portraits, both of famous people and relatives. Business picked up and we were kept quite busy for the rest of the decade and into the next decade just trying to keep up with the portraiture work. The portrait commissions began to slow down some toward the end of 2009, but Lilith and I both kept painting and actually got back to painting some of the subjects we loved best.

Some things never change and for artists like Lilith and me that was a good thing. People still enjoyed seeing and buying art and the local art museum was thriving more than it had ever done in the past. The local art school was bursting at the seams with students who wanted to be artists and make their living creating and selling their work, which is why Lilith and I were invited to the art school so often to do demonstrations and talk about our success as artists.

CHAPTER SIXTEEN

It was now January 1, 2011, and Lilith and I were returning to our house just after midnight after watching the
fireworks display on Sarasota Bay to bring in the new year.
Fireworks displays on New Year's Eve and the Fourth of
July were still two things that the general public could attend for free. We usually didn't stay out so late at night, but
we hadn't missed a fireworks display on these two holidays
since we met back in high school and we weren't going to
stop now. We have never gotten tired of this activity and
each year the display seems to be bigger and better. One of
our current patrons has a house on Sarasota Bay and for the
past several years has invited Lilith and me out to watch the
fireworks from their boat dock. Will and Cara Miason are
what my parents used to call "filthy rich." Will's father,
who had been a very successful business man selling yachts
to the rich and famous, had left him and Cara several million dollars when he died. Will's mother was still alive and
now ran the company, which Will and Cara would also in-
herit one day. In their late 30s, they thought that Lilith and I
were only a few years younger than them and they liked to
entertain us on occasion, mainly because they were patrons
of our art work. They must own at least two dozen of mine
and Lilith's paintings and they hold several dinner parties
every year mostly for our benefit, as they love to show off
their collection of original Morgans and talk others into visiting our gallery. Not wanting to be outdone by the Miasons,
many of their rich friends have come to the gallery within a

few days of one of their dinner parties and bought several of our paintings. And if the Miasons see something one of their friends has bought and they like it, they will then come to the gallery looking for something similar.

As usual, I digress. As Lilith and I were driving along Route 41 on our way home from the New Year's fireworks display, several police cruisers went speeding by us with their sirens blaring and their lights flashing. They seemed to be headed in the direction of the art school, so we headed over that way out of curiosity. We noticed that when we got close to the art school that it seemed to be surrounded by quite a few police cruisers along with several fire trucks and ambulances, all with their lights flashing. Being the curious individuals that we are, I pulled off into the driveway of a nearby business that was closed at this time of night so we could watch all the activity. We sat in the car watching from about 25 yards away and both of us tried to tune into the thoughts of some of the people closer to the scene. I managed to get into the head of one of the policemen and this is what I heard him thinking: *"Holy crap! Only two weeks on this job and I have to be the one to pull over a murderer that's on Florida's Most Wanted List. Now here I am in the back of an ambulance with a gunshot wound to my shoulder that hurts like hell! Man, mother is going to finish the job and kill me when she hears about this! Maybe she was right in not wanting me to follow in my father's footsteps and become a cop. I don't think she could continue living if she lost her son the way she lost her husband. Oh, she is definitely going to be one unhappy camper!"*

Lilith had picked up on the thoughts of a more serious person at the scene: *"Damn it! Everything was going fine until that damn rookie cop pulled me over for speeding.*

Probably didn't make his quota for last month. I had to shoot the mother f_____ or he would've found out who I am when he ran the license plate and found out my car is stolen. I should never have come into town to get drunk and see in the new year at Buzz Man's Bar. I only go there 'cause no one would ever recognize me. It's such a nice dark bar to go and get drunk at and pick up hot babes. I hope to hell that I killed that sorry rascal of a cop so the other coppers won't know that I'm hiding in this damn art school! This looks like some sort of art studio with these easels sitting all around. Oh crap! I think I hear them getting closer. Maybe I can hide under that there platform at the back of the room. Then if any of them coppers come in here I'll shoot them from under there and they won't know what hit them or where it come from!"

"James," Lilith said, "there's somebody hiding from the police in the figure painting studio under the model's platform and he plans to kill any policemen that enter the studio! I think he's hiding because he shot a policeman who had stopped him and it must be pretty serious if all of these police are here and he's ready to shoot them."

"It is very serious, Lilith," I said. "I was reading the thoughts of the policeman who was shot by a murderer on the state's Most Wanted List. The murderer must be the one who is hiding in the figure painting studio."

"Is the policeman going to be ok, James?" Lilith asked. "The guy in the figure painting studio hopes that he killed the policeman."

"The policeman is in a lot of pain," I said, "but he will recover just fine. He seems to be more worried about what his mother is going to do to him when she finds out than he has been shot. Seems his father was a policeman and lost his life in the line of duty."

"So, the man in the figure painting studio is the murderer on the Most Wanted List?" Lilith said more than asked.

"Must be," I replied.

"James, we have got to do something to help the police," Lilith said. "The man in the figure painting studio plans to shoot more policemen if they come in to the studio and we are the only ones who can prevent that from happening."

"Why don't you work on the minds of the policemen who are closest to the studio and keep them from going in there," I said to Lilith. "In the meantime, I will try to get the murderer to surrender to the police. Even if I can't convince the murderer to give up, maybe you can keep the other policemen from going in there blind."

"I'm on it, James," Lilith said. "This should be a piece of cake!"

I knew that Lilith wouldn't have any problem with changing the policemen's minds and at that, I started communicating telepathically with the murderer in the figure painting studio, *"You know that you are trapped and that you are going to die very soon regardless of how many cops you kill. You might as well surrender now and not die."*

"What the hell?" the murderer said out loud and then clasped his hand over his mouth just as two policemen were starting to come in to the figure painting studio. However, Lilith was at work on them and made them change their mind and they went to the next studio which was a first year drawing studio. *"Am I hearing things or did my dead old mama just contact me again? I wish you would leave me be you old hag!"*

That provided me with a perfect opening and I picked up where he left off, saying, *"This is your dear old dead mama, son, who still loves you very much no matter what you think of me. Please don't go and get yourself killed like your brother did in that bar shootout with the coppers a couple of years back. The cop you shot tonight is going to live, so they might go easier on you if you give yourself up, son.* " Of course, this fellow didn't know that he was actually being contacted by a real person telepathically.

"*Mama,* " he said, "*I don't wanna die either, but them coppers might go ahead and kill me anyways! I got to shoot them if they come in here after me! I'm sorry for calling you a bad name.* "

"*Son,* " I continued, "*I made them last two coppers skip on by where your hiding. The dead can do that you know. Now, you just put down your gun and go on out there and give yourself up like I told you! Please don't go and get yourself killed.* " I then went out on a limb hoping that there weren't any more of his clan still alive. "*You're the only one of the family left alive.* "

"*But, mama,* " he started, but got interrupted by "mama."

"*Don't you go 'but mama' to me youngin!* " I nearly yelled at him. "*You better give up now before them coppers come back and shoot you dead! I can't make them stay away forever!* "

"*Ok, mama,* " he said to who he thought was his dear old dead mama and he crawled out from under the model's platform, laid his gun on top of it, and slowly approached the door to the figure painting studio. "*I sure hope you're right, mama, about them not shooting me if I'm giving up.* " When he got to the door, he slowly opened it and stepped out into the bright search lights that were set up all around the area with his hands high above his head. His first thought at that moment was to look around and see if there was a way to escape, but he quickly realized that there were too many policemen to make a run for it. He just kept hoping that his "mama" was right when she said they would go easier on him if he gave up.

None of the policemen were paying any attention to this studio because of what Lilith had been doing with their minds, but she now released them all when the murderer stepped out into the open with both hands raised high above his head and yelled, "I'm giving up! Don't shoot me dead! Please don't shoot me dead! Don't make my mama mad at me!"

Lilith and I had gotten out of our car and moved in as close as we could so we could hear what was going on. When we heard what the murderer said when he came out of the figure painting studio about his mama, we got a good case of the giggles. The policeman closest to the figure painting studio yelled out, "There he is and he's surrendering!" He and about a dozen other policemen nearby then closed in quickly on the murderer with guns pointed at him and then two of them grabbed him and slammed him face first to the ground and put handcuffs on him.

"Please don't kill me! Please don't make mama mad at me!" the murderer said as he went to the ground.

Another policemen said, "Guess what buddy? You ain't on the Most Wanted List no more!" and he jerked the murderer to his feet and led him away to a waiting police cruiser.

"My dead mama come into my head and told me to give up," the murderer shouted at the policemen around him.

"Did she now?" said one of the policemen. "Is your dead mama some sort of spirit?"

"She sure did!" the murderer said. "I don't know if she's a spirit or not, but she said you would go easy on me if I gave up. She didn't want me getting' killed like my brother did. Hey, wait a dad burned minute!" At this point the murderer started trying to struggle to get free, but the policeman had too good of a hold on him for that to happen. "I ain't never had no brother!" he shouted. "That old biddy done went and tricked me! You are an old hag, mama! Damn your soul to hell!"

One of the policemen alongside the other policeman asked, "Sounds to me like that mother of yours was in that room with you? Maybe we should send a couple of officers back to investigate," and he nodded toward a couple of other policeman who headed back to the figure painting studio.

"Oh, hell no!" the murderer replied. "She was talking to me in my head. She died about ten years ago and she's goin' to hell for what she done gone and done to me today!"

"Sounds like they better put this one in a padded cell," the policeman said to another officer and he started laughing.

"Mother talking to him in his head," replied the other policeman. "I've never heard that one before."

"Well, I heard a lot of tall tales in my 23 years on the force," the policeman who had hold of the murderer said, "but this is a new one on me, too."

After the police shoved the murderer into a police cruiser and it pulled away Lilith and I went back to our car feeling good about probably saving several policemen's lives that night. The rest of the way home we discussed what we each had done in the minds of the policemen and the murderer and because we were so tired, we went fast asleep as soon as we hit the bed. Of course, if Lilith had wanted dessert I would have found a way to make her happy. As you know by now, I never turn down dessert. Our friends would certainly be talking the next few days about what happened at the art school that night, but they would never know that Lilith and I had anything to do with it. We had never revealed our little secret to any other humans after Sherry and Andy Chelltim had passed away back in the 1990s, actually within two years of each other. Although we had many human friends and loved them dearly, we never became that close with anyone else. It wasn't that we didn't trust our friends, but we had broken Voreshan rules when we revealed who we were to Sherry and Andy back in the late 1960s, and now that Lilith was the Head Elder we had to be more careful about such things.

We learned from listening to the news reports over the next few days that the murderer, whose name was Buck Franklin, but who was cleverly using the alias of Frank Bucklin, was wanted for killing his ex-girlfriend, Sandra Wedell, known as Saucy Waucy at the strip club in Gainesville where she worked. Old Buck had killed her in the cabin they had once shared up near Deadman Bay on the Gulf coast. Sandra had had enough of Buck's drinking and verbal abuse and had left him back in April of 2009. He had lured her back to the cabin with the pretense of them getting back together and him being a better person than he had been when they were together. When she showed up around 4:00 on a sunny Saturday afternoon in June of last year, he graciously invited her in and offered her a drink. As soon as Sandra had her drink in hand and turned her back to him to look out the front window thinking that maybe Buck had really changed for the good, Buck pulled out his .357 magnum automatic pistol and emptied all eight rounds into her back, including three rounds to the head.

Sandra Wedell was dead before she and her drink crashed to the floor.

Buck immediately fled the area, not even bothering to hide Sandra's body, and headed for Miami where he had a couple of buddies that he could stay with until things settled down some. He figured the cops would blame the murder on someone else since he hadn't been at the cabin for several months. When Saucy didn't show up for three nights for her late show at the strip club, the manager went to her apartment and discovered that she hadn't been home for several days. He immediately went to the police and filed a missing person's report and two days later her body was found by two officers from the Dixie County sheriff's department. It didn't take long for them to figure out that the murderer was Buck Franklin.

A statewide manhunt went out after that and when one of Buck's roommates heard about it on the news and that the authorities were looking for Buck Franklin for murder and offering a sizable reward, he ratted out his so-called friend so he could collect the reward. Well, this roommate was the type who couldn't keep his mouth shut and told several people what was going down and the word got back to Buck very quickly. While the police were on a stakeout at the apartment where Buck had been staying he was on his way across the state on Route 41, thinking that he would maybe disappear around Port Charlotte. However, Buck just kept on driving past Port Charlotte, past Sarasota, and then took Route 64 back inland thinking it would be easier to hide out somewhere away from a city. And the shocker for Lilith and me was that he had been holed up all this time in the Warders abandoned farm house and we had been out there twice while he was living there to check and make sure everything was ok. Fortunately for us, he was either not home or didn't see us prowling around. More than likely, he was sleeping off a drunk from the night before. Of course, we could have dealt with the situation if Buck had confronted us when we visited the farm, but it was better that it ended the way it did. It could have gotten really interesting if the police were to discover Buck murdered at the farm and the Warders were nowhere to be found!

CHAPTER SEVENTEEN

The rest of 2011 was relatively uneventful. Lilith and I seemed to have fewer and fewer run-ins with people who were angry, sad, depressed, etc. than we did back in art school in the late 1960s and early 1970s. Of course the competition between art students where their work was concerned was pretty intense and there was always some-one on campus who thought they were better than all the other students. In addition to that, jealousies ran high when it seemed that a few students, like Lilith and me when we were selected to go to Italy with the Cheltims, were getting preferential treatment. All that aside, we were still working at a steady pace to keep up with the demand for our paint-ings. Several gallery owners from other states often trav-eled through Sarasota looking for new talent and Lilith and I were now being represented in Miami, Atlanta, Santa Fe, Los Angeles, and San Antonio. Everyone thought that this was pretty remarkable for a couple who were barely 30 years old, but that was in Voreshan years. In reality we had been creating art for forty years since graduating from art school in 1971.

It was around Thanksgiving in 2011, however, that Lil-ith and I met up with a remarkably talented young student from the art school. For several years we had been inviting a handful of students from the art school, who were too far away from home to spend Thanksgiving with their families, to share Thanksgiving with us. Usually there weren't more than five or six and Lilith and I went all out and prepared a huge traditional Thanksgiving dinner so that the students would feel as if they were at home. As it turned out, there were seven students that Thanksgiving in 2011 who made it to our home to celebrate with us. Two were from New York, one from Washington state, three from the Chicago area, and one from New Mexico.

The student that I just mentioned was a new first semester freshman that the art faculty were as excited about as they were about Lilith and me when we were in school there. Her name was Evelyn Tibsen and she was the student from New Mexico. Evelyn had seen mine and Lilith's paintings in Santa Fe when she was on a high school trip from her home in Taos. When she went back home after the trip to Santa Fe she told her parents that she wanted to go to school in Sarasota, Florida. Evelyn's parents had hoped that she would go to college somewhere closer to home, but they had been told how talented their daughter was in art and that the school in Sarasota was one of the best. Thus, Evelyn's parents gave in and sent her off to Sarasota, Florida to study art.

We had not formerly met Evelyn, but when she showed up at our house for Thanksgiving that year we immediately recognized her as a student who had come to our gallery at least once a week to browse around. We always greeted her warmly and invited her to browse around and if she had any questions not to be afraid to ask. Evelyn didn't talk very much when she visited our gallery, but she seemed to intently study our paintings for a while and then slip quietly out the door and disappear down the street.

When I went to the door to welcome our first guest to Thanksgiving, Evelyn was standing there looking scared. "Hi," I said. "Welcome to our home and happy Thanksgiving! You're the young lady who comes to our gallery so often. I'm James Morgan and this is my wife Lilith," who had just come to the front door from the kitchen.

"Happy Thanksgiving to you two as well," Evelyn said. "My name is Evelyn Tibsen."

"Come on in and have a seat," Lilith said. "You're the first to arrive, but there are supposed to be about seven of you this year. Where is home for you?"

"I'm from Taos, New Mexico," Evelyn answered.

"Taos is such a lovely town," Lilith said. "James and I always love to visit there when we are in Santa Fe."

"We are represented by a gallery in Santa Fe," I offered, "so we get out there at least once a year."

"I know," Evelyn replied. "I saw your art last year when the art club at my high school took a field trip to Santa Fe. I really love your paintings."

"So that's why you're in our gallery so much?" I said. "Lilith and I are both very flattered that you come in so often. I wish we would have introduced ourselves sooner."

"That's ok," Evelyn said. "I'm kind of shy and I don't usually introduce myself either. It's something that my high school art teacher said I was going to have to work on if I wanted to be a successful artist."

"Well, don't feel too bad about it, Evelyn," Lilith said. "James and I were extremely shy when we first met, especially James!"

"We're not much better now," I added.

"But you are so successful!" Evelyn said. "I've been reading about you ever since I first saw your art work in Santa Fe. The gallery owner there said you are in galleries in Texas, Georgia, and Florida as well. She said that you were both widely known and had sold hundreds and hundreds of paintings."

"My goodness, Evelyn," Lilith said, "you certainly seem to know a lot about us. I guess we need to get to know you better as well."

About that time the doorbell rang and I went to answer it while Lilith and Evelyn got better acquainted. Three more of our seven guests had arrived together and I invited them in. Two more cars pulled up about that time and our other three invitees got out and came in. Lilith and I got all of the students to introduce themselves, especially since a couple of them were new freshmen and didn't know the other students who were there. We left them to their chatter and went to the kitchen to finish getting the Thanksgiving dinner on the table. We had a large dining room table and this was usually the only occasion that Lilith and I got to use it for something besides a spot for the mail and other things to collect. When everything was ready and on the table we called our guests into the dining room for the feast that we had prepared. They were all chatting simultaneously with each other including Evelyn.

Everyone seemed pleased with the dinner and a couple of them even said it was the biggest Thanksgiving spread they had ever seen. The two students from New York were juniors and currently a couple who planned to get married upon graduation. The other two females, from Washington and Chicago, and the other two males, from Chicago, seemed to hook up during dinner leaving poor Evelyn as the lone stranger in the group. It wasn't that she was being ignored or alienated by the other students, they included her in all of their conversations, but Lilith and I could tell when a female and male were attracted to each other. Because she was very attractive, Lilith and I were very surprised actually that Evelyn hadn't attracted the attention of at least one of the males during dinner. I actually sensed that the male student from New York, who was engaged, giving Evelyn the eye a few times during dinner.

Well, things wrapped up around 6:00 that afternoon and all of our guests gradually departed well fed and thankful for the opportunity to get to know Lilith and me better. Everyone except Evelyn, who hung back to talk with Lilith and me some more. Not ever having had a groupie before, at least that we knew about, we were glad to entertain Evelyn a little longer. Evelyn began, "You said earlier when I got here that you would like to get to know me better. Is that still true?"

"Absolutely," Lilith replied. "Although students have always seemed interested in our work, no one has ever been as enthusiastic as you."

"What would you like to tell us about yourself, Evelyn?" I asked.

"I'm not really sure how to start," Evelyn replied, "but I'll try this first."

"Go on," Lilith said. "What you have to tell us sounds somewhat serious."

"Well, not as serious as I'm making it sound," Evelyn communicated telepathically.

Lilith and I quickly looked at each other wide-eyed with our mouths open. "Evelyn, are you telling us that you are Voreshan?"

"Yes," was all she silently communicated.

"Ok," I began, *"But how do we know that you aren't something other than Voreshan? We have on occasion encountered less than friendly aliens who can communicate this way."*

"When I told my parents that I wanted to come to school here in Sarasota because I so admired your painting, they did a little investigating about you two. They found

plenty of information on the internet about you and your work and how you both graduated from art school here and how you are still involved with the school.." Evelyn paused for a few seconds to gauge our reactions.

"Go on," Lilith said. *"You have definitely got our attention."*

"Well," Evelyn began again, *"my parents decided that the best way to really find out about someone was to contact the Elder who represented our area. When Elder Semnag told us that one of the two artists I liked so much was Elder Lilith Morgan, my parents knew I would be ok here."*

"Elder Semnag recommended this art school because of who we are?" I asked.

"Yes, sir," was all Evelyn answered.

"This is certainly a strange turn of events, Evelyn, for James and me," Lilith said. *"What do you say to talking out loud, especially since no one else is around?"*

"I'm all for that," I said out loud.

"Ok," Evelyn said.

"I guess the first thing we should say," Lilith began, "is that you will always be welcome in our gallery and studio as well as our home."

"Thank you, Elder Morgan," Evelyn said.

"However, your interest in our work and our personal relationship with you needs to stay on a professional level where everyone else around here is concerned. Are you ok with that, Evelyn?" Lilith asked.

"Yes, ma'am," Evelyn replied. "I don't expect any special attention from either of you, but I would like for us to be friends if that is at all possible."

"Of course we can be friends, Evelyn," I said. "All Voreshans are our friends, just as all Voreshans should be your friends."

"That makes me very happy," Evelyn said. "I promise not to let our secret identity out. I was raised by two true Voreshan parents and taught all the rules that we must follow in our life on Earth. I would never compromise your position Elder Morgan. If I did my parents would probably banish me to Mars!"

Lilith and I both cracked up over that remark and assured Evelyn that her banishment would be to some remote locale on Earth and not Mars, at which she started laughing as well. We talked with Evelyn for about another hour, mostly concerning school and the opportunities that she had going to this art school. She was especially interested in when we would be doing future workshops and told her that depended on the school's administration. We usually did one or two workshops per academic year depending on the interest from both students at the art school and the general public.

After Evelyn finally left, Lilith said, "Well, James, that is certainly an interesting turn of events."

"I'll say," I responded. "I wonder if Evelyn has had any opportunities to practice her telepathic powers on any humans yet?"

"We'll have to ask her about that the next time we see her at the gallery," Lilith said. "I hope that her parents aren't expecting us to adopt her while she is in art school here."

"I don't know, Lilith," I said. "However, that wouldn't be the worst thing ever since we were never able to have any children of our own."

"I'm so sorry about that, James," Lilith said with a tear in her eye.

"There's absolutely nothing to be sorry about, my love," I said and wrapped my arm around her shoulders. "It just wasn't meant for us to have children. It was probably a good thing that we didn't considering all the dangerous adventures we've had over the years."

"Thank you, James," Lilith said. "You have always been so understanding about that."

"You know, Lilith," I said, "if Elder Semnag and Evelyn's parents had contacted us about her coming to school here before school started, we could have temporarily have adopted her and she could have lived here with us."

"That would have been a good idea, James," Lilith said. "We could have told people that she was our niece or some other relative."

"Oh well," I said, "it would look a little suspicious if we tried to do that now."

"I wonder if Evelyn would have enough spare time to work in our gallery with us, James?" Lilith suggested more than asked.

"That's a great idea, Lilith!" I exclaimed. "I'm sure that she would be trustworthy if Elder Semnag believes in her. Maybe we can talk with her about that idea the next time she is in the gallery."

"Let's plan to do that, James," Lilith said. "Well, it's getting a little late, dear, and we have a gallery to run tomorrow and a lot of dishes to wash tonight."

"I hope that doesn't mean I won't get my dessert tonight, Lilith," I said with that sad puppy dog look on my face. At that, Lilith started strutting her stuff up the stairs to our bedroom while shedding her clothes along the way.

Needless to say, I was close on her heels. I guess the dishes could wait until tomorrow.

CHAPTER EIGHTEEN

Lilith and I approached Evelyn about working some in our gallery the first day that she came by the next week. To say that she was excited about the idea would be an understatement and she started work the very next afternoon when she got out of school. Evelyn was quick to learn the ropes about running our gallery and Lilith and I were soon able to spend more time creating and less time selling. Nearly everyone who came into the gallery was impressed with Evelyn's story about how she came to the art school in Sarasota and many of them left with one of our paintings. We couldn't have picked a better salesperson for the job.

Christmas was approaching fast and our paintings were selling like hotcakes at a church supper. Evelyn had not seen her parents since school started and asked us if she could have about a week off over Christmas to go home to Taos. That was fine with Lilith and me as we had planned to close down from Christmas eve to after the first of the new year to take a little vacation of our own. Our initial plan was to hook up with Lilith's parents and spend the holidays in Key West. Lilith and I had never been to Key West, but the Lhuvs had gone a few years back to celebrate their wedding anniversary and loved it. But as often happens in mine and Lilith's lives, our plans took a different turn that Christmas, much to the dismay of the Lhuvs, who were really looking forward to spending some time with us.

Voreshans aren't really superstitious creatures, because we know that evil is real and exists not only on Earth, but

throughout the universe as we know it. If you have followed my story from the beginning back in the summer of
1963, you know that I have encountered several forms of
evil aliens both as a human and as a Voreshan. Lilith and I
have battled more of these evil beings than most Voreshans
ever know about. The Elders usually try to make sure that
most of our species can go about their normal day-to-day
tasks and only occasionally have to deal with bad humans.
Because Lilith and I have developed far stronger powers
than any other Voreshans, we are the ones called upon to
deal with the really bad aliens that prowl the earth. All that
said, essentially as a reminder, mine and Lilith's Christmas
plans for 2011 didn't come about and Key West would just
have to wait.

Evelyn had flown home to Taos two days before
Christmas and Lilith and I didn't expect her back until the
second semester of school started after the turn of the new
year. However, on December 27th, Evelyn's parents called
us just as we were getting ready to depart Sarasota for Key
West where Lilith's parents were waiting for us. It seems
that Evelyn had disappeared during the previous night. The
Tibsens told us that everything had gone quite well on
Christmas morning and into the rest of the day, but just
around dusk they had noticed a shadowy looking figure
seemingly darting from window to window around their
home. When Mr. Tibsen went outside to investigate he
couldn't find any evidence of anyone having been there. He
reported the incident to the local police and they cruised
around the neighborhood looking for anyone suspicious,
but turned up nothing.

Early on the morning of the 27th, Mr. and Mrs. Tibsen
were up early, but were letting Evelyn sleep in, something
that she didn't get to do very often at school since classes

always started at 8:00. Or so Evelyn's parents thought. Around 7:00 that morning their doorbell rang and when Mr. Tibsen went to the door he discovered an elderly Navajo man standing there with a very concerned look on his face. He introduced himself simply as Mosi and wanted to know if the Tibsen's daughter was ok. Mrs. Tibsen had come to the door by now and asked Mosi why he wanted to know. Mosi said that he had had a dream the night before and that in his dream their daughter had been taken by a yee naaldlooshii or skin walker, which was a person who could change into any animal that he or she wanted. Mrs. Tibsen told Mosi that was ridiculous and that his superstitions were not their beliefs and that Evelyn was still asleep in her bed upstairs. Mosi begged them to check on their daughter, because his dreams were seldom wrong. While Mr. Tibsen waited at the front door with Mosi, Mrs. Tibsen obliged the old Navajo man and went to check on Evelyn. She had been gone less than 30 seconds when Mr. Tibesn and Mosi heard a scream from upstairs. Mr. Tibsen told Mosi to wait there and he took the stairs three at a time and bursting into Evelyn's bedroom found his wife sitting on the edge of an empty bed with a bewildered look on her face and tears running down her cheeks.

When the Tibsen's went back downstairs they discovered that Mosi was gone and that made them very suspicious of him, so they immediately called the police. The police came out to their house, took down their story, and told them that their daughter was probably just playing a practical joke on them having probably learned about Navajo folklore in school. After the police left, the Tibsen's anxiously talked about what the police had suggested and dismissed that idea since Evelyn had never gone anywhere before without them knowing about it. Besides, practical jokes just weren't her style. They briefly considered contacting a local expert on Navajo folklore, but then decide to call Lilith and me to see if we could shed any light on the matter. And that is where our part in this little adventure starts and our plans to go to Key West end.

"Hello," I said when I picked up the phone.

"Is this Mr. Morgan?" the male voice at the other end of the line asked.

"Yes, it is," I replied. "Who am I speaking to?"

"This is Edward Tibsen, Evelyn's father," the man replied.

"How can I help you Mr. Tibsen?" I asked.

"Mr. Morgan," he continued, "it seems that Evelyn disappeared during the night and that is not like her at all. Ellen and I were wondering if you know anything about Evelyn's holiday plans that we don't?"

"No, we don't, Mr. Tibsen," I answered. "Have you tried contacting Evelyn telepathically?"

"Oh, we weren't sure if Evelyn had talked to you and your wife about that yet," he answered. "Evelyn keeps most of her private thoughts to herself and we respect that, but we did try and didn't have any luck."

"Well," I began, "if you've tried to contact Evelyn telepathically without any results it is beginning to sound pretty serious. Have you talked with anyone else about this, say Elder Semnag?"

"We did call the police in, but they passed it off as a prank," Mr. Tibsen said. "We didn't contact Elder Semnag because we've bothered him so much lately. We are sorry to bother you with this, but we know that you have taken a liking to Evelyn and are helping her out with some part-time work at your gallery. She respects you more than you can imagine."

"You're not bothering us," I said. "After all, Lilith is the Head Elder now and is always here for any Voreshans who need help in some way. Have you talked to anyone else?" I was picking up some thoughts from Mr. Tibsen about an elderly Navajo man.

"We didn't know Evelyn was even missing when we got up this morning," Mr. Tibsen said. "We were going to let her sleep in today, but then this elderly Navajo man came to our door early and asked about Evelyn. He claimed to have had a dream about her and that she had been taken away. Ellen and I had our doubts about him, but when we checked Evelyn's bedroom she was gone. When we came back downstairs the Navajo man who called himself Mosi was gone. He mentioned something about skin walkers."

"That's a new one on me," I said, "but it is quite possible that there are evil people among Native American tribes."

"I know that Evelyn said you had plans over the holidays, but Ellen and I were wondering if you could somehow help us out with this situation?"

"Mr. Tibsen, I am going to start communicating telepathically for security reasons and so that Lilith can participate in this conversation," I told him.

"Ok," he replied. "My wife is going to tune in, too, if that's ok with you."

"That's fine, Mr. Tibsen," Lilith chimed in. *"As James said, we are not familiar with Native American customs or folklore, but it wouldn't be that hard for us to find out more about these Skin Walkers that the old Navajo man mentioned to you. What do you think we should do, James?"*

"As much as I was looking forward to this little vacation trip to Key West, Lilith," I said, *"it sounds like we need to detour to Taos instead."*

"I agree, James," Lilith replied. *"Mr. and Mrs. Tibsen, James and I might be able to get a flight out tonight, but it will probably be tomorrow before we can get there. Will the two of you be ok in the meantime?"*

"My dear, dear Elder Morgan," Mrs. Tibsen put in, *"it isn't going to be easy to wait without knowing what is going on with our daughter, but knowing that you two are coming to help gives us hope at least."*

"Well, Mrs. Tibsen," Lilith said, *"James and I will do our best to get a flight out no later than tomorrow and we'll let you know when we will be arriving. In the meantime we will also look into these skin walkers and see what we might be dealing with when we get to Taos."*

"I don't know how we could ever thank you, Elder Morgan," Mr. Tibsen said.

"We'll worry about that at another time," Lilith said. *"For now, I want you two to stay put in your home and do not venture outside. You home may not be a safe haven against whoever or whatever has taken Evelyn, but it has to be better than going outside."*

"We'll wait right here to hear from you," Mr. Tibsen said and we stopped communication with Evelyn's parents.

"Well, my dear," I said, "there always seems to be something to interfere with our pleasure trips."

"I know, James," Lilith said, "but it is not only who we are and what we are charged with doing on Earth; it's also now who I am as Head Elder."

"I know, Lilith dear, but I am really going to miss you while I'm in Key West," I tried to say with a straight face. Instead, I said, "Ow!" as Lilith punched me really hard in the arm.

"The only way you would be going to Key West," Lilith said as seriously as she could, "is if I exiled you there, had you tied to the mast of a small boat, and shoved out to sea at the sign of the first hurricane."

"Isn't that called cruel and unusual punishment?" I asked and got punched hard in the other arm. For a sweet little redhead, this woman has always packed a powerful punch.

As we suspected at that time of the year, Lilith and I couldn't get a flight out of Sarasota on the 27th, but were able to grab two seats that someone had canceled the following morning early. We had to fly into Santa Fe via Dallas and didn't arrive at the Tibsens until late that afternoon. Mr. Tibsen met us at the airport so that we didn't have to rent a car and make the drive to Taos ourselves. The events that happened after arriving in Taos were the strangest to date for Lilith and me.

CHAPTER NINETEEN

After Lilith and I got settled into our room at the Tibsens we sat down to a delicious dinner that Mrs. Tibsen had prepared. We had talked briefly about Evelyn's disappearance with Mr. Tibsen on the ride from Santa Fe to Taos, but he really wanted to wait until we were back so that Mrs. Tibsen could be in on the conversation as well.

We had barely started dinner when Mr. Tibsen got the ball rolling. "So, Elder Morgan," he began, "were you able to find out anything about these so-called skin walkers?"

"Well," Lilith replied with a mouthful of food, "the first thing we did was to contact Elder Semnag and let him know about your situation."

"We really didn't want to bother him again so soon," said Mrs. Tibsen.

"I assure you," Lilith said, "that you will never be bothering him even if you contact him daily. If necessary, James and I will ask him to help out if things get too much for us to handle. Now, to answer your question about the skin walkers. I asked Elder Semnag to find out what he could, because I knew that James and I wouldn't get here until late in the day. Just prior to arriving in Santa Fe, Elder Semnag contacted James and me and reported his findings."

"This isn't going to be good , is it?" asked Mrs. Tibsen.

"We won't know how bad this situation might be until James and I have had some time to do a little investigating of our own," Lilith replied. "What Elder Semnag did find out is that most of what we know about the skin walkers is legend or myth. However, many of the Navajo people still believe that skin walkers are among us and that they are very evil individuals."

"Oh my God, our poor, poor Evelyn," Mrs. Tibsen said and began to cry.

"Now, now, dear," Mr. Tibsen said to his wife, "let's not get too upset. Let's listen to what Elder Morgan has to say and how she plans to deal with our situation."

"It is very important that you both stay as level-headed as possible under the circumstances," Lilith said. "Since we still don't know exactly what we are dealing with here I believe it is important not to get too emotional. We don't know how these creatures called skin walkers operate or what they can sense or know."

"Please go on, Elder Morgan," Mr. Tibsen said.

"Most of the extreme evil that James and I have had to deal with in our lives has been with other alien species, except for true earthly ghosts when we were in Italy," Lilith continued. "If we are dealing with humans here, then this problem will be relatively easy to solve. Even if this so-called skin walker is an alien species, James and I should be able to handle that as well. We have dealt with some very evil and powerful aliens in our short lives. However, if the legends about skin walkers are true, we may be dealing with an earthly evil far more dangerous and elusive than ghosts."

"What else can you tell us about these skin walkers?" asked Mrs. Tibsen now that she had better control of her emotions, although she was still sniffling.

"According to what Elder Semang found out, a yee naaldlooshii, or skin walker, is one of several kinds of Navajo witch."

"Oh my God!" said Mrs. Tibsen again.

Lilith just gave Mrs. Tibsen a look that could freeze an Eskimo and then continued. "Technically, according to Elder Semnag, the skin walkers are people who, using their super powers, can travel in the form of several different animals." Lilith glanced in Mrs. Tibsen's direction, but she remained quiet. "They can be men or women, but most are men, and they have attained a high level in their kind and are referred to as clizyati, which means pure evil. They are considered to be humans, but humans who have gained considerable supernatural powers. These clizyati, or witches if you prefer, primarily use their supernatural powers to move around from place to place faster than anyone trying to pursue them."

"Does that mean you might not be able to catch the one who took our daughter?" asked Mr. Tibsen.

"We don't know for a fact that that is the case, Mr. Tibsen," I replied. "If it is the case, then it might be harder for Lilith and I to catch the clizyati and, thus, harder to find Evelyn."

"James speaks the truth, folks," Lilith said. "However, James and I assure you that we will devote our full attention to this matter, but that means you are going to have to be patient and stay out of the way. We do not want to have to be looking for you two as well. Besides, if you get involved you could be risking not only your lives, but Evelyn's as well. If there really are humans who can shape shift or enter the body of other people then James and I are going to have to figure out a way to deal with them specifically. The telepathic and telekinetic powers that we have used before might not work on the skin walkers."

"Do you mean that these things could take over Evelyn's body?" Mrs. Tibsen asked with that horrified look returning to her face and one tear slowly creeping down her cheek.

"That is one of the legends that surround skin walkers," I said. "It is also rumored that skin walkers can read human thoughts. If that is so, Lilith and I might be able to do the same with it or maybe even communicate with it. But that remains to be seen as well."

"Can these things be killed?" asked Mr. Tibsen.

"Not easily," Lilith replied. "Our first priority is to try and find Evelyn. If we have to try and kill the skin walker or walkers in order to rescue her, then that's what we will try to do."

"When do you plan to get started with trying to find my daughter?" Mr. Tibsen asked.

"We were hoping to get a good night's rest first, so that we would be fresh in the morning," I said hoping that would satisfy the Tibsens.

"Seems like that's a waste of several good hours that you could be doing something to find our daughter," Mr. Tibsen replied coldly.

"I'm not sure that I like your attitude," I replied. "Lilith and I are no different than you when it comes to needing rest to be at our best."

"James is right, Mr. Tibsen," Lilith said. "Evelyn is our friend and we are just as concerned about her well being as you and Mrs. Tibsen, but we need to be at our best if we are to face great evil."

"Well, if you weren't the Head Elder I would be contacting him to find out what's up with you two," Mr. Tibsen replied raising he voice some. "You expect my wife and me to sit around doing nothing and worrying ourselves sick while you get your beauty rest. If you're not going to take any action, then maybe I'll get some of our friends together and form a search party tonight!"

"Are you thinking what I'm thinking, Lilith," I said.

"Absolutely, James," Lilith replied. "It's the only way we are going to be able to work effectively on this problem."

"What the hell are you two talking about now?" Mr. Tibsen yelled at us.

"Now, Lilith?" I asked.

"Now, James," Lilith replied and we both went to work on the Tibsen's minds. In a few seconds they were both slowing climbing the stairs to their bedroom where they fell into bed without changing clothes and went fast to sleep.

"How long do you think we should keep them knocked out?" I asked Lilith.

"Well, James," Lilith said, "as easy as that was I think we can keep them under control for as long as it takes to find Evelyn and deal with the skin walker."

"Should we try and get some rest as well or do you think we should get started now?" I asked.

"I'm still feeling pretty awake and still have some energy left after our trip out here, James," Lilith said. "If you're up to it, then I say the sooner we get started, hopefully the sooner we'll get finished."

"I'm definitely up for it if it means getting back to our original plans, love," I said. "Should we investigate Evelyn's bedroom first to see if we can pick up any clues to her disappearance?"

"That's a good idea, James," Lilith said. "Maybe whoever or whatever took Evelyn will have left us a clue by mistake."

Lilith and I went up to Evelyn's bedroom and went over it with a fine tooth comb, as human detectives say, and just as we were about to give up, Lilith found a big clue behind the bedside table. We moved the bedside table away from the wall and Lilith picked up Evelyn's diary. Flipping to the last entry Lilith read telepathically to me. *"It's 1:17 a.m. and I was awakened by what sounds like a dog whining. I went to the window and looked out and down in the yard below my window is a dog that is acting like it is hurt. I'm going to get dressed and go down to see if I can help it. The whining is getting louder, but mom and dad don't seem to be awake. I won't bother them until I see if the dog needs help."*

"That's her last entry, James," Lilith said. *"That leaves me to suspect that the legend of the Skin Walkers might hold some water."*

"Quite frankly, Lilith," I replied, *"those words pretty much convince me that there is such a thing as Skin Walkers."*

"Let's go down into the yard below Evelyn's window and see if we can find any trace of her or this Skin Walker," Lilith said and getting our flashlights out of our suitcases we made our way outside and to where Evelyn had indicated in her diary that she was going.

It didn't take but a few minutes to discover what appeared to be shoe prints of someone about Evelyn's size. The prints indicated that Evelyn, or whoever they belonged to, had struggled frantically with someone or something for a couple of minutes. Finally, the struggle seems to have stopped and the prints became drag marks leading away from the house. The odd part of this was that there were no other visible prints anywhere to be found. However, Lilith upon closer examination of the area did find a few drops of blood, but it didn't look bad enough to be too concerned about. We speculated that it was Evelyn's blood and that she probably got scratched in the scuffle with her attacker.

At least we were praying that it wasn't any worse than that. We followed the drag marks for about twenty yards away from the house and then they stopped as if Evelyn had been beamed into space, which would have meant that someone on the Enterprise was doing their job too well. Lilith and I just stood there looking at each other dumbfounded and wondering what we were really dealing with in this situation. We figured that whatever was dragging Evelyn probably picked her up and continued on its way to who knows where, but we were at a loss to explain why it didn't leave any tracks.

It was too dark to try and find any more clues with only our flashlights to guide us, so we decided to try and get a little sleep before continuing our search early tomorrow morning. We would inform the Tibsens in the morning about what we had discovered, but because they were under Lilith's spell, they wouldn't remember much about it. Lilith and I agreed that the Tibsens were both a little hysterical at times and didn't need to consciously worry about all of the little details, like the drops of blood. They could learn about all the details of our search for Evelyn after we had found her, if we found her. The other thing Lilith thought we should do was find this Navajo who called himself Mosi and see if he could spread any light on Evelyn's disappearance. What we would find out the next day was going to make this one of our toughest and strangest adventures yet, if you can call dealing with the evils of the world adventures.

CHAPTER TWENTY

Lilith and I were up and about early the next morning. The Tibsens were moving around slowly after the deep sleep that Lilith had put them into the night before. We had decided that they should go about their daily routine, but that they should remain in their home with the hope that they wouldn't become kidnap victims as well. Lilith had prepared a nice breakfast for all four of us and the Tibsens seemed grateful for that. We related to them that we had gone out last night to see if we could find any evidence of someone else having been prowling around their house, but that we hadn't found much to go on. We didn't see any sense in upsetting them any more than necessary. Lilith re-iterated that they were not to leave their house for any rea-son and that we were going to try and find Mosi and ask around to see if anyone had seen Evelyn since yesterday morning. Lilith and I left immediately after breakfast and headed out to the Taos Pueblo to ask around about Mosi, hoping that someone there might be familiar with him.

At first no one wanted to talk about this Navajo who called himself Mosi, but we finally found an older woman who was willing to tell us where he could be found. Mosi lived alone about 30 miles north of town up toward Ortiz Peak in the Carson National Forest. She told us to look for a traditional hogan on the Rio Costilla where it turned back north, but to be careful when approaching because "old Mosi" didn't like to be disturbed by strangers. It was ru-mored that Mosi was a skin walker and that he could talk to the wolves and would call them around his hogan when strangers came around. She said that she had heard that some people who went to Mosi's hogan never returned and thus must have been eaten by the wolves. She advised us that there could not be any reason worth risking our lives for to go to such an evil place as where Mosi lived. Lilith and I graciously thanked the old woman for her council and assured her that we would be safe no matter what we decided. Lilith and I had borrowed the Tibsen's ten-year old Land Rover and immediately headed off toward Carson National Forest in search of Mosi.

When we were on the outskirts of Taos I said, "Lilith, if what the old woman told us is true, then we might well be dealing with a real skin walker in Mosi. However, I find it hard to believe that he would make himself known before kidnapping Evelyn."

"I thought of that, too, James," Lilith replied. "I've been scared about some of the situations we have been in before, but if these skin walkers really exist it scares me more than ever. I, too, have been wondering why this Mosi would reveal himself and then kidnap Evelyn."

"I hope that what the old woman said about wolves being under Mosi's control is just a rumor," I said. "We have never really had to deal with animals that were under someone else's mind control."

"From what we have heard so far about these skin walkers, James," Lilith said, "wolves are going to be the least of our worries, mind controlled or not."

"You're starting to scare me now, Lilith," I replied. "Hopefully this Mosi character will welcome us and have some information about skin walkers and how to deal with them that we haven't already heard."

"James," and Lilith hesitated a moment.

"Yes, dear," I said. "What's bothering you now?"

"If this Mosi character, as you put it," Lilith began, "is a real skin walker himself and if he was the one who kidnapped Evelyn, we are going to have to be extra careful in how we both approach him and talk with him."

"How do you mean, Lilith?" I asked becoming more and more concerned about our safety.

"I think we need to act like we don't suspect him of anything," Lilith said, "at least not until we know for sure that he is the one we're after."

"Good thinking, Lilith," I said, "but then that is why you are the Head Elder of our species!"

"As you know, James," Lilith said, "flattery will get you everywhere with me, but you might just have to wait a few days this time."

"It will certainly be hard to wait, my dear," I replied, "but if we come out of this one alive it will be well worth it!"

We drove on in silence until we got to a dirt side road with a huge saguaro cactus next to it that the old woman had said would be there. Although saguaro cacti are not found in the wild in New Mexico, she said that Mosi had planted this one about 50 years ago and that it was now nearly 75 feet tall. We had asked the old woman how old Mosi might be so that we could better recognize him. She told us that some believed him to be nearly 300 years old, but that was impossible, so she guessed him to be approaching 100 years old. Little did she know that there were creatures on this earth who could live to be 400 earth years old, which put the question in mine and Lilith's minds about Mosi possibly being a Voreshan.

"Wouldn't it be funny if Mosi were a Voreshan?" I asked.

"We could only hope that that were true, James," Lilith said. "If Mosi were one of us, then that might make this whole experience a lot easier to handle."

"Maybe we should try to communicate with him telepathically when we first get there to see if he is Voreshan," I suggested.

"Good idea, James," Lilith replied as I drove the Land Rover down the somewhat rutted dirt road toward Mosi's hogan.

When we got to the end of the road, the old woman had told us that we would have to hike the last two miles back to where Mosi lived along the Rio Costilla. I parked the Land Rover behind some high brush so it wouldn't be as visible from the road in case someone else came exploring that way. The Rio Costilla was still about a mile away and then we would walk along it for about a mile until we got to our destination. Things were eerily quiet along our path to the Rio Costilla and if it was at all possible, even more quiet along the edge of the river. About 45 minutes later, Lilith and I spotted the old hogan where Mosi was supposed to be living.

We stopped and looked around to see if any wolves or other creatures were in the area, but seeing none I said telepathically, *"How do you think we should approach the hogan, Lilith?"*

"Not knowing what powers Mosi really has, James," Lilith replied, *"I don't know if we should sneak up to the hogan or just walk up and knock on the front door."*

"As dangerous as it might sound, Lilith," I said, *"I think we should just walk up to the front door like little lost tourists and if Mosi is in there, then we can explain our situation and see how he reacts. Sneaking around might not be to our benefit if he were to catch us."*

"Then that settles it," Lilith said. *"Might as well face whatever evil awaits us head on."*

And then out of nowhere, we both hear in our minds, *"There is no evil awaiting you at my home, my dear friends. Please come forward and I will greet you at the door."*

To say that Lilith and I were taken aback by this new voice in our heads would be an understatement. We were both literally frozen in our tracks and unsure whether to move forward or even communicate with each other again.

"Please, my friends, do not be afraid. I am a fellow Voreshan and would never attempt to do battle with legends such as yourselves."

Lilith spoke first to Mosi as we started toward the hogan, *"You don't know what a relief it is to find out that you are a Voreshan, Mosi. James and I thought about this possibility as we were coming to find you."*

"Yes, I heard you after you had gotten to the river," replied Mosi. *"Please forgive me for eavesdropping on your conversation, Elder Morgan. I am very old and sometimes forget the rules for Voreshans where the Head Elder is concerned."*

"If it makes you feel better," Lilith replied, *"I will forgive you, but I am glad that you did eavesdrop in this case."*

About that time we were almost to the front door of the hogan when it opened and out stepped a man who had to be at least 300 earth years old if he really was a Voreshan. The old Navajo standing before us looked to be at least 80 or 90 years old in human terms.

"Welcome to my humble abode," Mosi said out loud. "I hope your journey out here to find me wasn't too scary."

"Well, sir," I said, "not knowing what we were walking into always makes us a little nervous, especially if we aren't sure who or what we are going to encounter."

"I understand and once again apologize for not letting you know sooner that I am Voreshan," Mosi said, "but as you know, not all humans are friendly.

"Well, as I said before," Lilith said, "we are just glad that you are a Voreshan. Do you know why we are here to see you, Mosi?"

"I suspect that it has to do with the disappearance of Evelyn Tibsen," Mosi answered.

"That is exactly right, Mosi," Lilith said. "We wanted to ask you if you could shed any light on her disappearance. The only clues we have so far are somewhat confusing and, quite frankly, sound a lot like legends or myths."

"Please come into my home and let's sit down to talk about this," Mosi said and we entered his hogan. "Might I fix you some tea?"

"That would be lovely," Lilith said and we took a seat on a nearby old wooden bench.

After Mosi had put a pot of water on his wood burning stove and got a fire started under it, he came over and pulled up a chair to sit near us. Lilith and I sat in silence for a few seconds waiting for Mosi to speak and then he began.

"As you both know from your legendary adventures, there are many things in this world, both alien and of this planet, that are very evil. If any other Voreshans had come to fight the evil that I am going to tell you about, I would send them immediately away, but the powers that you two are known for might be able to defeat this evil that has kidnapped Evelyn Tibsen."

"Might be able to defeat?" I asked. "I'm really starting to get nervous now. Are you trying to tell us that skin walkers are real?"

"Being nervous is a good thing in this case, my young friend," Mosi said. "To have no fear when confronting this evil would give her an upper hand."

"Her?" Lilith said more than asked. "We were under the impression that skin walkers were mostly men and that a female skin walker was very rare."

"Not only very rare, my dear Elder Morgan," Mosi replied, "but ten times more dangerous than a male skin walker. This female skin walker may also be the last of her kind."

"Is the rumor true that only childless women can become skin walkers or witches?" I asked.

"That is true, James," Mosi answered.

"Why does that make them so much more dangerous?" Lilith asked.

"Because they are angry with the gods for making them childless and thus their anger is tenfold," Mosi answered.

"Mosi, do you think that this witch intends to harm Evelyn or is Evelyn even still alive?" I asked.

"Evelyn is very alive, James," Mosi answered, "and the witch, whose name is Dezba and means war, will keep her alive for as long as Dezba lives. But if you do not find Dezba and destroy her, Evelyn may never see her parents again."

"Will this Dezba just keep Evelyn confined or caged or will Evelyn be treated decently?" Lilith asked.

"The witch, Dezba, also has the power to enter the body of her captor," Mosi said more than answered. "Dezba will treat Evelyn like her own child, but because Evelyn made the mistake of looking into the eyes of the witch she will remain under Dezba's power until the witch has been destroyed by a person who is not a yee naaldlooshii."

"I hope that when you say 'person' that you are not excluding Voreshans," I said.

"If anything," replied Mosi, "it is better that you are Voreshan. Hopefully, being Voreshan will give you the powers and abilities to destroy this witch."

"You said that Dezba has the power to enter the body of her captor, in this case Evelyn," Lilith began. "Why would Dezba want to do that if she has Evelyn under her powers?"

"Dezba is no longer a young woman," said Mosi. "she has to be at least 60 years old and she has been angry about her childless condition ever since she was married at 16. Dezba did not find out that she could not have children until she was married and when she did find out she immediately killed her husband by stabbing him 666 times."

"Nothing like a little over kill," I said trying to lighten the situation.

"James!" Lilith nearly yelled at me.

"It is ok, Elder Morgan," Mosi said. "I was once young and full of humor, too."

"I apologize," I said. "Back to your story, Mosi."

"What Dezba did to her first husband made her tribe fear her and they labeled her a yee naaldlooshii and banished her form their camp," Mosi continued. "This made Dezba even more angry and it is said that she went immediately to the woods to find a male witch with which to mate, probably thinking that if she were believed to be a witch, then she would become one that way. We know that she did mate with a male witch, but that she did not become pregnant. What she did not know was that mating with a witch only turned you into a witch, much like the legends of vampires. The male witch with whom she mated was rumored to be the most powerful of all the witches, but his mistake was that mating with a human who was not already a witch would drain all of his powers and give them to the new witch. When Dezba realized that she still could not become pregnant and now had these new powers, she killed her mate and chopped him up into hundreds of pieces and fed him to the wolves. But to get back to your question, Elder Morgan, being older, Dezba would enter the body of the young girl to feel and act young again. In addition, other males, either witch or human, would then find her more attractive, as Evelyn is a beautiful young woman, and then Dezba could lure them into her trap and have her way with them before killing them. Then Dezba would leave the girl's body and Evelyn would go back to being treated like a daughter."

"So, it is true that a skin walker can control animals as well?" I asked.

"It is so, James," Mosi answered. "Unfortunately, however for Dezba and the wolf population around here, Navajo men have had to kill off the wolf population in order to protect themselves. That, however, hasn't stopped Dezba from attacking Navajo families and kidnapping their children. In these cases, Dezba slaughtered the children as revenge for killing all the wolves."

"She is certainly an evil one," Lilith said. "Mosi, do you think that James and I will really be able to destroy this creature?"

"If you cannot do it, Elder Morgan, then no one can," Mosi answered.

"Nothing like a little extra pressure on us," I said. "So, Mosi, where do we begin to search for Dezba and Evelyn?"

"The first part will be easy," Mosi said, "because she will come to you. She already knows that you have come here to find Evelyn and Dezba will come here or to wherever you might be to kill you. However, the second part of your question will be far more difficult. Dezba's reason for hunting you down first is to keep Evelyn's hiding place a secret. If you succeed in destroying Dezba, you may never find Evelyn and the witch will never reveal where she has the girl hidden."

"None of this is sounding like it is going to be an easy task," I said.

"The bravest warriors are afraid to confront a female skin walker," Mosi said. "They would rather fight a dozen grizzly bears at the same time than confront Dezba."

"Well, Mosi," Lilith said, "I think that James and I should find a different location to set up shop so that Dezba won't harm you."

"I have been on this planet for nearly 300 years, Elder Morgan," Mosi replied, "and have seen many types of evil and many horrible wars. In human years, my time is short and even in Voreshan years I don't have long for this life. I would consider it an honor if you stayed here with me and let me help in whatever way I can. To fight and, if necessary to die, alongside the two of you would be my greatest honor and accomplishment in life."

"It would certainly be easier for James and me if we were in more familiar surroundings," Lilith said, "and three against one like Dezba is certainly better than two. James and I accept your offer and help."

"Thank you, Elder Morgan," Mosi said. "May I live to tell others that I fought next to the bravest Voreshans on Earth."

CHAPTER TWENTY-ONE

The next few days were uneventful and the three of us went about the daily routine of life in a Navajo hogan on the Rio Costilla, at least the life that Mosi was living. Lilith and I talked a lot about how we might deal with the skin walker known as Dezba. We kept thinking about the things we had learned so far about female skin walkers and decided that maybe Dezba didn't have any powers that we couldn't at least match. We knew that humans shouldn't look into the eyes of a skin walker, but did that mean Voreshans as well? We knew that a skin walker, especially a female skin walker, could enter the body of her captor for whatever reason she wanted, whether it was to lure young men for sex or simply to look at herself in a mirror in an effort to reclaim some semblance of her youth. We are all vain to some extent and most of us don't want to believe that we change that much as the years pass us by. I was still getting used to the idea of looking so much younger than I should have looked after living over 60 earth years.

After about a week had passed, Lilith and I began to wonder if we were on a wild goose chase and that all of what we had been told really was a myth. And as I have indicated before, just when Lilith and I think things have settled down and we can lead normal Voreshan lives, all hell breaks loose! We were actually considering packing up and leaving Mosi's to head back to Taos the next morning when we were all three awakened around 4:00 in the morning by what sounded like a wolf being tortured. Imagine the noise that would result in combing the yelping of a dog be-ing beaten and a cat's tail being stepped on at the same time. That was all I could think of when I first heard the howling, screeching, sound that seemed to be penetrating my entire being.

"What the devil is that?" I said when I realized every-one was sitting straight up in their beds.

"A devil it is, James," said Mosi. "The she-witch has come for you and Elder Morgan."

"Should we be communicating telepathically?" I asked silently.

"It matters not, James," Mosi replied. "Skin Walkers are said to be able to read your thoughts."

"How close do you think she is, Mosi?" Lilith asked.

"From the sound of it," Mosi answered, "not more than a 100 yards, maybe 150 yards."

Foolishly, Lilith and I had come unarmed to do battle with the skin walker believing that out telepathic and tele-kinetic powers would be enough like they had been in the past. Of course, we should have known better since we were dealing with an entirely new kind of evil. What we didn't know was that one was supposed to kill a skin walk-er by shooting her or him with a bullet dipped in ash.

"I am sorry to say that I do not own a gun, my friends," Mosi said, no doubt reading our thoughts.

"Does that really make a difference, Mosi?" I asked

"Supposedly," Mosi said. "It is believed that the only way to kill a skin walker is by shooting her with a bullet dipped in ash."

"Are you saying that there is no other way to destroy a skin walker other than shooting her or him with a bullet dipped in ash?" Lilith asked.

"Supposedly," Mosi said again and this time hung his head.

"Damn!" was all I said.

"James," Lilith began, "we will just have to fight as we usually fight and if that doesn't work, the ride has been a great one so far."

"I'm not ready to call it quits, my love," I said. "I've got a lot of dessert coming and I don't plan on missing out on it because of some woman who thinks she can change into a wolf or some other critter!"

"Always the same thing on your mind, James," Lilith said. "Now, we need to come up with a plan and fast! That howling or whatever you want to call it is getting closer!"

"About 50 yards away," Mosi said.

"Well, dear," I said, "We can't sneak up on our enemy this time and since there is only one witch to fight we can't turn her against herself!"

"James!" Lilith exclaimed loudly.

"Whatever it is, I'm sorry," I said.

"No, dummy!" Lilith said. "You're a genius! We have turned humans against themselves before and since Dezba is basically a human, maybe we can do the same to her!"

"That would be an amazing thing," said Mosi. "Do you really think that it would work?"

"All we can do is try, Mosi," I said.

I was desperately looking around Mosi's hogan for something we might use as a weapon against Dezba and was just about to give up when I noticed a baseball bat tucked away in one corner near Mosi's bed.

"Mosi," I said, "is that baseball bat a Louisville Slugger?" and the howling now sounded like it was just outside the hogan.

"Yes, it is, James," Mosi replied. " I used to play some baseball on the reservation in my younger days. Why do you ask?"

"I don't think trying to fight off Dezba with a bat is going to do much good, James," Lilith said.

"Well, call me crazy," I said, "but those bats are made from Northern white ash. How important is that bat to you, Mosi?"

"It is just something I have kept around for protection from intruders," Mosi answered. "I agree with Elder Morgan, James. I do not think it will be of much use against this witch."

Grabbing the bat, I headed for the fireplace where Mosi had a small fire going to help keep off the cold during the night. "Do you have a sharp knife, Mosi?"

"I will get my knife I use for cleaning fish," he replied and brought it to me where I was kneeling in front of the fire with the small end of the bat stuck into the flames and beginning to slowly start burning.

What Mosi handed me looked more like a machete than a fish scaling knife. "You must catch some awfully big fish," I said and Mosi just laughed a little.

Not knowing what I was up to, Lilith was now trying to telepathically communicate with Dezba.

The screeching stopped all of a sudden and Dezba silently communicated with all three of us. *"I know what the three of you are and the troubles you have caused yee naaldlooshii over the centuries, but let it be known that all Voreshan attempts to defeat us have failed!"*

"Well, my dear old witch," Lilith said, *"that was before James and I came along. We have confronted and defeated evil much more powerful than you."*

"There is no evil greater than a yee naaldlooshii!" Dezba nearly screamed. *"Now you will all die and the girl will be mine forever!"*

At that, the screeching outside Mosi's hogan seemed to jump from one side to the next and even sounded at one point like it was on the roof.

"What's wrong, Dezba?" Lilith said. *"Can't you use your powers to get inside the hogan?"* and the screeching became even louder and seemed to surround the hogan.

"I will kill you and feed you to the girl before the dawn breaks!" screamed Dezba.

"I don't know what you had in mind with that bat, James," Lilith said out loud, "but if you have a plan it might just be time to put it into action!"

I had just finished burning the knob off the bat and had whittled the end down to a point. "If we are going to face this witch, Lilith," I said, "I would rather do it in this confined space than try and out maneuver her in the open, especially in the dark."

"You're probably right, James," Lilith said. "Should we let her in now or do you need more time?"

"I'm as ready as I will ever be," I replied. "If you and Mosi can keep her distracted when you let her in I will hide in the shadows and then attack her from behind."

"Open the door, Mosi," Lilith instructed him.

Reluctantly, Mosi went to the door and started to slowly open it, but it slammed wide open knocking Mosi to the floor.

When Dezba entered the hogan, she screamed at Lilith, who stood her ground and calmly said, "Welcome to your funeral, Dezba."

Dezba screeched again loud enough to be heard back in Sarasota and started toward Lilith. I had been hiding in the shadows near the door and rushed out toward Dezba's back hitting her in the head from behind with all the strength I had. I had hoped to knock her to the floor, but my blow didn't even faze her and she turned and screeched at me with yellow glaring eyes. Then Dezba rushed at me with her hands extended to choke me and finger nails long enough to decapitate me with one swipe, but I held my ground and turning the pointed end of the bat toward her I let her run straight into it at about chest height. The pointed end of the bat sank deep into her chest and came out her back having pierced her heart on its path. Dezba eyes grew wider and she screamed so loud I thought I would be deaf afterwards, if I lived. The yellow glare in her eyes began to fade and she staggered backward, turned toward Lilith, opened her mouth to say something and then collapsed on the floor dead.

"James," Lilith exclaimed, "how did you know you could kill her with the bat?"

Mosi, who had been temporarily stunned, had gotten up off the floor and spoke before I could answer and said, "Elder Morgan, you are married to a genius!"

"Well, I don't think I would go that far," Lilith replied with a smile on her face.

"James knew that the bat was a Louisville Slugger and that it was made of ash," Mosi explained.

"Lilith, Mosi is right about that part," I said. "However, I could only hope that Dezba could be killed in the same way as one would kill a vampire by stabbing her through the heart with an ash stake."

"Bullet dipped in ash, ash baseball bat, brilliant, James," Lilith said.

"Well, I don't know about that," I said, "but one thing my father taught me was a little bit of common sense.

Sometimes when you put two and two together it actually comes out to be four. The legend about dipping a bullet in ash could have meant the ash of any wood. Since Dezba was really a human, we could have probably killed her by simply stabbing her with Mosi's knife. This way just added a little more drama to the situation, besides the end of the bat still had some ash on it from the fire. Maybe it was just the ash that is fatal to these witches."

"Well," said Mosi, "maybe when the word of what happened here today gets around, the yee naaldlooshii will think twice about kidnapping children or harming anyone."

"Oh my God, James!" Lilith exclaimed. "What about Evelyn? How will we ever find her now with Dezba dead?"

"I was wrong, Lilith," I said, "two and two aren't adding up to four after all. Maybe we can try to contact Evelyn telepathically."

"That's probably going to be our best hope, James," Lilith replied. *"Evelyn, if you are able to hear me, please reply."*

There was no response for the next several minutes, so Lilith tried again. *"Evelyn Tibsen, this is Elder Morgan. Please respond if you are able."*

"Elder Morgan?" a faint reply came through to both Lilith and me. *"Is that really you? Is Mr. Morgan there, too? Please help me!"*

"Do you know where you are located?" I asked.

"I don't know where I am, but Dezba has me tied up and gagged," Evelyn said. *"I can't get up and look around, but I know that I am in a dark place somewhere, maybe a cave."*

Mosi had tuned in to the conversation as well and said, *"There is a cave not too far from here that is large enough for someone to live in. It was used as a place of refuge from the white man many, many years ago. It is high up in the mountains in a cliff face that is difficult to get to."*

"Elder Morgan," Evelyn interrupted, *"it is awfully cold and damp wherever I am. Maybe this is a cave."*

"Can you take us there, Mosi?" I asked out loud.

"I can show you where it is located, but I am too old to climb up to the cave," Mosi answered.

"Evelyn, have you ever used your telekinetic powers before?" I asked.

"No, Mr. Morgan," Evelyn answered. *"I wasn't aware that I could do anything more than read people's minds and communicate telepathically with other Voreshans."*

"Well, I doubt if we could train you long distance," Lilith said, *"so James and I are going to get Mosi to show us where the cave is that he has mentioned and we will then try to reach you. Don't panic and hopefully we will be there soon."*

"Ok, Elder Morgan," Evelyn said, *"but please hurry! I'm awfully scared!"*

"We are leaving right now, Evelyn," I replied, *"and you don't have to worry about Dezba anymore. She is dead."*

"Oh, thank you both," Evelyn said. *"That does make me feel better."*

Mosi had plenty of rope if we needed it, but he didn't have any other kind of climbing gear. Not that Lilith and I had ever done any real rock climbing, meaning never.

After we had removed Dezba's body from Mosi's hogan and properly disposed of her according to Voreshan methods, the three of us headed off with the hopes that this cave that Mosi knew about was where Evelyn would be located. Mosi led the way and we walked along the Rio Costilla for about two miles before he led Lilith and me up a rather steep incline for about another 100 yards. The sun was starting to come up when we left and it was now nearly full daylight, so the climbing wasn't that hard. Yet! When Mosi stopped, he pointed up a near vertical rocky ridge to a large, dark opening about another 50 yards up and to the right of our current position.

"You have got to be kidding me!" I exclaimed. "Lilith and I have never tried to climb anything this steep. I don't know if we can do it or not."

"James," Lilith said, "do you think we could use our telekinetic powers to levitate ourselves up to the cave opening?"

"I don't know, my dear," I replied. "It's one thing to move around a foot or two off the ground, but it sounds pretty scary to try and make it so far up that way."

"It's either that or we do it the hard way, James," Lilith replied. "I say we give it a shot anyway."

"You're the boss, boss," I said. "I'm ready when you are."

"Do you mean that we Voreshans have the ability to levitate?" Mosi asked.

"I believe that all Voreshans can do it," Lilith said, "but for most it probably takes some practice. James and I have done this in the past, but not to such heights as this," and Lilith pointed up to the opening of the cave far above.

"I will watch carefully," said Mosi. "One is never too old to learn."

"Ready, James?" Lilith asked.

"Ready as I will ever be," I said and concentrating together we began to slowly rise from the ground where we were standing and moved upward toward the cave opening.

Lilith and I didn't communicate while we were rising slowly upward at the rate of about six feet every 30 seconds, because any lapse in our concentration could send one or both of us plummeting back down the cliff. We were moving slowly, but we didn't want to take any chances and try to move faster not knowing if we could maintain our collective concentration that way. We had to stay on the same telekinetic wave length or risk falling. About 25 minutes later Lilith and I found ourselves hovering at the entrance to what appeared at first to be no more than a large, deep hole in the side of the cliff. We moved forward now and settled back down to the ground.

"This doesn't look like a real cave from here, James," Lilith offered.

"No, it doesn't, Lilith," I said, "but maybe we should see how far back it does go before we give up on this spot."

Switching to silent mode, Lilith tried contacting Evelyn again. *"Evelyn, can you still here me?"*

"Yes, Elder Morgan," Evelyn replied, *"and you sound closer unless I'm imagining things."*

"James and I may be at the entrance to the cave where you are trapped, Evelyn," Lilith said. *"We are going to investigate further and hopefully we are very close to you now."*

"Oh, I do hope so, Elder Morgan," Evelyn said.

"Shall we begin our exploration of this cave, my dear?" I asked out loud.

"We shall," Lilith said and turning on our flashlights we started walking back into the depths of this large opening in the cliff.

From the looks of it, the opening to the cave appeared to be manmade and probably thousands of years old. The large opening quickly narrowed down to about ten feet wide and eight feet high and took an abrupt turn to the right, which completely eliminated the light from outside after only a few feet. Fortunately, Lilith and I had brought along some very strong flashlights and our way was well illuminated. We probably went along this corridor for about 500 yards, not realizing that it was very gradually turning back to the left and descending ever so gradually downward. At this point Lilith and I thought we had come to a dead end as we ran into what appeared to be a solid wall. Shining our flashlights all over the wall in front of us and back along the corridor we had just come down didn't show any indication of the route changing or there being another opening.

"James," Lilith said, "do you think we missed a turn somewhere?"

"I don't know, Lilith," I replied, "but this certainly looks like a dead end to me."

"Well, I guess we might as well start back along the corridor and see if we missed a turn somewhere," Lilith said.

"I'm almost sure that we didn't miss any turn or other corridor cutting away from this one, Lilith," I said.

At that moment Evelyn communicated with us telepathically, *"Elder Morgan, I think I can hear you. You must be getting closer."*

"Evelyn," Lilith said, *"we seem to have come to a dead end. How could we possibly be closer to you?"*

"That's what I thought when Dezba brought me to her lair," Evelyn replied. *"There is some sort of lever somewhere in the wall that opens a sliding door into her lair where she has me trapped."*

"We are going to look around and see if we can find this lever, Evelyn," I said.

"Well, James," Lilith said out loud, "if there's a lever or some other device that opens a secret door, then start pulling and pushing on every square inch of rock."

"Already ahead of you, my dear," I replied as I was feeling around on the wall trying to find any protrusion that might be the lever.

After feeling up and down the wall for about 20 minutes it was obvious that Lilith and I weren't making any progress in finding the lever that Evelyn was talking about.

Evelyn contacted us again, *"Elder Morgan, have you found the lever for the door yet?"*

"No, Evelyn," Lilith replied. *"I'm beginning to think that there isn't a lever here. Are you sure it was a lever that Dezba used to open the door?"*

"I can't be sure, Elder Morgan," Evelyn replied. *"It was very dark even though she was carrying a lantern. When we seemed to have come to a dead end, Dezba made me turn away from her and then I heard a sliding noise and when she let me turn around there was an opening into a large room where she tied me up and gagged me."*

"Why didn't you make a run for it when you turned away from her, Evelyn?" I asked.

"The old witch had my ankles tied together with a short rope," Evelyn replied. *"If I had tried to run I would have fallen down."*

"Seems like Dezba covered her basis pretty good," I said out loud.

"That it does, James," Lilith said, "but right now we need to find out how to get the secret door open."

"Maybe we're looking in the wrong place," I said. "Maybe the lever or other device for opening the secret door is on the floor or maybe on the ceiling."

"I doubt that it is on the ceiling, James," Lilith replied, "because the ceiling has to be at least eight feet high and Dezba was simply not tall enough to reach that high."

Shining my flashlight around the edges of the floor where we were standing I saw an outcropping of rock about twelve inches wide and two feet high. Running the light from my flashlight up the wall from there and up onto the ceiling I spotted what appeared to be a stalactite about six inches long.

Lilith was watching me all this time and said, "James, do you think that's the lever?"

Stepping up on the rock I said, "Well, my dear, let's give it a try."

I first tried pushing the stalactite-like piece of rock back and forth in every direction, but it did not result in the secret door opening.

"Nothing is happening, Lilith," I said. "This doesn't seem like the lever that opens the door."

"Did you try pulling on it, James?" Lilith asked.

"Duh, no," I said and gave it a hard tug. It gave way and I lost my balance falling on my skinny little rump on the hard rock floor.

In the meantime the secret door started slowly sliding to one side. When Lilith had helped me to my feet, we shone our flashlights into the opening and discovered a large room with a variety of furnishings including a large cage where Evelyn was sitting bound and gagged.

"Elder Morgan," Evelyn communicated telepathically, *"is that you? Did you find a way in to Dezba's lair?"*

"Yes, Evelyn," Lilith replied, "we are here and will have you out of your cage shortly."

"The cage is only held shut with this piece of wood," I said and I quickly removed the piece of wood and started freeing Evelyn from her bindings and gag.

Throwing her arms around my neck, Evelyn started crying and saying thank you over and over.

"You're safe now, Evelyn," I said. "You'll be back with your parents soon."

CHAPTER TWENTY-TWO

When the three of us got back down to where Mosi had been patiently waiting for our return we found him practicing levitation. He had a great big smile on his face and seemed to almost be dancing on air. Evelyn was weak from her confinement in the cave and Lilith and I had to use our telekinetic powers to not only get ourselves back down the cliff, but to also levitate Evelyn down as well. She tried to levitate herself, but she was just too weak from her ordeal with Dezba.

"Oh, Elder Morgan," Mosi said, "this is the best fun I've had in many, many years! I may never walk on my own two feet again!"

"You certainly seem to have already mastered the levitation thing," I said.

"Oh, and you have returned with Evelyn!" Mosi exclaimed and gave Evelyn a big hug.

"Mosi has been very helpful in trying to find you, Evelyn," Lilith said. "I don't know if James and I could have done it without him. His knowledge about yee naaldlooshii was very valuable to us in dealing with Dezba."

"Thank you all so much for finding me," Evelyn said and gave Mosi another big hug. "If there is ever anything that my parents and I can do for you, please do not hesitate to ask."

"That is very kind of you, my dear," Mosi replied, "but I have all I need in my little hogan and now my life is complete, because I have helped the Head Elder with your rescue and the elimination of the yee naaldlooshii. This shall be a warning to all yee naaldlooshii to not terrorize Navajo or Voreshans ever again."

"Well, I think it's time we started back and returned Evelyn to her parents," I said. "They have really been very worried about you, Evelyn."

"Agreed, James," Lilith said and we headed back to Mosi's hogan with him floating along above the ground all the way and laughing at his new found skill.

After Lilith and I had packed up our few belongings, the three of us said our goodbyes to Mosi and thanked him again for all of his help in finding Evelyn. He told us that we were always welcome at his place and didn't need an invitation. Lilith and I actually did visit with Mosi several times over the next few years before he finally passed away. Having no family, Mosi left his hogan and land to Lilith and me and we go there at least once a year just to get away from the hassles of modern life. However, we have modernized it some by using a generator to create electric lights, a refrigerator, and a small stove. Other than that, we haven't changed anything else about Mosi's old home, as we want it to remain as authentic as possible as a tribute to him.

When we got back to Taos and the Tibsen's house, Lilith released them from their semi-stupor that she had put them under and Evelyn and her parents had a very emotional reunion. Mr. and Mrs. Tibsen thanked Lilith and me about a thousand times during the course of the rest of the day. Mrs. Tibsen prepared a huge celebration feast for Evelyn's homecoming and Mr. Tibsen invited about 50 of their closest friends and neighbors over to celebrate with us. The celebration lasted until after midnight which didn't give Lilith and me very much time to rest up before having to fly back to Sarasota. It was now the fifth of January and school would be starting back up soon for Evelyn in just a few days, provided her parents let her go back. Mr. Tibsen managed to pull a few strings and Lilith and I were scheduled to fly out the next day, and surprisingly Evelyn was coming with us. The Tibsen's were perfectly happy with that arrangement and felt that Evelyn would always be safe in our company, besides the fact that Evelyn wouldn't have had it any other way. The plan was for Evelyn's parents to come to Sarasota and spend Spring Break with her and see some of the nearby sights, including mine and Lilith's favorite spot at the carillon park.

Although Lilith and I didn't think that this had been our most dangerous event to date, it had certainly turned out to be one of the most interesting, if not the most dangerous. Just when one thinks there isn't anything much different in the world to experience, the powers that be send a new kind of experience, good or bad, your way. Fortunately for Lilith and me, we are usually able to figure out how to handle the bad and best enjoy the good. We were certainly looking forward to getting back to Sarasota, our home and gallery, and, hopefully, back to a more normal life, at least as normal as life can be for Voreshans on Earth.

Life did return to normal for most of the semester at school for Evelyn and she seemed to spend more and more time at our gallery. We didn't mind and actually enjoyed her company very much, often thinking of her as if she were our daughter, too. Spring Break came and went at the art school and while the Tibsens were in town to visit with Evelyn we took them to the carillon park one day and then left them on their own to explore other areas in and around Sarasota. Lilith and I still went out to the beach almost every weekend to swim and stroll along where we were married. It was still hard sometimes for me to believe the life that I was living as a Voreshan and being married to the most beautiful Voreshan woman in the universe. Of course, I'm sure that other Voreshan men would argue that their wives were the most beautiful as well, but I doubt if their lives had been or would ever be as exciting as mine and Lilith's had been so far.

The end of the spring semester at the art school rolled around and Evelyn was making plans to head back to Taos to spend the summer with her parents and working in the gallery there that carried mine and Lilith's paintings. Evelyn was a terrific sales person and had sold quite a few of our paintings while working in our gallery after school and on weekends. She was doing so well, in fact, that she was now on commission instead of a set hourly salary and making much more than she would have as a wage slave. Because her art work was improving so much, we even let Evelyn show some of her paintings in the gallery as well.

Lilith and I were seriously thinking about taking a second honeymoon, but instead of going back to Italy we were considering spending at least a couple of weeks in Paris, maybe even a month. When we told Evelyn about our plans, she begged us to let her stay in Sarasota and keep our gallery open while we were gone, even if it was for a month. She said that she would even be glad to house sit for us while we were away since she couldn't stay in her dorm room at the art school over the summer. We only agreed to her idea if she checked with her parents to make sure it was ok with them. Lilith even suggested that her parents might come and spend the month with her in Sarasota and share the responsibilities of house sitting. She was so excited that the Tibsens couldn't refuse and they actually sounded quite excited about it as well. They had thoroughly enjoyed their short stay at Spring Break and had even been talking about the possibility of moving to Sarasota. So, it was all set and Lilith and I would be off to Paris for our second honeymoon in June.

As usual, something always seems to come up when Lilith and I are trying to make plans for ourselves. A few days before we were getting ready to fly out of Sarasota and head to Paris, the art school called and asked us to come by and talk with them about something. They wouldn't be any more specific than that and Lilith and I were afraid that they weren't going to ask us to do any more workshops for them. We both really enjoyed doing the workshops and had decided that if we hadn't been so successful as working artists that we might have actually gone into teaching instead.

We went to the art school the next day and met with the Dean in his office to discuss the matter that he had called us about.

"Welcome, welcome, James and Lilith," we were greeted by the Dean when we arrived. "Please, have a seat and make yourselves comfortable."

Lilith and I were looking at each other and thinking that the Dean wouldn't be so congenial if he had bad news for us.

"I know you must be wondering why all the secrecy in asking you to come in today without telling you why," the Dean said, "but I thought it would be better to present our little proposition to you in person."

"Sounds kind of serious," I said.

"Well, yes and no, I guess you could say," the Dean replied. "I'm glad that I caught you two before you headed off to Paris. You said something about a second honeymoon?"

"That's right," Lilith said. "We have been so busy since our trip to Italy when we were in school here and with our growing gallery business that we wanted to go back to Europe and see something new."

"You two are undoubtedly two of our most successful graduates where working artists are concerned," the Dean said. "Well, let me explain why I have asked you here today."

"We're all ears," I said.

"You see, the thing is," the Dean began, "the head of our painting department is finally retiring after all these years."

"You're kidding," I said. "Les Peppers has always been one of our best friends and a really great teacher over the years. It will be a shame to see him leave the school."

"I second that," Lilith said.

"And it is because of both your relationship with Les and your success as artists here in Sarasota that Les has made a recommendation to us," the Dean said and paused briefly to see if we had a reaction to his statement. Hearing none, he continued. "When Les told us he was retiring, we essentially told him that it would take a while to replace someone as good a teacher as him. His response to that was, and I quote him here, 'That's where you're wrong, Dean Meacroft.' I asked him what he meant by that and he said that there were two artists right here in Sarasota who could do as good a job as him if not better."

"I think I see where this is going, Dean Meacroft," I said.

"I didn't think it would take long for you to catch on," the Dean replied. "Les highly recommended that you two take over from him. He suggested that you could probably split up the teaching responsibilities and still be able to keep up with your art work and gallery."

"I was getting ready to turn you down," Lilith said, "but James and I have talked about the idea that we would have probably gone into teaching if we hadn't been as successful as we have. What do you think, James?"

"Well, my dear," I said, "we both enjoy teaching the workshops here and I can't imagine getting a better recommendation than one from Les. How would we be compensated for this kind of a situation, Dean Meacroft?"

"Well, since Les has been at the school for so long, he is making a pretty good salary," the Dean said. "His salary has been enough so that his wife hasn't had to work outside of the home. As you know, she has a part-time interior design business that she runs from their home."

"James and I have used her expertise a couple of times when we couldn't decide how to decorate a couple of rooms," Lilith said.

"Yes, well," the Dean began, "as you know, Les teaches our upper-level students in both figure and landscape painting each semester and one course per year in beginning portraiture. I was hoping that you might consider adding the beginning portraiture class every semester."

"So," I said, "we are talking about three courses each semester?"

"That is correct," the Dean said. "How the two of you divide up the teaching load would be entirely up to you and we would pay each of you half the salary Les was making or pay you as one if you prefer."

"The extra money would certainly help out a lot," I said, "especially when things were slow at the gallery. In addition, we might actually be able to start saving some for our retirement some day."

"That was what I was thinking about in particular, too, James," Lilith said. "Should we think it over some more or go ahead and give it a try in the Fall semester?"

"I say let's give it a try, my dear," I said.

"Marvelous!" the Dean exclaimed. "I was so hoping that you two would agree to this idea. I can't tell you how happy the President and Board of Trust are going to be about this. Everyone here at the school hold you two in the highest regard."

"Well," I said, "Lilith and I are always proud to represent the art school wherever we go and we always enjoy teaching the workshops."

"Seconded again," Lilith said.

"Well, if you have a little more time today," the Dean said, "we can get your paperwork filled out and you won't have to worry about anything until you get back from Paris."

CHAPTER TWENTY-THREE

Lilith and I booked an overnight flight to Paris and arrived at the Charles de Gaulle Airport early on Monday morning, June 4th. We had made reservations at a small hotel in Montmartre and rented a top floor room with a great view of the Eiffel Tower and a panorama of Paris. Although hesitant at first, the hotel manager agreed to rent us the room for three weeks and even gave us a 15% discount. I'm sure that Lilith's flirtatious eyes had something to do with that as the hotel manager seemed to take to her immediately while eying me up and down like some ordinary criminal. There was a Metro stop that wasn't too far away and there were numerous little restaurants and cafes in the area where all the food turned out to be delicious. We were actually within walking distance of the Sacre-Coeur and St. Pierre de Montmartre, where we were anxious to see some of the little known stained glass work of Max Ingrand. We spent the rest of the day lounging around, eating, and sleeping hoping to get rid of our jet lag before our first real day in Paris. We wanted to get as much rest as possible so we would hopefully be refreshed for our first venture into Paris the next day. Lilith was so excited that she hardly slept at all that night.

The very first thing we wanted to do was to go down to the Seine and see some of the sites there. Many artists of the 19th and 20th century are supposed to have gotten much of their inspiration from the Seine and we wanted to have that experience as well. We had read about such artists as

Camille Corot, Henri Matisse, Claude Monet, Édouard Vuillard, Alfred Sisley, Raoul Dufy, and J.M.W. Turner being inspired by this famous river running through the heart of one of the greatest cities in the world associated with art. To be honest, Lilith and I were starting to feel a little stale with our art work since it mostly centered around landscapes from the Sarasota area and a few other places in Florida, not that we disliked the Florida landscape, but the old Florida we knew when we were growing up was rapidly disappearing. For many years we had hoped to return to Italy for both our second honeymoon and inspiration for our art, but as you know that has never happened. We had seriously talked about going back to Italy instead of making the trip to Paris, but we were hoping that there wouldn't be as much evil to contend with in France as we had encountered in Italy.

Back to the Seine. For most people who have seen the great works of art reproduced in books and magazines, the painting that is probably the most famously associated with the Seine is Georges Seurat's *Sunday Afternoon on the Island of La Grande Jatte,* done around 1884-86. However, it has never been one of mine and Lilith's favorites because we aren't really fans of Seurat's work. Being the "realists" that we are, we have gravitated more toward artists like Carl Fredrik Hill, *Seine Landscape in Bois-Le-Roi,* done in 1877, and Alfred Sisley, *The Terrace at Saint-Germain, Spring,* done in 1875, and *View of the Canal Saint-Martin,* done in 1870. We had brought a couple of sketchbooks and some cheap watercolors with us to use as we prowled around Paris as well as our cameras to record those fleeting moments that were impossible to sketch. Lilith, being as hopelessly romantic as me, had suggested that we go down to the Seine in the afternoon and not come back until after dark, because she thought we could find a romantic little place to have dinner before retiring to our hotel for dessert. And as you should know by now, when it comes to having dessert with Lilith, I'm like a hungry little puppy dog on a leash!

So, on our first full day in Paris, Lilith and I took the Metro down to the Tuileries Gardens to start our little excursion along the Seine. I had suggested that we skip the Louvre for now and catch it later when we could spend most of the day browsing through all of the galleries. This idea was fine with Lilith because she really wanted to see if we could find the approximate spot from where Sisley did his *Saint-Germain* painting, then to head on to the Pont Neuf, because she had seen a photograph taken from there and thought it was so beautiful, and then on to the Notre Dame Cathedral, with any spur of the moment side trips as necessary.

As Lilith and I walked along the Quai du Louvre I had a very strange and eerie feeling that we were being watched. I mentioned this to Lilith and she said that she felt it get a little colder as we walked between the Rue de l'Amiral de Coligny and the Pont Neuf Bridge, but just figured it was her imagination or that it was a spot where a cool breeze swept up from the Seine. Dismissing it to our vivid imaginations, and hoping that was all it was, we continued along and discovered a quaint little café along the Quai du Louvre and decided it would be where we had our romantic dinner that evening. After we had made the first two stops on Lilith's agenda we headed on toward the Notre Dame, but came across Sainte-Chapelle, something that we were not familiar with, but which to this day is probably our most favorite piece of Gothic architecture. Although damaged during the French Revolution, it was restored in the 19th century and has one of the most extensive in-situ collections of 13th-century stained glass anywhere in the world. This royal chapel is a prime example of a phase of Gothic architecture called "Rayonnant," which refers to its feeling of weightlessness and high vertical emphasis. Our next stop on the Ile de la Cité was the Notre Dame Cathedral.

Lilith and I had actually gotten a slow start on the day, probably still suffering some from jet lag, and had been taking our time as we explored the Ile de la Cité. We had spent a considerable amount of time stopping every few feet and shooting more photos than your typical tourist since we were especially paying particular attention to details we could incorporate into our art. We no doubt spent way too much time in Saint Chapelle and not enough time in the Notre Dame Cathedral and a lot of extra time casually circumnavigating the island. We were especially interested in taking as many photos as possible along the waterway around the island, because we saw so many possibilities for future paintings. The sun was starting to set and the shadows were getting longer and longer across the Seine, so Lilith and I decided it was time to head back to the café we had seen earlier for our romantic dinner. Quite frankly, I was much more interested in dessert and would have been willing to skip dinner, but I would just have to be patient and hope that Lilith wasn't too tired when we got back to our hotel.

As soon as Lilith and I had stepped off the Pont Neuf Bridge and back onto Quai du Louvre, we both felt a cold shiver run down our spines and Lilith nuzzled in close to me and said, "Does it seems strange to you, James, that this particular area seems colder than the other places we have been?"

"I'm sure this time," I answered, "that it isn't our imagination working overtime. Let's get into the café and hope that it is warmer in there."

"I'm with you, love," Lilith replied and we hurried on to the little café we had seen before when passing that way.

When we were just inside the door we were quickly and politely seated by the host who immediately recognized us as Americans and spoke to us in fluent English.

"Welcome to our humble establishment, my friends," he said. "May I get you something to drink?"

Lilith and I both ordered a glass of wine and he hurried off to get it and a couple of menus. He returned shortly with our wine and menus and pointed out a couple of specials for the evening. After he had left us to pour over the menu I said, "Lilith, I'm glad that it is warmer in here. Maybe, when we leave we should head up the Rue de l'Arbre Sec and avoid going back along the Quai du Louvre."

"Did you have that feeling of being watched again, James?" Lilith asked with a little fear apparent in her voice.

"I did, love," I replied. "It was eerie the first time, but it was almost overwhelming this time as soon as we stepped off the Pont Neuf Bridge."

"There has to be something to this, James," Lilith said. "Do you think there is some sort of evil about this particular area?"

"As much as I don't want to think about such things, Lilith," I said, "it wouldn't surprise me in the least where we are concerned. I just hope that it doesn't have something to do with this café."

"Well, James," Lilith began, "I'm all for taking a different route back if it means avoiding trouble on our second day in Paris. I'm still hoping that we don't have to deal with any evil while we are on our second honeymoon. Quite frankly, it's getting to be a little bit annoying."

About that time the host returned to take our order for dinner. Lilith and I both ordered one of the specials, which were more American than French. Our host, who now introduced himself as Diodore, looked at us in a questioning way and said, "My new friends, you seem to be upset about something. Have I done something wrong?"

"Absolutely not, Diodore," Lilith replied. "It's just that it seemed so cold on the Quai du Louvre just before we came in and we are glad that it is warm here in your café. You have a very pleasant establishment and you seem very nice."

"Thank you. You are very kind. However, I have not been out since early this morning," Diodore said. "You are telling me that it is cold out there now?"

"It seemed that way to us," I said, "but it was only while we were walking along the Quai du Louvre."

"Oh, this is not good!" Diodore exclaimed loud enough for the few other patrons to hear. "No, this is not good! Not good at all! This is bad, very bad!"

"Take it easy, Diodore," I said. "Why is this cold feeling out there so bad?"

"I will bring your food immediately," Diodore said. "I do not mean to seem rude, but as soon as you are finished you must leave!"

"Why?" Lilith asked. "Why are you acting so strange toward us? What have we done to offend you?"

"No, no, my friends," Diodore said. "You have not offended me. But your presence has no doubt brought out the ghost of l'Inconnue de la Seine and I don't want her in my café. If I had known about her before I opened my café, I would have not done so in this location."

"Ghost?" Lilith asked. "Are you saying that you believe in ghosts?" Remembering Italy, we knew that ghosts did exist, but it was rare to run into someone who actually believed in ghosts.

"My beautiful new friend," Diodore began, "I wish that I could say no to your question, but I cannot. Not being a handsome man, l'Inconnue de la Seine will not bother me, but she might take out her wrath on my café and patrons if she doesn't claim your husband for her own."

"Whoa!" I said. "Why would this ghost woman you're talking about want to 'claim' me as you put it?"

"Because you are so handsome, my friend," Diodore said, "and please do not be offended by that. There has not been a report of l'Inconnue de la Seine in many years. The last time this happened was when a young Danish student came into my café. He didn't believe in ghosts and said it was just a myth. After he left my café no one ever saw him again. The young girl's ghost took him into the Seine where she has kept him ever since."

"Did you or someone else see this happen?" I asked.

"No," Diodore answered, "but that is what must have happened since he disappeared right after leaving here. I forgot to thank him for his business and when I looked out the door only seconds later, he was gone!"

"What exactly do you mean by 'young girl,'?" Lilith asked Diodore, "and why would she be interested in older men?" and I gave Lilith my squinty little "What is that supposed to mean?" look.

"It is believed by many that she was only 16 years old and that she committed suicide," Diodore answered. "Her body was pulled out of the Seine at this location over 100 years ago."

"So, what you are saying is that she is attracted to handsome young men?" I asked.

"I do not believe that the men have to be young," said Diodore, "just handsome. You must leave now. Please!"

Our dinner had been brought out while we were talking with Diodore about this so-called ghost of a young suicide victim. Lilith and I had eaten very fast, more out of anxiety than being rushed by Diodore, and we were ready to leave the café as requested. When we had paid our bill we got up from our table and started for the door when Diodore began apologizing profusely while also thanking us for being so considerate of him and his café.

"Please be careful out there my friends!" Diodore said as the door closed and locked behind us.

When Lilith and I were back out on the Quai du Louvre the chill set back in on us and Lilith said, "James, I think we may be in for a little confrontation with a ghost before the night is through."

"As much as I hate to admit it," I replied, "I think you may be right. Maybe, because she is supposedly younger, she will be easier to deal with than the one we confronted in Italy."

We had just turned around and were starting for the Rue de l'Arbre Sec in order to avoid the Quai du Louvre if at all possible when I felt a tugging on my right arm. The one closest to the Seine.

"What the . . ." was all I got out before I was pulled down to the ground by an invisible force and started being dragged across the Quai du Louvre. Fortunately there wasn't any traffic coming as I was moving along slowly. I kept trying to grab hold of something to stop whatever was dragging me along, but I couldn't get a good hold on anything.

"James!" Lilith yelled and running out into the street, grabbed my left arm and started pulling in the opposite direction. I wasn't sure which arm was going to be ripped from my body first, but I felt sure that one of them was going to go pretty soon if one of my admirers didn't let go. Although Lilith is very strong for her slight build she was losing this tug of war to whatever had hold of me and that was moving in the opposite direction.

"Lilith," I yelled back, "I feel like I'm going to be ripped apart!"

"Hang on, James," Lilith said. "I'm going to try and communicate telepathically with this ghost or whatever it is that has hold of you."

"Hurry, Lilith, before you two rip me in half!" I said and at that the invisible entity gave an extra hard jerk at my right arm. "Ow!" I literally screamed out loud.

"Ghost of the Seine or whoever or whatever you are," Lilith started, *"release my husband before I call all the wrath of my kind down on you and banish you to a worse hell than what you now live in!"*

Surprisingly enough a voice came back to us both, *"But your husband is young and beautiful and I want him to join me in the river forever. You do not deserve such a man,"* and she pulled even harder on my right arm.

"Ok," said Lilith a little more calmly and the pulling from the ghost's side seemed to let up a little, *"but you have no right to take another woman's man regardless of what you may think or have been used to."*

"That is the way it always is with you women who claim to be married to my choices," replied the ghost, *"but so far I have never lost and I don't intend to lose this time either!"* and the ghost jerked even harder at my poor right arm.

I had now been pulled across the Quai du Louvre and we were under the trees between it and the Voie Georges Pompidou. Next stop? The Seine! *"Do something, Lilith!"* I yelled.

"I am not going to warn you again," Lilith said. *"Let go of my husband you pathetic bitch!"*

"Yes, let go of her husband!" I said. *"I thought the l'Inconnue de la Seine only liked younger men. I'm Voreshan and over 50 years old and I don't perform well in water!"*

Both Lilith and the ghost had now let up on trying to rip my arms off, but neither had completely released their hold on me. The way my shoulders ached I was sure that both shoulders were dislocated by now. I could see me now walking around Paris with both arms in casts and looking like Frankenstein!

"My name is Harmonie," said the ghost in a softer tone.

"Oh, crap!" I exclaimed out loud. "Not another one!"

"What does your man mean by that?" this Harmonie asked Lilith. *"Does he not like girls named Harmonie?"*

"Oh, my man has had problems with women named Harmony before," Lilith replied, *"and he isn't terribly fond of that name. So, you would both probably be miserable if you took him into the river."*

"Besides which, I'm over 50 years old," I tried to remind the ghost.

"How can that be?" asked the ghost, Harmonie.

"We are an alien species known as Voreshans," replied Lilith, *"and we age much slower than humans and can live to be 400 earth years old. Do you really want to deal with me or my kind for the next 300 years?"*

"That explains your ability to communicate with me," said Harmonie, *"but why didn't your kind try to stop me many years ago when I committed suicide to escape the abuse of my father?"*

"I do not know the answer to that question, Harmonie," Lilith replied. *"My husband and I are not from your country and our kind might not have been here at that time. I'm very sorry to hear that your father abused you."*

"I think you speak the truth," said Harmonie, *"but I have not had a new man in many years. I sometimes wish that I could age like normal people, but I am forever stuck at 16 years old."*

"We do not wish to harm you, Harmonie," Lilith said, *"but if you don't let go of my husband right now I am going to make your existence even more miserable than it already is!"*

At that moment the ghost let go of my right arm, which flopped to the ground numb, and said to us, *"I am not familiar with the concept of aliens and I am only interested in human males. Because of that and the love you have for your man, I will leave you alone now and go back to my home in the river."* A couple of seconds passed and Lilith and I heard a splash in the nearby Seine.

"Well, my love," I said as I still sat on the ground, "once again you have come to my rescue, even though I may never be able to use my arms again. My right arm is so numb I may have to learn to write left handed."

"No need to keep count, James," Lilith replied. "It's part of my Voreshan duty as your mate and leader to protect you and I have a feeling those arms will work just fine when we get back to the hotel."

"I don't think that I would have been able to convince the ghost as well as you did, if at all," I said. "Gee, look, my arms are feeling better already."

"She was rather easy to convince after I mentioned that we were aliens," Lilith said, "even though she had never heard of such a concept. Now get your cute little butt up off the ground and let's get back to our hotel before some other ghost vixen tries to abduct you."

I got back to my feet and was rubbing my arms to make sure everything was in the right place, even though the pain in my shoulders indicated differently. As we started walking along the Quai du Louvre to head back to our hotel, I said, "Well, my dear, that was certainly a trying ordeal, but I hope you're still up for dessert."

"You're impossible, James!" Lilith said and gave me a little punch in the right arm and I feigned intense pain. "Well, my love, if your arms hurt that much I guess you won't be able to perform properly tonight, so I guess dessert is out of the question."

"I'm not impossible," I said, "just horny. You know how much I always like my dessert! Besides, I think my arms are getting much better already and should be fine by the time we get back to the hotel."

"Men!" Lilith exclaimed and we picked up our speed as we headed back to the hotel.

CHAPTER TWENTY-FOUR

Because the Sacre-Coeur and St. Pierre de Montmartre were so close to our hotel, Lilith and I planned to spend the next day exploring those two churches. Our first stop was St. Pierre de Montmartre, because we were very excited about seeing the stained glass designs of Max Ingrand in the apse and aisles of the church.

Lilith and I had first seen images of Ingrand's stained glass in this church when another teacher at the art school had shown us some slides he had taken back in the late 1970s. St. Pierre de Montmartre is the oldest church in Paris, dating all the way back to the 11th century, but Ingrand's stained glass windows were designed by him in 1953. Although the windows were very contemporary for the time and nothing like traditional stained glass windows of the great cathedrals in France, the colors and designs were awe inspiring for Lilith and me. Seeing them in person was one of the highlights of our visit to Paris. We spent a couple of hours in the church both sketching and taking some photographs of the designs and images of the stained glass windows. We both thought that our painting might take a turn in that direction, especially toward Ingrand's color palette. Our next stop was the Sacre-Coeur.

The Sacre-Coeur is one of Paris' best known landmarks, but is not loved by all Parisians. From the photographs that Lilith and I had seen of it in books and the slides taken by the aforementioned teacher at the art school, we were very excited about not only seeing it, but also taking in the views of Paris and the surrounding Île de France area from high up around the inner dome of the cathedral. We wanted to find out for ourselves why Maurice Utrillo loved drawing and painting the cathedral so much. Lilith and I can't imagine why anyone wouldn't like the architecture with its white domes and the interior with its fabulous mosaics. It, too, was just as awe inspiring to Lilith and me as St. Chapelle and St. Pierre de Montmartre, even though it might be considered a "modern" piece of architecture since the construction of it wasn't started until 1876. Lilith and I spent several hours in the area sketching and doing quick watercolors, à la Ingrand, to take back home to Sarasota and turn into larger paintings. When we figured that we had enough drawings and watercolors to last us for a while, Lilith and I decided on the spur of the moment to detour to the Saint-Vincent Cemetery to see where the Demon of Montmartre, Maurice Utrillo, was buried. Maybe not the biggest mistake of our stay in Paris, but it had to rank right up there with the others.

The Saint-Vincent Cemetery was only a short distance from the Sacre-Coeur and along the way we came across the Clos Montmartre, a small vineyard tucked away along the Rue des Saules. Since neither Lilith nor I had ever seen a real vineyard, we decided to see if we could get in. The vineyard just happened to be open and Lilith and I enjoyed seeing and taking pictures of the grapes growing and a few people working in the vineyard. One of the female workers asked where we were going next and Lilith told her that we were headed over to the Saint-Vincent Cemetery to see where Maurice Utrillo was buried, because he was one of our favorite artists. She was an older woman and looked around to see who was listening and then in a low voice told us to be very careful when we were in the cemetery.

Lilith asked if there were bad people hanging out there and the old woman, again looking around carefully, said some of her friends had recently seen the Cernunnos in there.

"Very bad!" she exclaimed in a loud whisper. "You must be careful! He is very bad!"

Being typical American tourists without a clue, I asked, "What is a Cernunnos?"

"How do I explain?" the old woman said. "Cernunnos is Celtic god with horns who preys on young women."

"What do you mean by 'preys on young women'?" Lilith asked her.

"He is very old, hundreds of centuries old, but he still lives and is very, how you say, horny," she replied. "He has been living in the cemetery for many years now and is known to make young women pregnant with his kind."

"I seem to remember reading about this myth in one of the guide books, Lilith," I said. "Sounds like the kind of guy who likes to take his dessert with more than one woman."

"No myth!" the old woman exclaimed out loud and then quickly glanced around to see if anyone was nearby. "Real! You will see!" she said in a lower voice and then scurried off toward the other workers at the far end of the vineyard, but then she stopped a few paces away and turned around to stare at Lilith. "Young woman, you must not go in the cemetery or Cernunnos will surely rape you!" She then turned and headed back to the group of workers.

"Wait!" Lilith yelled after her and the other workers looked up, but the old woman kept going while motioning them to get back to work.

"Well, Lilith," I said, "maybe we should skip the cemetery. I don't know what I would do if something terrible happened to you."

"I know we have run into some things in the past that were supposed to be myths that turned out to be real, James," Lilith said, "but I have a real hard time believing some old superstitious woman. Besides, if what she said about Cernunnos making women pregnant was true, wouldn't there be a lot of little Cernunnos' running around?"

" Well, Lilith, I can see that you have made up your mind. Shall we then proceed on to Maurice's grave and wish him well, my dear?" I asked.

"We shall, my minion," Lilith replied and I pretended to hang my head in shame and dropped back about ten feet behind her.

"Get your butt up here next to me," Lilith said in a demanding voice, "if you want dessert tonight, besides, it's your duty to protect me."

At that I caught up with Lilith and we headed on over to the entrance to the Saint-Vincent Cemetery, which was probably about 400 yards away from where we had been standing in the edge of the vineyard. When we looked back to see if the old woman was watching us, what we saw gave us a little bit of a start. The old woman and the other workers in the vineyard were down on their knees praying and I thought that if it kept Lilith and me safe, then so be it!

"Do you think they are praying for us, Lilith?" I asked.

"That would be nice, James," Lilith replied, "but my guess is that they are praying that this Cernunnos doesn't come out of the cemetery to get them."

"If we run into this Cernunnos, Lilith," I said, "we'll just ask him to not bother the nice people in the vineyard."

"Very funny, James," Lilith said, but she definitely wasn't smiling.

"Maybe it's just the ghost of Utrillo running around with the mask of a horned god to scare visitors," I continued flippantly.

"James!" Lilith exclaimed. "If we never run into another ghost for the next three hundred years I will be a very happy camper! Now stop with the jokes!"

"Yes, dear," was all I said until we got into the cemetery.

We immediately started taking pictures of the statuary in the cemetery and looked around for Utrillo's grave. By now it was getting to be late afternoon and the shadows were getting long in some areas of the cemetery, but there was enough daylight to still get some good pictures with excellent light and dark contrasts. When we found Utrillo's grave we sat down and did a couple of quick sketches of the statue next to his tombstone. This didn't take us very long and when we got up to leave and head back to our hotel we heard what sounded like someone grumbling close by on the path we had taken into the cemetery. Looking at each other quizzically, Lilith and I just shook our heads in unison hoping that the old woman had been out of her gourd when she said Cernunnos had been seen in the cemetery. Actually, I thought to myself that it might be a cemetery worker grumbling about the late visitors.

Going to silent communication, Lilith said, *"I didn't see anyone else in this cemetery when we came in, James, did you?"*

"Not a soul, dead or alive," I replied and I got punched in the right arm again. *"Ow!"* I said silently.

"Maybe someone came in after we did," Lilith said.

"That or maybe it's someone who works here in the cemetery," I replied, but about that time we heard the

sound again, only this time it was closer and sounded more like a growl.

"*Maybe they have a watchdog in here, James,*" Lilith said.

"*Dogs we can handle, horned gods I'm not so sure about,*" I said.

Then someone or something said behind us, "Cén fáth a bhfuil tú anseo?" (Irish translation: Why are you here?)

Spinning around, we were within a few feet of what at first appeared to be a human male, a very large muscular human male, but upon closer examination the thing standing before us was naked and had horns!

"*Oh my God!* Exclaimed Lilith. "*It is real, James! And get a load of that huge magic wand!*" meaning his enormous third leg.

"*Oh, great! That's a real romantic thing to say in front of your less endowed mate!*"

"*No harm in looking,*" Lilith said.

"*Maybe it's just someone with a mask on who tries to scare tourists,*" I said trying to remain calm. "*And get your eyes off that enormous heat-seeking love missile!*"

"Freagra dom!" whatever this was roared at us and came a couple of steps closer. (Irish translation: Answer me.) Then it looked at Lilith lasciviously with its eyes glowing red in the dusk that was setting in on us rapidly and said, "Tá sí go hálainn." (Irish translation: She is beautiful.)

"*I don't know what it just said, Lilith,*" I said, "*but I don't like the way it is looking at you either!*"

"*Me either, James,*" Lilith replied even though her eyes were still affixed to this creature's third leg. "*Maybe we should get out of here fast!*" although Lilith wasn't making a move to do so as she seemed to be genuinely transfixed.

What we were now assuming to be the Cernunnos said, "A dhéanamh liom ag iompar clainne tú! (Irish translation: I make you pregnant.) Cas timpeall agus bend thar." (Irish translation: Turn around and bend over.)

Right then the old woman appeared next to us waving a pitchfork in the air and hollered at the Cernunnos, "Leave them alone you demon or I will run this pitchfork through your penis!"

"Do you know what he said?" I asked the old woman.

"He want to make your woman pregnant," she answered.

"Over by dead body!" I shouted at the creature and took a couple of steps toward him.

"That probably happen," the old woman said and at that moment the Cernunnos stepped forward and grabbed the old woman by the arm and tossed her aside like a rag doll. Flying through the air she struck a tombstone close by very hard and appeared to be knocked out, but the pitchfork remained tightly grasped in her hand.

I then stepped between Lilith and the Cernunnos and staring him directly in his red glowing eyes I yelled, "Go back where you came from monster or suffer your final death at the hands of Voreshans!"

His eyes got bigger and glowed more red than before, but he took a couple of steps back and bending over took a good look at Lilith and me. "Voreshans!" he screamed loud enough to awaken Utrillo and the rest of the dead in the cemetery and he took a couple of more steps backwards.

"That's right," Lilith said to him now that she seemed to be out of her trance, "we are Voreshans and we will destroy you if you don't leave us alone!"

Once again he screamed, "Voreshans!" and then turned to walk away from us, but then he stopped and looked back over his shoulder and roared loud enough to wake all of Paris.

We weren't sure whether or not the Cernunnos understood us, but it was certain that he understood the word "Voreshan." He then bent over like an ape and quickly disappeared among the tombstones, hopefully not to be heard from again, at least not while Lilith and I were in the area. Lilith was now bending over the old woman and lifted her bleeding head up to see how badly she was injured. Fortunately for the old woman, her wounds didn't look too serious although she did have some scrapes and the back of her head was matted in blood. She was breathing and starting to come around and I helped Lilith to get her into an upright position against the tombstone.

When she had opened her eyes and seemed to be aware of where she was and who we were, she faintly said, "You must run away. Do not let the Cernunnos get you."

"You do not need to worry about the Cernunnos anymore for now," Lilith said. "We have chased him off and I do not think he will be back for some time."

"How?" the old woman asked. "He is a huge monster!"

"My husband chased him off with your pitchfork," Lilith answered and which she had removed from the old woman's hand. "It seems he does not like sharp things."

Looking at me, the old woman said, "You are very brave man. Maybe you walk me back to the vineyard? I am still afraid and feel dizzy."

"It will be our pleasure to walk you back to the vineyard," I said. "After all, if you hadn't come to our rescue with the pitchfork, I would not have been able to chase the Cernunnos away."

It was now almost dark and after we had walked the old woman back to the vineyard and reunited her with her friends, Lilith and I headed on back to our hotel for the evening deciding we had had too much excitement for one day to go out that evening or, unfortunately for me, to even have dessert.

CHAPTER TWENTY-FIVE

The next morning before Lilith and I got out of bed, I said, "Well, this seems to be a typical adventure for us, my dear, what with a ghost and a mythological creature just happening to come our way on our first two days in Paris. Kind of reminds me of the days when you weren't the Head Voreshan Elder."

"You can say that again," Lilith responded. "I really thought that being the Head Elder would mean giving these paranormal jobs to other Voreshans, but it's like we're magnets for this kind of thing. I just don't think I can handle this excitement everyday for three weeks."

"Well, this seems to be a typical adventure for us, my dear," I said again as instructed and immediately got punched in the arm. "One thing is for sure, I will have a nicely bruised arm by the time we get back home to Sarasota. Maybe you should start on the other arm for a while, my dear."

After rolling me over and punching me in the other arm, Lilith asked, "What sort of adventure would you like to go on today, James? Got any long lost girlfriends who might pop by, 'handsome man.'"

"I wouldn't be surprised if the Voreshans who headed back to Voresha didn't kick Harmony Beckham off the space ship before they took off. That aside, I thought we might stay in bed all day and wait for the action to come to us," I said, "as long as it doesn't interrupt our action."

"You can lounge around inside all day if you like," Lilith said as she tried to punch me in the other arm again, "but I intend to explore more of Paris on my second honeymoon with or without you. I'm sure you probably know how to give yourself all the action you need. Who knows, maybe I'll find a handsome Frenchman who would like to spend the next two weeks with me showing me the sights, both his and Paris'."

If our gender roles had been reversed, I would have punched her in the arm, but, being the gentleman I am, instead I said, "Sorry, love, but you are going to have to settle for an old, though handsome, and less endowed American instead."

"Well, since it's you, I guess I can suffer through it," Lilith said in her sexiest voice and planted a big kiss on me, whereupon she immediately jumped out of bed and started to get ready not giving me a chance for some morning action.

"Did I ever tell you what a tease you are, my dear?" I asked and got out of bed to get ready as well.

Totally ignoring my comment, Lilith said as we were getting dressed, "There are three museums that I want to visit today."

"Tease!" I exclaimed.

"Just get ready, James," Lilith said, "or I will tease you the rest of this trip!"

"You sure know how to hurt a fellow. Anyway, which museums are you thinking about?" I asked hoping that we weren't going to try and crowd the Louvre into a three-museum day. I wanted to go to the Louvre, but after Italy a few years back there just wasn't that much that I wanted to see in the Louvre.

"First, I thought we would head over to the Victor Hugo Museum since it is small," Lilith said. "You know how I love *Les Misérables,* besides which he was a pretty good artist, too. After that, I want to go to the Monet Museum at one end of the Tuileries Garden and finish with the Impressionist Museum just across the Seine from there. I know that we aren't the biggest Impressionist fans, but I think it is something we need to take in while we are in Paris, especially since they have some of our favorite works of non-impressionist art as well."

"Sounds like a plan to me, Lilith," I said. "Hopefully we won't spend part of our third full day in Paris fighting off some new ghost or mythological creature. I'm beginning to think that we should wear tee shirts with VORESHANS emblazoned across both the front and back! It seems that some of these paranormal creatures that we have encountered are quite familiar with the species."

"If we run into any major trouble today, James," Lilith said, "we are going to run as fast as we can in the opposite direction regardless of our mission on this planet! I like the tee shirt idea except that every human we come in contact with would want to know what it meant. Oh, that's the name of the alien species we belong to and who first came to Earth 2,000 years ago. Then they would lock us up in their most heavily padded cell!"

"You are right about that and I feel the same way you do about running in the opposite direction, my love," I said, "but I really don't think we are meant to run from trouble and I don't think it's in your blood to do so. Besides, a padded cell would certainly be safer."

"You're right, of course, James," Lilith said, "but let's try to stay on the beaten path today and maybe trouble will not find us or, if it does, maybe it will simply be some disgruntled human."

"I remember not long ago when we were in a museum in Florida and trouble found us," I said, "even though it was an Elder searching us out for help."

"That's true, dear," Lilith said, "but it came looking for us and the past couple of days here in Paris we have just been in the wrong places at the wrong times or so it seems. Besides, we have come to a city of romance and the paranormal entities that have found us the past two days were looking for mates. You really can't blame Harmonie or the Cernunnos for coming after two such attractive people as us."

"You're right as usual, my love," I said, "especially you. Are you about ready to get underway on today's adventures?"

"Well, James," Lilith said, "let's hope our adventures today only involve looking at and studying great art and maybe taking a few more pictures around Paris. I was also hoping that we might go out to the Palace of Versailles tomorrow. It looks so beautiful in all the pictures I've seen and hopefully there isn't anything there to try and do us in."

"I don't know, Lilith, I can see it now," I said. "The head of Marie Antoinette chasing us all around the palace with the other tourists wondering what was wrong with us because they couldn't see it. And then, the Dean at the art school would have to fly to Paris and bail us out of jail."

"Oh, James," Lilith replied, "your imagination gets away from you sometimes. There have only been sightings of the beheaded Queen," and she started laughing and came at me with a mirror hiding her head so that all I saw was my reflection coming toward me.

"You won't think it so funny when it actually happens to us," I said matter-of-factly taking the mirror away from her.

"Get your camera scaredy-cat and let's get going," Lilith told me and she was out the door of our room and halfway down the hall before I could get my camera and get the door closed.

Our third full day in Paris went without a hitch. Well, except for one little non-threatening event around lunch time. I'll get to that in a minute. Lilith and I followed her plan to go to Victor Hugo's place first, then to the Monet Museum, and finally to the Impressionist Museum. It was a glorious day and we took many pictures along the way as well as sneaking a few shots in the galleries when the guards weren't watching. Lilith's sexy charms could always keep the guards occupied while I got the shots we wanted. We didn't have anything to eat that morning and had done a lot of walking by the time we got to the Musee D'Orsay. There was a little outdoor café near the Museum and we parked ourselves at one of the tables and ordered some lunch and a couple of coffees. If you will remember, Lilith and I are big coffee drinkers and to start the day without a couple of cups is like facing a lion and a crocodile coming down the street. As we were waiting for our lunch, the third chair at our table all of sudden seemed to pull itself back and we heard something that sounded like someone sitting down.

Lilith and I looked at each other and I communicated silently, *"Must be some sort of trick they play on American tourists. Should we act scared?"*

"That would be my guess, James," Lilith replied. *"At least I hope that is what is happening. I think we should*

just ignore it and pretend like nothing happened. If asked, you can say that you shoved the chair with your foot."

"*Well, my friends,*" a somewhat familiar voice said in our heads, "*you would be wrong about the café playing the trick on American tourists."*

"*Ok,*" Lilith said" *who are you and what do you want?"*

"*Do you not recognize my voice?"* the invisible person sitting across from us asked.

"*Wait,*" I said. "*Is this Harmonie, from down the river?"*

"*Very good, handsome man,*" Harmonie replied. "*If only you were not married."*

"*What do you want from us this time?"* Lilith asked the empty chair rather impertinently.

"*Please forgive me and please do not be angry with me, but I saw you crossing the Place Solférino Bridge from down the river and I just wanted to say hello,*" Harmonie said. "*I want to thank you for teaching me about true love. When I saw how much the two of you love each other and how you would sacrifice everything to save the other one, I knew then that I had been very bad over the years. Because of my miserable life growing up, I thought love was a myth. I no longer plan to drag unsuspecting men into the river with me, but I only want to help people from now on. Maybe I can help couples who have problems get back together somehow. I just want to do good so people will not hate me anymore."*

"*That is very admirable, Harmonie,*" Lilith said. "*James and I are very glad to hear you say that and hope that your existence from now on will be happier. James and I are here on Earth to do good, but sometimes the bad we encounter is so evil that we have to deal with it severely. If you only search out those people you can really help, we will let all Voreshans know that you are a good ghost and do not mean them any harm."*

About that time our lunch showed up and the waiter looked curiously at the vacant chair that had been moved away from the table. "Is someone else joining you?" and he pointed to the empty chair.

I couldn't help myself and said, "Just our friend, Harmonie, here," and I pointed at the empty chair. "She is our friendly ghost friend."

"Ah, the American jokester," the waiter said. "I get it now. Ha ha," as he looked at us with his raised eyebrows and no smile and then walked away. "Crazy Americans!"

"That was terrible, James!" Lilith communicated.

"No, James, that was very funny," Harmonie said and I noticed Lilith was giggling just a little. *"Well, my new friends, I must go now. Maybe I see you again before you leave Paris."*

"We would like that very much," Lilith said.

"Bye, now," Harmonie said and we heard a splash in the river soon after.

"Well, that was certainly interesting, my dear," I said. "I hope the waiter doesn't call the folks with the butterfly nets on us."

"You've got that right, James," Lilith replied. "You never know how some people view foreigners. However, it sounds like this is one ghost that is going to be good from here on out and be much happier."

"If so," I said, "we will have accomplished at least one good thing on this trip."

As soon as we had paid our bill and apologized to the waiter for teasing him we got up to leave. Although we left the waiter a good tip, he picked it up, looked at it, then at us, sighed deeply and walked away without saying thank you, go to hell, or anything else. Lilith and I looked at each other, sighed deeply, and went on to the museum. The Musée d'Orsay had a lot to offer and Lilith and I found ourselves spending the rest of the afternoon exploring the collections and especially looking for some particular artists' works. As far as the so-called Impressionists were concerned we wanted to see Manet's portraits of Berthe Morisot, his *L'évasion de Rochefort*, and, of course, *Le déjeuner sur l'herbe*. I probably spent an hour gazing at the 12 Adolphe-William Bouguereau's in their collection, especially *Naissance de Vénus* and *Les Orádes*. Lilith was especially interested in seeing the three Edward Burne-Jones paintings in the museum, as well as Edith Rackham's *Portrait de femme*. Lilith and I were both very interested in seeing Ford Maddox Brown's *Haydée découvrant le corps de Don Juan*. Of course there are many wonderful works of art in the Musée d'Orsay, but these were the ones in particular that Lilith and I wanted to see and study.

It was getting late in the afternoon when Lilith and I finished our extensive tour of the Musée d'Orsay, so we decided that we would hurry on back to the hotel and then maybe get something to eat for dinner close by. There was a quaint little tavern across the street from our hotel that the manager had been raving about and we had decided to try it that evening. However, before getting back to our hotel, Lilith wanted to stop by a store along the Rue la Vieuville that she had read about in one of the magazines in the lobby of our hotel. It was supposed to have all kinds of designer things and it stayed open until 7:30, so we had plenty of time provided there weren't any obstacles to hurdle before getting there. Little did we know that this obstacle lived beneath us in the sewers of Paris, had a tough hide, four short legs, a long narrow mouthful of razor sharp teeth, and was over 20 feet long! Having a pleasant day without encountering any sort of evil just wasn't in the game plan for us.

CHAPTER TWENTY-SIX

Back in 1984, workers in the sewer system under the Pont Neuf Bridge came across a Nile crocodile (now known as Eleanor and that some say was an alligator) which had somehow found its way into the sewer system. In one way, this was an excellent place for such a beast since it had plenty of rats and who knows what other kind of varmints to feast on. If it had been bigger at the time of its discovery it might have even had one of the sewer workers for lunch, but it was reported to be a "baby" and is supposed to still be in an aquarium in Paris. No, that one didn't escape back into the sewer system, but if there was one "baby" crocodile or alligator in the sewer systems there might have been more. Right? It's a logical conclusion. At least in the mind of someone who grew up in Florida. Anyway, in this story there was one as previously described. There are any number of ways the first one or ones, since these creatures aren't normally asexual, got into the sewer system, but the one that Lilith and I encountered on our trip to Paris must have eaten every rat that ever existed in the sewer system there to get to its enormous size. Of course, there were probably a few humans who for one reason or another, as you will soon see, "wandered" into this crocodile's territory and who probably gave the creature a few extra growth spurts. I have often thought that some of the missing persons around the world might have been some creatures next meal.

Anyway, back to our story. When Lilith and I entered the little shop that she wanted to see, the middle-aged woman working in the shop was very friendly and welcoming. I actually felt that she was a little too welcoming, because she stayed very close to us pretending to show us all the latest styles and accessories that she claimed were all the rage of young Parisian girls. I initially got the feeling that she was watching us closely to make sure that we didn't steal anything. I didn't communicate my feelings to Lilith, because she was thoroughly enjoying all of the attention the woman was giving her, something that we didn't often encounter back in the states. Most of the time back home we were lucky if we could find anyone to help us when we were out shopping. There wasn't anyone else in the shop and the woman excused herself for a couple of minutes saying she had something to tend to, but that she would be right back. Lilith kept taking in all the "fashionable" clothes and oohing and aahing appropriately as she went along, but being the suspicious person that I am I kept an eye on the woman to see what she was up to. She hurriedly went back to the front door, opened it and appeared to look up and down the street, then closed and locked the door. I didn't see her do it, but she also flipped the open sign around to read closed. Now, I figured there were only two reasons why she would lock the door to keep other patrons out of the shop. One, she didn't want to be interrupted while she was trying to sell as much as she could to these two "rich" Americans, or two, she was up to no good. Based on our encounters so far, I'll take door number two.

When the woman returned to Lilith's side, she said that she wanted to show us some new items in the basement that weren't supposed to go out until the next month, things that she was sure Lilith would love. She even mentioned that she had locked the door so that no one would come in and steal anything while we were downstairs. Lilith looked at me and I just shrugged my shoulders like any good obedient husband and then followed them down the stairs into the basement, although my first impression was that this was some sort of a dungeon since it was poorly lit and very dark around the sides. Fortunately, I didn't see any machines of torture or sense that anyone or anything was watching us.

"You certainly have an interesting basement," I offered. "Where are the styles that you wanted to show us?"

"Over this way," the woman said and took Lilith by the arm. "Just follow us young man and you will have a big surprise to see what awaits you."

"Quite frankly," I said, "It's kind of dark down here and hard to see anything. This feels more like a dungeon than a place to store clothes. Don't the clothes get kind of musty smelling?"

"There is more light back here," the woman replied ignoring my comment about the basement feeling like a dungeon. I was becoming more and more suspicious as she continued to lead us deeper into one corner of the basement where the dampness seemed to soak right through my clothes and into my skin. There was also an increasing odor that I can only describe as putrid and rotting and I started to think about the sewers and wondered if they ran under her shop. "Just around the corner now and you will see. I have a big surprise for you."

"You know," I said, "you could definitely use a dehumidifier down here," and the woman continued to ignore me as she led us along.

Lilith had been quiet all this time, but I could tell she was getting a little suspicious, too. Communicating with me telepathically, Lilith said, *"James, this is starting to seem a little strange, don't you think?"*

"Absolutely, Lilith," I replied. *"I don't think you are going to see any more clothes down here. I just wonder what this woman is up to. Do you think she has someone down here waiting to rob us?"*

"She better hope not, if she knows what's good for her!" Lilith said.

"Here we are, my dears," the woman said as we found ourselves standing in the darkened basement in front of a closed curtain. "The surprise is behind here."

"Be prepared, James," Lilith said.

"I'm right here next to you, love, and ready for anything," I said, or so I thought.

The woman quickly opened the curtain, moved behind us with the speed of a cat chasing a mouse and shoved us both into a dark hole that was probably about 10 feet deep. Lilith and I didn't have time to respond to her actions and we landed on what felt like a thick, soft bed of very damp and smelly leaves. Jumping to our feet quickly, Lilith yelled up at the woman, "What the hell? What do you think you are doing?"

"It is dinner time for my pretty little pet," she answered. "He will enjoy a nice, young tender meal for a change."

"Oh, crap!," I said. "I bet her pet isn't a cute little mouse either!"

If Lilith and I weren't discombobulated enough, a blindingly bright light came on above us and we saw that the distance we had fallen was actually about 20 feet. If it hadn't been for the soft landing we might have broken something. As it was we were covered in something that didn't smell too good. Looking up into the light we could see the silhouette of the woman at the edge of the hole we were now standing in and she was eagerly clapping her hands and dancing around like a little child.

"What do you mean by dinner time for your pet?" I yelled up.

"You will see soon, because I hear him coming now," she answered and kept clapping. "I just love to watch him eat his dinner."

"You are crazier than you look," Lilith said, "if you think we are going to be anything's dinner." Lilith then went to silent mode, *"James, it's time to levitate,"* as the noise that the woman mentioned was getting closer and closer and sounded like someone shuffling along and dragging something heavy behind them.

We both concentrated together and began to rise off the floor of the hole as the fast shuffling noise seemed to be right below us. Lilith and I had risen about five or six feet off the floor of the pit just as a 20 foot crocodile came crashing into the hole for his dinner with his mouthful of razor sharp teeth snapping at our feet. His powerful rear legs must have sent him upwards of ten feet toward us, but we had just barely risen high enough to avoid the crocodile's snapping mouth. I later discovered that the heel of my shoe was missing and nearly fainted.

"No!" the woman screamed as we came up level to where she was standing. "You must go back down for my baby's dinner!" and she swung at us with a flat edge shovel while the crocodile kept leaping up at us.

"Not this time," Lilith said as we avoided the shovel and moved toward her while still levitating. "This time you will be his dinner!" and with her emotions running at a human fever pitch, Lilith grabbed the woman by the arm and slung her into the pit, but jerked the shovel from her hand.

We didn't stay to watch, mostly because we didn't want to see the carnage that was about to take place. When we had settled back on the floor of the basement, I said, "I hope the crocodile likes tough old women!"

"I have a feeling that he will have to chew on her for some time," Lilith replied. "Remind me to never trust store clerks again!"

As I started to walk away, I said, "Never trust store clerks again," and got poked in the butt with the shovel handle.

The screams that started coming from the pit didn't last long as we heard the crocodile munching away on what would hopefully be his last human meal as we were sure that he had been fed many by the woman who used to run the shop. Lilith and I hurried back up the stairs as quickly as we could and noticed that several people were standing outside the front of the store expecting it to open back up soon. We dove behind a counter and crawled along toward the back of the store hoping that there was a back door we could sneak out of before being seen by anyone in the crowd. There were just too many people walking by for us to put to sleep the group waiting to get in, besides some of those people walking by would no doubt notice that something wasn't quite right. I could see the headlines in tomorrow's paper now: "AMERICAN COUPLE ARRESTED FOR MURDERING STORE CLERK BY FEEDING HER TO A CROCODILE!" I could only imagine that French prisons weren't all that comfortable. We kept crawling along behind the counters until we came to a small back room. Once we were out of sight behind the wall we stood up and looked around for that back door and seeing it fled quickly out and hopefully away from the store. However, we found ourselves enclosed in what could be called the

backyard of several buildings. A couple of these were restaurants that faced an adjoining street, so we slipped an
open back door of the one on the corner away from the
shop. The open door brought us into the rear of the kitchen
area, but no one seemed to pay any attention to us, even
though we were covered in smelly gunk and resembled
some of the homeless people we had seen around Paris. We
figured it was a fairly common practice for patrons from
the adjoining shops to come in that way. Lilith and I quickly made our way to the front of the restaurant and looked to
see if anyone was particularly interested in us and, seeing
none, then slipped out the front door. It's amazing how little people pay attention to what is going on around them.
It's a good thing we weren't the Cernunnos, because he
could have found a number of good looking mates in the
restaurant. Reading my mind, Lilith punched me in the arm
again, which wasn't as bad as getting poked in the butt with
a shovel handle. We found ourselves on the street that was
perpendicular to the street the shop was on, so we headed in
the other direction and circled around the block away from
our "crime" scene. As we got safely back to our hotel we
heard what we were sure were police sirens not too far
away. Fortunately, the manager at the front desk was busy
with another customer and neither noticed the filthy couple
that slipped past them. We had taken our shoes off so that
we could hopefully sneak quietly back into the hotel. Once
we were back in our room and had settled down a little, we
decided to not venture out for the rest of the evening.

    We had barely said anything to each other while we
were fleeing the scene of the "crime," but Lilith now spoke
up and said, "James, I know that we have had to kill other
aliens when necessary, but I'm not sure how I feel about
tossing that woman to the crocodile. I just did it in an emo-

tionally charged rage, because of what she was trying to do to us."

"Well, Lilith," I said, "it may be my human callous side coming out, but I have no regrets whatsoever about feeding her to the critter that she has obviously used for who knows how long to feed who knows how many tourists to. I doubt if the local police would have believed us instead of her about what had happened if you hadn't disposed of her."

"I guess it's the Voreshan side of me that opposes violence that's coming out right now," Lilith said. "This is the first time I've had to kill a human. I could have done something to her mind to make her be a good person and never feed anybody to the crocodile again, but I reacted more like an angry human."

Lilith," I responded, "we didn't have time to do work on her mind like that. If we had hesitated for even a few seconds, the woman might have attacked us in some other way and we could have ended up in the pit again. She only missed clobbering us with the shovel by a few inches. It all happened so fast that we just weren't thinking in our normal mode. And you know that we wouldn't have had time to deal with the crocodile before it chomped off a foot or two. If you hadn't thrown her in the pit, I can promise you that I would have done so."

"But it wasn't you that threw her in the pit, James," Lilith said and I could hear the depression and anguish in her voice now.

"We are in this together, my love," I said, "and I could have done something different, too, if I had wanted to. However, I still have no remorse for eliminating this woman, who was essentially a serial killer. The police might have found us guilty of feeding her to the crocodile, but they would surely have discovered her crimes of the past and let us go for defending ourselves."

"When you put it that way, James," Lilith said, "it does make me feel a little better."

"Besides, Lilith," I said, "you can't tell me that former Head Elders, or maybe even some of the other Elders, have never killed a human over the centuries."

"It is one of those things that would never be talked about, James," Lilith said, "because if information like that ever got out to the general Voreshan public it could cause all kinds of trouble."

"Well, as far as I am concerned, Lilith," I replied, "this is our little secret and no one is to ever know. Quite frankly, Lilith, I would have felt worse if we had killed the crocodile and let the woman get away with her crimes."

"James, I don't know what I would do without you," Lilith said. "You always have a way of comforting me in bad times and I am ever so thankful for that."

"Even if you weren't the Head Elder, Lilith," I said, "I would always stick by your side and do whatever it takes to protect you from anything, human or alien or reptile that comes our way, even though it is usually the other way around."

"Well, maybe we can get some sleep tonight and hope that tomorrow will be a better day," Lilith said.

"After what we have been through so far, Lilith," I said, "I'm hoping that the next two weeks will be better. I don't know what's going on in this old world, but it can stop sending the most evil of evils our way anytime now!"

After we showered and got ourselves cleaned up, Lilith and I got a large garbage bags from the housekeeper and bagged up our filthy clothes that we had been wearing when we were pushed into the pit where the crocodile lived.

We told her that we were going to take our dirty laundry to get it cleaned. We had seen some trash bins not too far from the hotel and planned to discard the clothes there the next day. Hopefully no one would discover the bags before they went off to wherever the Parisians sent their garbage. We then decided to go to bed early and try to get some rest and hopefully some sleep before the next day arrived. Just as we were climbing into bed there was a knock at our door and Lilith and I gave each other that, "Oh crap, we've been caught" look. Whoever was at the door was a little impatient and knocked again, harder this time. I got out of bed, went to the door, and asked who was there.

"This is the manager, my friends," came the reply.

Since it certainly sounded like him, I opened the door a little and asked, "Is something wrong?"

"I am so sorry to disturb you," the manager said, "but I thought it necessary to let my guests know that there has been a horrible crime only a few blocks from here."

"Oh my God," I said trying to sound as surprised as possible. "What has happened?"

"A nearby shop clerk's remains were found just a short time ago in the basement of the shop and the police think someone killed her," he replied. "They said all that was left of her was her head and right arm. They said it was terrible to look at and that it looked like she had been eaten by something, but they suspect a serial killer. The police wants everyone to stay inside and keep their doors locked for the rest of the evening."

"That's terrible," I said. "We went to three museums today and are really tired. We planned to stay in this evening anyway, but we will certainly do so now."

"Thank you," he said. "Again, I am sorry to disturb you, but my guests need to know to stay in tonight." At that he walked away and I shut and locked the door back.

Communicating silently, Lilith said, *"That was a close one, James."*

"You've got that right," I said. *"Do you think we dare stay in Paris any longer, Lilith?"*

"I really want us to have a nice vacation, James," Lilith replied, *"but I am beginning to wonder if this was the right place for us to come."*

"Well, if we stay in Paris for the duration of our vacation," I said, *"I think we should only communicate silently when we are around others."*

"I agree, James" Lilith said, *"unless, of course, we are being spoken to by others."*

"Right," I agreed. *"Right now, we need to get some rest. Maybe we will sleep in late tomorrow and see what the news is about the 'horrible crime' when we go downstairs."*

"Sounds like a plan to me, James," Lilith said and we went back to bed and fell fast asleep, not waking until around 10:00 the next morning.

CHAPTER TWENTY-SEVEN

The next morning when Lilith and I went downstairs to the lobby we discovered that the hotel staff along with all the guests were being gathered there. When we asked the hotel manager what was going on, he told us that the police were arriving soon and wanted to talk to all of the guests and staff of the hotel concerning the murder in the neighborhood that had been committed the day before. It seems that the police had followed a trail of slimy stuff to the front door of the hotel that resembled what was found in the basement of the shop where a woman was murdered. They found it to be suspicious enough to find out why the trail ended at the hotel. If their questioning didn't produce any answers that they found satisfactory, then they were going to do a thorough search of the hotel room by room. If all of that didn't produce any results, the police would put a watch on the hotel to see if anyone tried to dispose of any evidence that might implicate them. So, Lilith and I were going to have to join the other guests and wait for the police to arrive.

Going to silent mode, Lilith said, *"This isn't good, James."*

"No kidding!" I exclaimed. *"We should have removed our shoes sooner and disposed of them somewhere on the way back here. If they search our room they are going to find the bag of dirty clothes and our shoes that will put us in the basement of the shop. I know that we can alter the*

minds of everyone here, including the police when they arrive, but that isn't going to make the crime go away."

"I think we can take care of the bag of dirty clothes, James," Lilith said, "if all of the guests and staff are in the lobby. True Voreshans can telekinetically move objects from distances that are far away, so getting rid of the bag of dirty clothes shouldn't be a problem. Remember how Harmony made you trip when she wasn't around?"

"Please don't remind me of anything that had to do with that vixen!" I replied.

Although I haven't done this is many years, I think I can take care of our garbage bag so that it won't implicate us."

"Have at it, love," I said. "What do you plan to do with the garbage bag?"

"I'll have to figure out a way to get it out of the room and as far from here as I can before the police start to question me," Lilith answered. "I think there was a dumpster over past the Sacre-Coeur, so I will try to get it that far."

"That would certainly help us out in the short term," I replied, "but how are you going to get it out of our room in the first place without someone seeing it go floating by?"

"There's a window at the back of our room, James," Lilith said, "and I am pretty sure that it is easily unlocked and opened telekinetically. If that works, then there won't be a problem of getting the bag out of the hotel so that no one sees it."

About that time several police officers were entering the hotel and motioning for everyone to gather around in a line in the lobby. In the meantime, Lilith was telekinetically unlocking and opening the window on the back side of our room and floating the bag of dirty clothes out the window and high up into the air, so that no one would notice it, and then literally made it fly across toward the Sacre-Coeur where she let it fall into the dumpster she had seen near there. What we didn't know is that it nearly scared to death a somewhat inebriated homeless man sleeping behind the dumpster. It scared him so badly that he stumbled off to find some of his buddies and tell them that a piece of the sky must have fallen into the dumpster he was sleeping be-hind. While Lilith was taking care of disposing of our bag of dirty clothes, the police had started asking their general questions of the group gathered in the lobby. Their questions were the normal ones: "Where were you when this murder happened?" "When did you return to the hotel?" "Did anyone see you return to the hotel when you say you returned?" "What were you wearing the day before and can you produce those clothes? "Would you object to us searching your room?" Lilith and I answered their questions honestly, except for what we were wearing the day before and agreed to them searching our room.

Before the police got to us, I asked Lilith in silent mode, *"What were we wearing yesterday, love? I think we should get our story straight before they get to us."*

"Right, James," Lilith replied. *"I don't think anyone saw us returning to the hotel yesterday including the hotel manager, so I was wearing my blue jeans and red blouse. What were you wearing?"*

"Well, I always wear blue jeans and I will go with my blue and white striped shirt," I said.

"Good, that should take care of it," Lilith said as the police were just coming up to us. *"I'm sure that we un-packed those clothes and hung them in the armoire. If not, I will create a little more magic."*

The questioning of everyone went on for about an hour, in which we all had to stay until the police were finished. Being satisfied that everyone was telling the truth, they let all of the guests go on their way, but watched closely to see if anyone immediately returned to their room. However, guests were told not to return to their rooms until later in the day, just in case they had to search the rooms for evidence. Everyone who was a guest immediately left the hotel including Lilith and me. We learned later when we returned to the hotel that the police had questioned all of the staff and had actually taken one of the men who worked there to the police station for further questioning. It seems that he had a criminal assault record when he was a teenager and he seemed to the police to be a likely suspect in the murder case, especially since he worked so close to the murder scene. However, he was eventually able to prove he wasn't anywhere near the shop when the murder happened and was released. It seems that he was off yesterday, but that he was at his apartment making time with the hotel manager's 16 year old daughter. When the hotel manager found this out a couple of days later, he fired the man on the spot and threatened to kill him if he ever caught him with his daughter. The man reported this threat to the police saying that if the hotel manager could kill someone that he might just be the one who killed the woman at the shop. With this information, the police returned to the hotel and grilled the hotel manager again, but finally left convinced that he was innocent.

As soon as we could get away from the hotel, Lilith and I headed off to the Metro and made our way toward the Eiffel Tower. It wasn't exactly what we had originally planned for the this day, but we wanted to get as far away from the area of the hotel as possible, just in case the police happened to find the garbage bag with our dirty clothes in it that Lilith had telekinetically deposited in a dumpster near the Sacre-Coeur. Fortunately, the dumpster was emptied shortly after Lilith had made the deposit of our clothes and taken off to who knows where. That, of course, made the old drunk look silly when he brought his friends back to see what had fallen from the sky into the dumpster.

When we arrived at the Eiffel Tower, Lilith and I decided that we would spend some time walking around the area surrounding the tower doing some sketching and a few quick watercolors and taking many photographs that we might use later for our art work. Since we got a late start on the day, it was early afternoon when we decided to climb the stairs to the first level where we took more photographs. The climb was fairly exhausting, so we took the elevator to the second level, where we would later have a romantic dinner at the restaurant on that level. After spending some time looking at the views of Paris from every side at this level, as well as taking more photographs, we took the elevator to the top for the most spectacular view of Paris. It was late afternoon when we returned to the restaurant for our romantic dinner. This was probably the most romantic place we had ever been for dinner, although we normally liked smaller, more quaint type of places. The food and service was good and we had a table with a great view. We talked a lot about what we had seen and done in Paris so far, except that we didn't mention anything about the evil we had thus far encountered. We both wanted to forget about such things and simply enjoy being together in such a romantic city.

By the time we returned to ground level it was getting to be early evening and the shadows were getting longer and longer. Going back to silent communication, I said, *"I hope that we haven't stayed out too late, Lilith. Being out late seems to draw the paranormal, among other kinds of evil, to us."*

"I was thinking the same thing, James," Lilith said. *"We'll just have to take our chances on the Metro and get back to the hotel as soon as possible. With any luck, it won't be too dark when we get back."*

The closest Metro stop to our hotel was near the shop where the "horrible crime" had been committed and we were reluctant to take that route as long as the police investigation was ongoing. However, the next closest Metro stop to our hotel was north of the hotel and in front of the Saint-Vincent Cemetery where we had encountered the Cernunnos.

Since no one was around to hear us talking, I asked, "Well, my dear, which Metro stop do you want to get off at? We might run into the police who are investigating the incident at the shop if we take our usual route, while the other stop is in front of the Saint-Vincent Cemetery."

Carefully looking around to be sure no one was listening, Lilith replied, "I think I would rather deal with the police, James. We can at least control human minds if necessary and make them forget they ever saw us. I'm not so sure about the cemetery monster."

"You're right as usual, Lilith," I said, "but I think we should get going before it gets too dark. The next ghost that we encounter might not be as understanding as Harmonie."

"Ghosts do seem to have an extraordinary power over us for some reason," Lilith said. "That's something I'm going to have to question the other Elders about when we get back home."

When we got off at the Abbesses' Metro stop there were several police officers in the area who seemed to be watching everyone who got off at that Metro. No doubt they were going on the assumption that criminals always returned to the scene of the crime.

Going back to silent mode, I said, *"Lilith, let's head off in the opposite direction and do a wide circle back to the hotel. Maybe that way the police won't be too suspicious of us."*

"Good idea, James," Lilith said. *"They are only doing their job and I hate to make them lose their memories about the situation unless it becomes absolutely necessary in order to protect us. Those aren't the same officers who were at the hotel, so they shouldn't recognize us."*

Instead of going in the direction that we had fled the previous day, Lilith and I headed in the other direction and circled way back north of our hotel and came in from that side. All seemed much more quiet at the hotel when we got back and the hotel manager seemed very glad to know that we were back safely. We related our trip to the Eiffel Tower and told him about our romantic dinner there and he related that the police had been in and out all day, but that they had not searched any of the rooms. He said that they seemed more interested in the staff than the guests, but that they were also going door to door and questioning everyone within a half mile radius of the shop where the woman was murdered. The police were hoping to talk to someone who might have seen the person or persons who committed the crime. The hotel manager had found out from the police that a couple who were standing outside the closed shop when the crime was committed thought they had seen a couple of shadowy figures inside. However, when they strained to see through the front window, which hadn't been cleaned in some time, the shadowy figures seemed to disappear into thin air. The police thought that because the couple were teenagers that they had probably been smoking too much dope.

"Oh crap!," I thought silently and Lilith picked up on it.

"I'll second that, James," Lilith replied.

"Do the police think these people actually saw someone?" I asked the manager.

"They believe there was more than one person involved," he replied. "The woman who was murdered was a little on the heavy side, if you know what I mean, and it would have taken a very strong person to throw her in the pit in the basement of the shop. That is why they think there were two murderers. The trail left by the murderers went out the back door of the shop and they followed the trail to the front door of my hotel. That is why they were here questioning everyone."

"But, they seemed satisfied that no one here committed the crime," Lilith said. "Have their suspicions changed since this morning, because everyone here seems so nice?"

"They did arrest one of my employees," the hotel manager told us, "but they let him go because he had a good alibi. I hope to find out where he was when he comes in tomorrow. They cannot seem to explain why the trail led here and then stopped at the front door. I'm beginning to think they suspect me and, admittedly, I am often here by myself so I don't always have an alibi."

"Oh, that's ridiculous!" I exclaimed. "You're probably the nicest person we have met since we have been in Paris, especially the way you care about your guests."

"You are very kind to say so, my friend," he said. "You may have to be a witness for my character before all of this is finished."

"It would be our honor to do so," Lilith said. "I think we are going to retire to our room now and maybe go to bed early tonight. We are very tired from all of the day's activities."

"Good night, my friends," the hotel manager said and Lilith and I went up to our room.

Not being the trusting type in situations like this, Lilith and I went into our silent communication mode. Lilith said, *"James, do you think that the police could end up identifying us based on what those two people saw at the shop?"*

"I really don't think they have enough solid information from those two 'witnesses' to place us at the scene, Lilith," I answered. *"That doesn't mean that they aren't looking into the matter more closely, however. Why do young people do drugs anyway and why are all young people suspected of doing drugs? I remember that when I was in high school we were all suspected of drinking, but I never touched the stuff."*

"Well, my love," Lilith said, *"if they get to close to the truth we will just have to erase their memories and anyone else's memory of the whole event. With any luck, we won't have to do that and this will become a cold case that never gets solved. If the police are smart, they will figure out what the woman at the shop had been doing and maybe solve a few unsolved disappearances in the process."*

"That could end up being a rather interminable task," I said. *"We might not be able to ever leave Paris!"*

"Paris is a wonderful place, James," Lilith replied, *"and there are many wonderful things to see and do, but if it means dealing with the worst kinds of evil every day, then I'm ready to get back to quiet little Sarasota."*

"I'll second that one, my dear," I said. *"At least today seemed to be fairly normal, aside from the inquisition this morning."*

"If the police keep coming around here every day," Lilith said, *"then we might want to consider coming up with an excuse to go back home early. I'm sure the hotel manager would understand a couple of mild-mannered Americans being scared off by all of this and hopefully the police wouldn't get suspicious and hold us here."*

"I really hate to end our second honeymoon, Lilith," I said, *"but maybe things will be better for the remainder of our stay in Paris."*

"We can certainly hope so, James," Lilith said. *"are you too tired for dessert tonight my shining knight?"*

"I think you always know the answer to that question, my princess!" I said and we got undressed and hopped into bed.

After about an hour of the most intensive love making that we had ever done, Lilith and I were lying back really exhausted this time and propped up on our pillows. *"Lilith, my love,"* I said, *"you are the most incredible lover in the universe!"*

"And just how would you know that, James?" Lilith asked in her most sexy and coy voice. *"I thought I was the only one you have ever been with."*

"You know you are, Lilith," I said, *"but I can't even imagine there ever having been a better lover at any time in history or there being a better lover anywhere now."*

"You always know how to make a girl feel special, James," Lilith said even more coyly.

"Is that an invitation to a little more dessert tonight?" I asked.

"No!" Lilith said emphatically. *"I really am tired now and we both need to get some sleep if we are going to keep up the pace we've been going the past few days."*

"Darn!" I said. *"But, of course, you are right as usual."*

CHAPTER TWENTY-EIGHT

The first thing on Friday morning, Lilith and I called Evelyn at our gallery in Sarasota to check in and see how things were going back home. Normally, at this time of the year sales of our paintings slowed down some and then picked back up as the tourist trade increased over the summer months. Evelyn sounded excited to hear from us and wanted to know everything that we had been doing, but we told her that she would get the full story when we returned, or that part of it that she should hear. Overseas phone calls were expensive and we would rather spend our money on other things while in Paris. Lilith did most of the talking and assured Evelyn that we were having a great time. We didn't want to worry Evelyn with our little side adventures. The surprise that Evelyn had for us was that she and her parents had been kept quite busy with sales of our art work and she informed us that the "inventory" was starting to get a little low. Lilith told her to let customers know we would be back in a couple of weeks and that we would start producing some new work based on our trip to Paris as soon as possible. If by some miracle, the gallery sold out of our art work, Evelyn was to start a waiting list of patrons who would be contacted as we produced work. Evelyn told us that nothing weird had happened and that all was running smoothly and then wished us a good time for the rest of our honeymoon. Lilith thanked her for running the gallery for us while we were gone and for all of her good work.

Lilith and I had decided to take in the Louvre Museum that day and figured that would probably be all we could handle in one day, provided ghosts and mythological creatures stayed away from us. There were many specific works of art that we wanted to see and we of course wanted to take in everything since this would probably be the only time we would ever visit Paris. Some of the paintings that we wanted to especially see were Dürer's *Portrait of the Artist Holding a Thistle,* Van Eyck's *The Virgin of Chancellor Rolin,* Poussin's *The Rape of the Sabine Women,* La Tour's *The Cheat with the Ace of Diamonds,* Vermeer's *The Lace Maker,* Murillo's

The Young Beggar, Ingres' *La Grande Odalisque,* Géricault's *The Raft of the Medusa,* Delacroix's *Liberty Leading the People,* Veronese's *The Wedding Feast at Cana,* Titian's *Woman with a Mirror,* and *Portrait of a Woman Known as L'Europeenne* from the second century A.D. Of course, we explored all of the galleries that were open to the public at that time taking in all that we could. Although mine and Lilith's preferences, where art was concerned, were stuck mainly with the realists of the latter half of the 19th century, we had had enough art history courses to both understand and appreciate a wide variety of eras and techniques.

The rest of the day was thankfully uneventful and Lilith and I managed to drag our tired old bones back to the hotel before dark. Being out after dark hasn't always proven to be the best of ideas for us, especially since we had been in Paris, because it seemed that some sort of evil was always waiting right around the corner to introduce itself to us. Our first weekend in Paris had finally arrived and the only plans we had were to casually stroll around Montmartre sketching and taking photographs of things that both interested us for possible paintings and just simply peeked our curiosity. The weather was pleasant and a lot of people were out and about and many would stop and watch us sketch. Several people offered to buy some of our sketches, so we picked up a little extra and unexpected spending money.

Lilith and I discovered several small eateries where we had lunch and dinner as well as some smaller galleries where local artists exhibited their art work. It was always great to see what other contemporary artists were doing, especially in other countries. We always carried a small photographic portfolio of some of our work with us and a couple of galleries feigned an interest in showing our work. I say "feigned," because we never heard from them again even though we wrote to them several times as a reminder. Like most retail establishments, they probably figured that if they were nice and encouraging to us that we might buy someone else's art. However, the prices on the works displayed would have temporarily bankrupted us. If our patrons only knew what a bargain they were getting on our work back in Sarasota, they might even buy more. After dinner at a nearby café late on Sunday afternoon, we crashed back at the hotel for dessert. If you will remember, I am never too tired for dessert!

Because Lilith and I had decided to communicate telepathically while at the hotel, in case the walls were thinner than we thought and someone had a glass stuck to the other side of the wall, after dessert was over and we were resting quietly in each other's arms, I said, *"Lilith, as usual that was fabulous!"*

"Dinner was very good," Lilith said.

"Lilith, you know that isn't what I meant!" I exclaimed.

"Oh, James," Lilith replied, *"you would say our love making was great even if I was as cold as an ice cube and responsive as a log."*

"Well, dear," I said, *"there have been a few times when you came close to being that cold and nearly as responsive as a log, but it was still great!"* whereupon she punched me in the arm.

"Sometimes I don't know whether to beat you up or kiss you!" Lilith said.

"Either way is ok with me," I offered with a big grin on my face and I got punched in the arm again.

"Have I ever told you how terrible you are?" Lilith asked.

"Only about a million times," I answered.

"Well, mister smarty pants," Lilith said, *"add another million to that and you might have caught up!"* whereupon she rolled on top of me and planted a very long and passionate kiss on me.

"Does that mean you're ready for some more action?" I asked when I could come up for air.

"No! I'm really tired this time," Lilith said in her best matter-of-fact voice and rolled off me to her side of the bed. *"However, I would like to talk about how the past three days have been uneventful where evil is concerned."*

"I know," I said. *"It kind of scares me a little."*

"How do you mean?" Lilith asked.

"Well, the uneventful past three days makes me wonder if all the evils of Paris are getting together to attack us at the same time," I said. *"I know that I always seem a little paranoid, but I'm actually worried about going out tomorrow. Or any day for that matter."*

"That sounds kind of crazy to me, James," Lilith said. *"I would almost be willing to bet that we haven't seen the*

last of our encounters with evil while we are in town, but I can't imagine that all the evils of Paris would gather together to try and harm us. I would hope that our reputation for dealing with evil would precede us and evil would turn tail and run."

"I would like to think that, too," I said, *"but that never seems to be the case. There always seems to be something out there that has never heard of us before."*

"Yes, I know, James," Lilith said. *"I wish I had an answer for you, my love, but I don't."*

"I wonder if our ghost friend, Harmonie, would have any ideas about this," I said.

"What a good idea, James," Lilith said. *"I'll try to contact her right now and see if she has heard anything."*

"Do you think ghosts have the same long distance telepathic abilities as Voreshans?" I asked.

"I don't know, James," Lilith said, *"but it can't hurt to try. We know that they do communicate with each other telepathically and have done so with us in the past."* Then, concentrating as hard as she could, Lilith said, *"Harmonie, if you can hear me, please answer. We have a question for you."* We waited a couple of minutes, but there wasn't a response. *"Harmonie, it's your friends Lilith and James. Can you hear me?"*

"Lilith, it is good to hear from you," Harmonie chimed in. *"Are you near the river? I looked around when I heard your voice, but I did not sense you nearby."*

"No, Harmonie," Lilith answered, *"we are in our room at the hotel. We were wondering if you could help us with a concern we have?"*

"I will try," Harmonie said, *"but first, you must tell me, was your man a good lover tonight?"*

"That is kind of personal, Harmonie," Lilith said, *"but if you were to ask James, he would say he was great."*

"But, what do you think, Lilith?" Harmonie asked.

"Well, for a former human, he is ok," Lilith replied and there was giggling at both ends of their communication.

"Ok, ok," I chimed in, *"if the two of you are through having fun at my expense, could we get back to our real concern?"*

"Yes, dear," Lilith said looking at me with that sexy "I'm sorry" look. *"Harmonie, the past three days have been, how shall I say this, without any evil coming our way. The way our visit to Paris started out this past week, we were worried that all the evil things out there in Paris were gathering to attack us en masse. Have you heard of any such thing going on?"*

"I have not, my friends," Harmonie answered, *"but I will let you know right away if I do hear of such a thing, especially now that I know I can reach you this way no matter where you might be."*

"Thank you, Harmonie," Lilith said. *"We really appreciate you watching out for us like that."*

"It is my pleasure, my friends," Harmonie said. *"I saw you go into the Louvre Museum today, but I did not want to disturb you while you were there. It is so big and there is so much to see."*

"Harmonie, my dear," Lilith said, *"you can bother us anytime when we are near the Seine, because we know you are our friend and can be trusted not to harm us."*

"You are very kind, Lilith, Harmonie said, *"but I will leave you now and let you get back to what you were doing. And, James, I know you are a great lover! I sensed it the first time I saw you. Goodnight, my friends."*

Goodnight, Harmonie," Lilith and I said in our familiar two-part harmony.

"Gee, maybe I should have let Harmonie take me into the river," I said as straight faced as I could and got punched in the arm again.

"Maybe I'll just call Harmonie up and let her have you," Lilith said as straight faced as she could manage.

"Well," I said *"at least we have one friend out their among the paranormal and evil. Quite frankly, my dear,"* I said in my best Clark Gable imitation, *"I don't give a damn if we never get a report from Harmonie."*

"I'll second that, Rhett," Lilith replied in her best sexy Georgia accent. *Gone with the Wind* was one of Lilith's favorite movies, although I didn't care much for it. *"But, on a more serious note, James, we need to be extra diligent and watch our backs for the remainder of our stay in Paris. I don't think we should let our guard down for a minute, but at the same time I want us to really enjoy this trip."*

"I'm with you on both accounts," I said. *"I don't mind helping people with normal problems or turning bad humans into good humans, but fighting the unknown evils of the world is starting to get to me. Just my human side coming out I guess."*

"That's perfectly understandable, James," Lilith said, *"I sometimes feel bad for bringing you into this mess I call my world."*

"You should never feel bad about that, Lilith," I replied. *"I made the choice to cross over to the Voreshan side and would probably never have met you if I hadn't."*

"Well, I don't know about that," Lilith said. *"I had picked you ,too, and would have probably found some way to win you over even if Harmony Beckham hadn't turned out so bad."*

"*You know that I am very glad that things turned out the way they did, Lilith,*" I said. "*If I had had to stay with Harmony, I probably would be dead or residing somewhere in Siberia by now.*"

"*Harmony and her parents were that evil, James,*" Lilith said. "*I think it was a shock to everyone, especially the Elders, that there were Voreshans who could be so despicable. Hopefully there won't be any more Voreshans who turn out to be so bad.*"

"*Lilith,*" I began, "*I have a proposition for you.*"

"*No, James,*" Lilith said, "*we can't stay in our room having sex for the next two weeks!*" I want to experience more of Paris while we have this opportunity to be here. Besides, you wouldn't be able to get past the first day.*"

"*As appealing as spending the next two weeks in bed with you sounds,*" I said, "*that's not what I had in mind and I bet I could last for at least two days.*"

"*Well, then, what's your proposition, James,*" Lilith asked trying not to laugh out loud.

"*What if we finished up our exploration of Paris tomorrow,*" I said, "*and then checked out of the hotel and caught a night train to Venice to finish up our honeymoon trip?*"

"*Seriously?*" Lilith said more than asked and her faced seem to light up.

"*Seriously!*" I said emphatically. "*I did a little research and found a great bed and breakfast near the Grand Canal in Venice where we can stay. As a matter of fact, I made a phone call when I went down to the desk last night and made our reservation with the hope that you would agree to my plan.*"

"*Going back to Venice for our honeymoon is what I dreamed of all along, James!*" Lilith nearly shouted in my head. *"Do we have to wait until tomorrow night? Couldn't we leave first thing in the morning?"*

"I thought about that, too," I said, *"but I am afraid that if we leave too soon it will draw too much attention to us. However, if we approach the hotel manager tomorrow morning with our idea, simply saying that we don't feel too comfortable with a murderer roaming around the neighborhood, I think he would understand and forgive us for leaving so soon."*

"That's probably a better plan, James," Lilith said. "Besides, that would still give us nearly two weeks in Venice and I don't think we will run into as much really bad evil there as we seem to be encountering here in Paris."

"That's what I was thinking," I said. "I know we had some interesting encounters with evil when we were there before, but we also had more good times than bad."

"Oh, James," Lilith said, *"you really did make reservations for us in Venice?"*

"Great!" I exclaimed. "I did and come Tuesday morning, we'll be in Venice to finish our second honeymoon!"

"I know I have said this many times, James," Lilith said, "but I love you more and more each and every day!"

"And that goes double for me for you, Lilith," I said.

CHAPTER TWENTY-NINE

"This was Venice, the flattering and suspect beauty - this city, half fairy tale and half tourist trap, in whose insalubrious air the arts once rankly and voluptuously blossomed, where composers have been inspired to lulling tones of somniferous eroticism."

Thomas Mann, *Death in Venice*

Our last day in Paris went without a hitch and the hotel manager completely understood our concerns about recent events and why we wanted to leave. As a matter of fact, he said he would probably have left Paris immediately if he had been there as a visitor and knew that a murder had been committed just around the corner from where he was staying. He apologized to us on behalf of all the people of Paris because mine and Lilith's second honeymoon had been marred by such violence. We pretended to be disappointed, but still felt like we should be on our way. Lilith and I stayed in the nearby neighborhood to the hotel that day and tried to find some more interesting places to photograph and sketch that we could use for future paintings. It turned out to be a very relaxing day, especially since nothing out of the ordinary happened. When we returned to the hotel we packed up our things, said our goodbyes to the hotel manager and his staff, and headed off to catch an overnight train to Italy. Look out Venice, Lilith and James were coming back!

We hadn't much more than settled into our compartment on the train when we fell fast asleep listening to the sound of the train moving along the tracks to our next destination. Lilith and I got a really good night's sleep for the first time since we had been on our trip and arrived at the Venezia Santa Lucia train station well rested and ready to go the next morning. We couldn't believe that we had had a peaceful night's sleep without interruptions by ghosts or other paranormal things or just disturbed people in general. Just being back in Venice put us in a better mood and Lilith was literally jumping up and down with joy as soon as she stepped off the train. She threw her arms around my neck and wrapped her legs around my waist, causing me to do a 360 right there on the train station platform to keep from falling down, and told me how much she loved me. Several passersby stopped and applauded, which made us settle down and thank them for their kindness while we both turned a rosy shade of red. As soon as we had collected our baggage we were off to our B&B.

It was a little less than a mile to our B&B and we were allowed to check in early per my arrangements with the B&B manager when I had called him from Paris. After Lilith and I had freshened up and changed clothes, we decided to browse around our new neighborhood and see what we could find to eat. We had skipped dinner the night before and we felt like we were starving and couldn't wait to sink our teeth into some good Italian food! There were several small cafes near one of the universities that were recommended by one of the guests, who happened to be from Miami, we met while checking in and which was only a short walking distance from our B&B. From there it was a short walk over to the Grand Canal where we planned to spend some of our first day back in Venice sketching and taking photographs and just simply enjoying being back. Over lunch Lilith and I had a conversation about what we had been through so far on our second honeymoon.

"James," Lilith began after scarfing down a big slice of pizza, "I love you so much for getting us out of Paris and arranging for us to come back to Venice. As much as I enjoyed what little time we had in Paris not fighting evil, this is where I have wanted to come for a very long time. I know that we haven't traveled to very many places, but I do so love Venice. To sing the line from the Pointer Sisters song, 'I'm so excited and I just can't hide it, I'm about to lose control and I think I like it'."

"I know we saw a lot of great art in Paris and we have some super photographs and sketches to work from when we get back home, Lilith," I replied, "but all I ever wanted was for you to be happy on our second honeymoon. I'm sorry that I insisted on going to Paris instead. And for the record, I'm really excited, too! I'm glad that I am here with you, Lilith, but wouldn't it be nice if Sherry and Andy could have been here, too? And, by the way, you need to work on your rhythm a little when singing."

"My poor ability to carry a tune aside, don't be silly, James, about going to Paris" Lilith said. "It would have been crazy if we hadn't spent some time in Paris at some point in our lives, although I could have done without encountering ghosts and other forms of evil, especially the one who tried to take you away from me. And, yes, I still miss Sherry and Andy being in our lives, but if they were here they would be taking up all of our time together."

"You're right in both cases, as always, Lilith," I said, "but as it turned out, Harmonie wasn't such a bad ghost once we got to know each other. I wonder how ghosts or spirits or whatever you want to call them feel and if they are all as lonely as Harmonie seemed to be."

"No, she wasn't all that bad, James," Lilith said, "but I'm glad you didn't get pulled into the Seine never to be heard from again! I believe that Harmonie was lonely, but she was also a really good spirit."

"Well, my dear," I said, "if you hadn't been there I would be swimming with Harmonie and the fish right now and that does not sound too appealing to me!"

"I'm not convinced that you wouldn't have been happier with Harmonie and the fish," Lilith said with that coy little grin spread across her face, "even though we have no idea what she looked like in real life. I would like to imagine that she was a very pretty young woman when she was alive."

"For what it's worth, Lilith," I said, "if it's named Harmony, I don't want anything to do with it, regardless of how it's spelled or what it looks like! You're all the woman I have ever wanted since the day I met you!"

"Thank you for the compliment," Lilith said. "You always know the right thing to say to save your butt," continuing to grin, knowing that I was always trying to salvage things that came out of my pie hole.

"It never seems to come out quite right," I said. "I'm starting to get used to the taste of my foot!" and we both broke up laughing which brought a few stares from some of the patrons at the café.

"You know what I like the most right now?" Lilith asked.

"The idea of going back to the B&B and having dessert right after lunch?" I asked and got punched in the arm across the little café table where we were sitting, which also drew some strange looks from the patrons.

"No!" Lilith said. "My mind isn't always on sex like yours!"

"Darn!" I replied. "I Wish there was some way I could fix that."

"May I now tell you what I like the most right now?" Lilith asked very seriously.

"Yes, dear," I replied hanging my head down in shame.

"That's better," Lilith said. "It's about time you had a little more respect for your Head Elder." I raised my head and saw that Lilith was smiling from ear to ear and she almost started laughing out loud, but put her hand over her mouth so as not to attract the attention of the patrons in the café again. Whispering, she said, "What I like the most right now is that we don't have to communicate in our usual secretive way."

"Wow!" I said. "You are absolutely right! I hadn't even given it a second thought. Let's hope that we can keep it that way for the rest of our trip."

"I'm with you, James," Lilith said. "If you're finished stuffing your face with pizza, let's get on over to the Grand Canal and take some photographs. If you're lucky, you might get dessert before bedtime tonight."

"This is my last slice," I said and finished off the extra large pizza we had ordered. "I've been trying to keep up with you, but you ate like you were starving!"

"I felt like I was starving. Now, there are two things I want to see while we are out today, James," Lilith said. "Both are near here and shouldn't be too much for us to take in before dark."

"What are they, Lilith?" I asked.

"Well, I want to go to the Frari, which is the second largest church in Venice," Lilith said, "and then we just have to take in the Scuola Grande di San Rocco, which is supposed to have the largest collection of Tintoretto's work anywhere."

"Sounds pretty exciting to me," I said. "You know I'm a Tintoretto fan."

"I've read so much about his *Crucifixion* and *The Bronze Snake* that I just have to see them while we are here," Lilith said. "We saw a lot when we were here back in art school, but we also missed a lot of things."

"Maybe if we had concentrated more on the art in Venice and less on the tourist attractions, we wouldn't have run into the evils that we did," I said. "What's so special about the Farri?"

"We never studied it in our art history classes," Lilith said, "but I read about it after we were here when we were back in art school. Two of Titian's masterpieces are there as well as a famous triptych of the Madonna and Child by Giovanni Bellini. And if that isn't enough to peak your interest, Titian's and Canova's tombs are supposed to be there!"

"Well, you certainly sound excited about it and it sounds great to me," I said. "Shall we get going? I know that it's a while until bedtime, but if we stay occupied in the meantime, I might not think about sex so much."

"We shall get going and I doubt your mind will wander far from sex," Lilith said and we took off for the Grand Canal to take some photographs.

After taking way too many photographs, Lilith and I meandered our way on over to the Frari to see the Titians and Bellini's triptych. After taking our time to marvel at and study the Titians and the Bellini, we stumbled upon and interesting wood carving of St. John the Baptist that we didn't know about. As it turned out, this piece was by Donatello and that made the visit to the Frari even more special. The Scuola Grande di San Rocco was right behind the Frari, so we didn't have to go very far. I think I was more excited about seeing Tintoretto's work than Lilith and we spent most of our time there looking at and studying the masterpieces. There's nothing quite like seeing famous artists' work first hand, especially those that one has admired so much in art books.

Our B&B was nearby and Lilith and I were getting pretty tired from our first day back in Venice, so we decided to head on back and catch a few winks before dinner. The B&B manager had suggested that we try a little bar and café for dinner near where we had lunched, claiming that they had the best cannoli and chianti in Venice. The food was good and the chianti average, but we later found out that the B&B manager was getting a little cut on the side to recommend the café to his guests. As it turned out, the café was run by a distant cousin of his. Tomorrow we would head over to the Piazza San Marco and spend more time exploring the San Marco Basilica than we had back in art school. After that Lilith wanted to explore some of the shops in the piazza, especially the tourism shop because she wanted a really tacky souvenir from our second trip to Venice.

CHAPTER THIRTY

The next morning Lilith and I skipped breakfast at the B&B and headed on over to the Piazza San Marco hoping to find a little café that we had visited on our last trip to Venice many years ago. To both our surprise and pleasure the café was still there and still serving the great pastries and wonderful espresso that we had experienced on our first trip to Venice. When we had finished with our breakfast we strolled over to the San Marco Basilica to explore in greater depth the wonderful mosaics and other treasures that can be found there. The cupola at the transept crossing is one of the most beautiful that we had ever seen and will always be one of our favorites. The upper order of the interior is completely covered with bright mosaics containing gold, bronze, and a huge variety of stones. Both Byzantine and Gothic influences can be recognized in the Saints from the 11th century between the windows of the apse. In the vault above is a mosaic with Christ the Almighty. From the apse towards the entrance one can contemplate the history of Salvation in the domes: the Prophets, the Ascension and the Pentecost. The domes over the transept are called St John's and St Leonard's. In the vaults between the domes are represented episodes of Jesus' life. We hoped to find a picture book in one of the gift shops that showed all of these things in color, as this would mean far more to us when we got back home than looking at them in art history books.

After spending close to two hours wandering around inside the Basilica, we wandered back across the piazza to find the tacky souvenir shop where Lilith wanted to buy her little treasure to commemorate this trip. It only took her a few minutes to find something just kitchy enough to suit us both. What Lilith found was a colorful little gondola about 12 inches long and eight inches high that was resting on a little pedestal that was supposed to represent water. Upon the little gold colored waves floats a black gondola propelled by a gondolier in a blue and white striped shirt and yellow hat. He is standing at the back of the boat propelling it with a yellow and red striped oar instead of a pole. There is a couple in the boat, one with blond hair and one with black hair, although I'm not too sure that both aren't female. The boat has gold accents and comes complete with a little red sign at the bottom that says "Venezia." It's new home is sitting on the mantle over our fireplace in our house in Sarasota where everyone who visits can see just how tacky we really are, but with one little change. I had painted the woman's hair red to match Lilith's after we had returned home.

After our little shopping spree, Lilith and I walked back down by the Grand Canal where we spent a good part of the afternoon taking photographs, doing some sketching, and just being together watching the gondolas and other boats coming and going. This day was turning out to be one of the most relaxing we had had on our trip overseas and I could tell that Lilith was thoroughly enjoying being in Venice. We had gone all day since our small breakfast at the café without eating anything and were now starting to feel those hunger pangs again. We decide to go back to the same café in the piazza since it was so close by and have a sandwich and some more espresso for an early dinner. It was a pretty good ways back to our B&B from the Piazza San Marco, especially since we couldn't go back in a straight line, so we decided to head on back and maybe turn in early. We had been out after dark when we were in Venice the first time and, if you remember, it didn't turn out to be the best of experiences.

Our route back to our B&B led us across the Grand Canal at the Academy Bridge, which wasn't too far from our destination. The sun was going down and it was sometime around dusk when we started across the bridge and discovered that we were alone. Lilith and I had been enjoying a very pleasant and peaceful arm-in-arm walk along through the streets, often stopping for a brief kiss or two or three or four. Things couldn't have been going better since we arrived in Venice. However, by now you know what that statement means: trouble just ahead. Just as we were getting to the other side of the bridge, we heard a man and woman arguing, but it sounded like the woman was crying between barely audible screams.

"Please stop!" the woman yelled at the man in Italian.

"You sorry little tramp," the man replied in English, "I'll teach you to never rob a client again!" and we heard what sounded like someone slapping another person.

Lilith and I hurried along and stopped just before getting to the end of the bridge and looked over the railing to see a medium sized motor boat sitting just under the edge of the bridge. We then saw what was going on as the man, who both sounded and appeared to be American, slapped the woman again and she fell backwards on the floor of the boat.

"Please no, no more," the provocatively dressed woman begged the man through her tears. "I not try to rob you. Just want what is mine," she continued in English.

"You told me one price before I did you and then you doubled it afterwards," the man said. "You prostitutes are all the same," and he spit on her. "No matter where I travel, your kind always tries to take advantage of foreigners, especially Americans. You all think we are a bunch of idiots, but I'm familiar with your thieving kind!" He then reached down and grabbed her by the underarm and pulled her back to her feet and started to slap her again.

"Don't you dare hit that woman again!" Lilith yelled at him.

Stopping in the middle of his swing, the man looked up and saw Lilith and me bending over the railing. "Who the hell are you to tell me what to do?" he yelled up at us. "You just better go on along and mind your own business if you know what's good for you!"

We're a couple that you don't want to mess with," I yelled back. "Now, let the woman go."

"Oh, yeh," the man yelled back. "If you think you can stop me you scrawny little crapper come on down here and try!" and he started to slap the woman again.

"Now, James?" Lilith asked.

"Now!" I replied and through our telekinetic abilities we made the man let go of the woman and then we threw him into the Grand Canal head first and about ten feet from the boat.

"The woman looked up at us with wide eyes and said, "Thank you. You are my guardian angels. I think he might have killed me."

"Run," Lilith said. "Get away from here as quickly as possible! We'll deal with this guy when he comes out of the water."

Whether the woman understood everything Lilith had said or not, she obviously understood "run" and jumped from the boat onto dry land and disappeared into the shadows between some nearby buildings. Just before she vanished into the early evening she stopped, turned back toward us and threw us a kiss.

About that time the man surfaced in the Grand Canal and as he looked up at us he waved his fist and yelled, "I'm going to kill you both when I get out of the water! You'll not interfere with anyone ever again!"

"Come on out and give it a try if you dare," I yelled back, whereupon he swam over to the boat and climbed back in. When he stood up, Lilith, using her super telekinetic powers, ripped all of his clothes off right down to his birthday suit and threw him back into the canal. She then caused his clothes to float up to where we were standing and, looking around to make sure no one was watching, threw them onto the nearest rooftop, which was three stories high. We then walked away and headed back to our B&B while the man splashed around in the Grand Canal cursing loud enough to be heard back in Sarasota. However, all of a sudden he stopped cursing for about 20 seconds and then started up again.

"Maybe that monster will think twice before he tries to beat up another woman," Lilith said. "If he doesn't shut up I'll dunk him again."

"We can only hope so, my love," I replied. "You were at your best back there when you stripped him down and threw him back in the water."

"Well, James," Lilith said, "I didn't want to hurt him too badly and I certainly wasn't going to let him hit the woman again, even though she is a prostitute. If you men have to pay for sex, I pity you."

"I've been paying for it for a long time now," I said trying to make a joke and got punched really hard in the arm.

"You think about that little love tap when your begging for your dessert tonight," Lilith said and we walked on in silence for a while, but could still hear the cursing man in the distance.

"The prostitute did seem grateful," I said after about 10 minutes of silence. "After all, you did save her life, Lilith."

"I'm sorry I hit you so hard, James," Lilith replied. "Not sorry that I hit you, just that I hit you so hard."

"I deserved it," I said.

"It just made me so angry to see a man strike a woman," Lilith said.

"Me, too," I said. "Prostitute or not, I would have probably hurt him a lot worse if you hadn't acted so fast, my dear."

"I know you would, James," Lilith said. "I'm a very lucky woman to have someone like you who would never ever even think about hitting me."

"You know I would never hit you, Lilith," I said. "Even the human part of me would never do that. Hitting women was something that my parents taught me was wrong and if they ever found out that I had, they would have turned me over to the police immediately. Do you think we should have called the police on to that man? It wouldn't hurt for him to spend a few nights in a Venice jail."

"Oh, he will run into the police soon enough, James," Lilith said. "He won't get far from the bridge in his birthday suit before they find him. I have already set that in motion while we were being silent. He will be charged with indecent exposure, being intoxicated, and resisting arrest when he tries to run away from the police. In addition, I have put it into his head to confess to beating up the prostitute."

"Always thinking ahead, my dear," I said. "That's why you're the head honcho of the Voreshans!"

"And don't you forget it!" Lilith said with a big smile on her face.

"By the way, am I forgiven for what I said earlier?" I asked in my most pathetic voice.

"There's nothing to forgive, James," Lilith replied. "I know you were just joking around, but I was really angry with that slob who was beating up that woman on the boat and your arm was close by."

"Thanks, love," I said. "Does that mean I get dessert tonight?"

"Only if I get to be in charge," Lilith said.

"You can charge whatever you want, my dear," I replied. "I'm willing to pay your price any time," and I got punched again in an already sore arm. "However, I don't know if I can support myself with only one good arm," and Lilith stepped around me and punched me in my other arm.

"You are so bad!" Lilith exclaimed, "but I love you just the same. I wouldn't know what to do if you didn't have a sense of humor."

"I'm just glad that you find my humor just a tiny bit amusing, my love," I said, "but I would probably not have sore arms if I didn't have a sense of humor."

"Oh, I would find a way to punish you, my dear," Lilith said and we both started laughing.

CHAPTER THIRTY-ONE

"A splendor of miscellaneous spirits."
John Ruskin on Venice

Lilith and I were now approaching our second weekend in Europe, the first in Venice since our last trip many years ago, and the last week of our second honeymoon trip. I'm happy to report that the remainder of our time in Venice had been uneventful as far as ghosts and other forms of evil are concerned except for one minor, but pleasantly surprising incident involving a previous acquaintance. It happened on our last day in Venice and in the public area just across the narrow canal that runs in front of our B&B. Lilith and I were sitting at a table in front of a wine bar right after lunch enjoying one of their fine cabernets We had just finished browsing through a nearby workshop, having purchased one more souvenir. It was a quiet, peaceful afternoon with only two other couples in the immediate vicinity who were also enjoying a glass of wine along with some fairly heavy petting and giggling.

Communicating silently, because I didn't want anyone to hear what I was talking about, I said, *"Lilith, this has been the best vacation ever being here with you in Venice and not having to deal with the evils of the world all week."*

"It has been wonderful, James," Lilith replied. *"I guess the ghosts and mythological creatures that roam the canals of Venice decided to give us a break this week.*

Maybe word got around about how we dealt with them the last time we were here."

"I just hope that they don't decide to follow us back home to Sarasota," I said. "I'm actually looking forward to getting back to our normal routine."

"I'm sorry to hear you say that, James," a different voice chimed in interrupting our conversation.

"What the devil!" I exclaimed.

"Who's there?" Lilith asked in a demanding voice.

"It is I, Harmonie, from Paris," the voice replied.

"What in the name of God are you doing here?" Lilith demanded.

"I am sorry if I have offended my friends," Harmonie said, "but I am tired of Paris and living along the Seine. I have decided to see the world and so I follow you here."

"You could see the world without following us," I said.

"But you are my friends," Harmonie said. "I know you think ghosts are fearless, but that is only true when they have other ghosts to rely on. I have no one. Other ghosts in Paris don't like those who have committed suicide."

"I'm sorry for sounding so rude, Harmonie," Lilith said, "but you kind of shocked us just now."

"You are not rude, my friend Lilith," Harmonie said. "I have been here since yesterday trying to find you, but I didn't want to scare you by trying to contact you before I found you."

"Well, since you are here, what can we do for you?" I asked.

"Yes, Harmonie," Lilith said, "are you in some sort of trouble or do you just need suggestions for where you should travel in the world? Besides our own country, James and I have only been to Italy and Paris."

"The only trouble I have is the trouble I cause my dear friends," Harmonie answered. *"Meeting you and James made a big difference in my existence and I thought it would be nice to leave my old existence in Paris to seek a new existence. I want to be happy for a change. Kind of like Casper the Friendly Ghost."*

"Good old Casper," I said for no good reason.

"Well, Harmonie," Lilith began, *"I think that is a wonderful idea. You must have been very miserable all these years being in the same place and suffering the persecution of the people of Paris. However, James and I didn't know that ghosts could actually leave the surrounding area where they died. I guess that comes from watching too many American movies about ghosts."*

"From what I know, few ghosts have ever wandered far from their place of death," Harmonie said. *"Regardless of what the living may think of ghosts, we are very afraid of humans. However, we cannot always help making our presence known when the living invade our spaces."*

"Really?" I interjected. *"I haven't always believed in ghosts, but since I found out they were real many years ago here in Venice, I have always thought it was the other way around. As Lilith said, probably too many American movies about ghosts."*

"Yes," said Lilith, *"our only encounter with ghosts, until we met you, were rather scary and even the encounter with you was scary at first!"*

"I am so sorry for that," Harmonie said. *"You and James taught me so much about love that I decided after you left Paris to change my ways. I no longer seek live human males to drown for companionship. Besides, none of them ever stayed with me anyway. If I must exist alone forever, I will do so to be a good ghost and not frighten the*

living anymore. However, since I am a ghost, I am sure that I will unintentionally frighten a living person sometimes."

"Well, Harmonie," I said, *"having once been alive, anytime you make your presence known you are going to scare the living. I think it is just in human nature to be frightened by the unknown, especially ghosts. We can probably attribute that to books and movies as well."*

"No doubt," Lilith said. *"Anyway, Harmonie, what would you like to know about the world that we can help you with?"*

"I want to travel to your country with you," Harmonie said and Lilith and I looked wide-eyed at each other.

"Can't you simply fly on over to America?" I asked reluctantly feeling I knew the answer already after making such an assumption.

"No, James," Harmonie said. *"Those who believe in ghosts also believe that about ghosts. The only way I could fly anywhere in the world would be on an airplane. Ghosts cannot fly like in the cartoons."*

"Are you saying that you want to fly with us to America when we leave tomorrow?" Lilith also asked reluctantly.

"Only if you and James will allow me to do so," Harmonie said. *"I could go on the plane without you or anyone else knowing, but that would not be right and I want to do what is right."*

"We are very proud of you, Harmonie," Lilith said, *"for wanting to do the right thing, but are you sure you want to leave Europe?"*

"Yes, I do," replied Harmonie. *"If you allow me to go with you to your country you call America, I will travel your country on my own and not bother you ever again. Although, that would make me very sad to never talk with you ever again."*

"*Harmonie,*" Lilith said, "*you would not be bothering us as long as you weren't always around. However, if you were to get into trouble somewhere we would want you to contact us for help if you needed it and you are always welcome to come and visit once in a while.*"

"*We would? She is?*" I asked and got punched in the arm really hard.

"*Don't pay any attention to him, Harmonie,*" Lilith said. "*He likes to stick his big foot in his mouth a lot!*"

"*I didn't mean that the way it sounded, Harmonie,*" I said. "*Just the human side of me coming out again. Please forgive me. For a ghost, you are very cool!*"

"*I forgive you, James,*" Harmonie said. "*I know you do not mean to be bad,*" and she and Lilith started giggling.

"*Just promise to not try and drag me into a river ever again,*" I said and the giggling got more intense with Lilith actually starting to laugh out loud, which got me going as well. The other two couples in the vicinity were so into kissing and fondling each other that they didn't even hear us.

"*Does this mean that you will let me go to America with you?*" Harmonie asked.

"*Yes, dear Harmonie, we will let you go to America with us,*" Lilith said, '*but you must promise to behave yourself on the plane.*"

"*I promise,*" Harmonie said. "*I will go now and let you two be alone. I will meet you at the plane and let you know that I am there without scaring you.*"

"*That would be nice,*" I said. "*See you tomorrow for the trip back to America. Well, we won't 'see' you, but I guess we will hear you.*"

"*Foot in mouth?*" Harmonie asked Lilith.

"Yes," Lilith said, *"but we call it 'hoof-and-mouth disease,"* and Lilith laughed out loud at her little joke.

"Do I look like a cow?" I asked very seriously managing not to crack a smile.

"You do not look like cow to me," Harmonie said and Lilith laughed even harder and louder, this time attracting the attention of the other two couples who just smiled and then went back to seeking third base.

"Maybe I should go find a nice Italian girl with whom to finish my wine," I said out loud with an air of pomposity.

"I go now," Harmonie said and we didn't hear any more from her until the next day.

"Maybe you should go back down to the Academy Bridge and look for your girlfriend," Lilith said.

"If you insist, my dear," I said and started to walk away.

"Get your pompous ass back here!" Lilith exclaimed silently and I immediately obeyed to keep from getting punched in the arm again.

When I had parked my "pompous ass" back in my chair, I looked over at Lilith and we both cracked up and couldn't stop giggling for several minutes. *"Well, my love,"* I said, *"it is certainly going to be an interesting experience having our own personal ghost along."*

"You've got that right, James," Lilith said. *"But, on the bright side, she might just become a tremendous ally in our fight against the evils of the world. After all, she could help and no one would know what was going on."*

"I hadn't thought about it like that," I said, *"but you, as usual, are absolutely right."*

The next morning Lilith and I were all packed and headed off to the airport to catch a flight that would begin our journey back home to Sarasota, with an additional guest that we hadn't planned on taking back with us. We had to take a small plane into Munich where we caught our main flight back to the states. When we arrived in Munich we discovered that the plane was not full, so Lilith and I paid for an additional seat next to us for a couple of reasons: one, since the plane had one aisle and three seats to each side of the aisle we didn't want to be bothered by someone who would no doubt talk all the way back to the states or sleep and snore all the way; and two, we were reserving a seat next to us for Harmonie. Laugh if you must, but Harmonie was very appreciative for keeping a space just for her. As Lilith and I found out when Harmonie tried to drag me in the river, the living can feel a ghost when touched by one.

Everything was going along smoothly until what Europeans call an "ugly American" boarded the plane in Munich. Although the plane wasn't full, this rather large and somewhat muscular man roamed up and down the aisle a couple of times before stopping next to where Lilith and I were sitting. I was sitting in the aisle seat with Lilith next to me and Harmonie was in the window seat. Neither Lilith or I cared to sit next to the window as flying was not one of our favorite activities, except, of course, on our first flight to Italy when we joined the mile high club, which was the only thing we ever really enjoyed about flying. The man kept standing there and we kept ignoring him until he grabbed my shoulder, shook it, and said, "Scoot over, buddy. I want to sit here."

I turned away from Lilith and looked up at this giant of a human who had to go about 6'8" and weigh in around 300 pounds if he was an ounce. "These seats are taken," I politely told him and removed his hand from my shoulder.

"Oh yeh," he said grabbing my shoulder again and giving me his most menacing look while squeezing a little harder. "Looks to me like that one over there by the window is empty, so get your ass over before I pick it up and throw it over there! Besides, I wouldn't mind sitting next to that hottie you're with."

At that moment Lilith and I both heard in our heads, *"Why don't you just go away before you mess yourself in your pants you big ass!"*

"What the hell!" the man exclaimed loud enough for everyone to hear him. Everyone around us was already staring to see what happened next. "Who said that? You a ventriloquist or something, smart boy?"

About that time one of the attendants approached and said, "Said what, sir? No one said anything bad to you. I was standing close by and didn't hear anything."

"Somebody just told me to move away!" he replied. "I ain't going nowhere, cause I want this seat here!"

"I did not hear anything, sir," the attendant said again. "Did you hear anything, sir?" she asked me touching me lightly on the shoulder.

"My wife and I did not hear anything of the sort," I said. "I tried to explain to this gentleman that these seats were taken, but he won't leave us alone."

"Sir," the attendant said to him, "I am going to have to ask you to take a seat somewhere else on the plane. There are plenty of available seats toward the rear of the plane and they are just as good as this one."

"Well, you listen to me my little pretty," the man said to the attendant, "I'm going to sit here and this little fart is going to move over or else! If the seat's taken, then where's the other person?"

'Sir, this couple paid for the seat and it is their choice not to let anyone else use it," the attendant said.

"Leave my friends alone or I am going to rip your penis off and stuff it in your mouth!" Lilith and I heard Harmonie tell him and our eyes got big as we glanced at each other.

"There it is again," the man said. "one of these people here just threatened me again!"

"I don't know what you think you heard, sir," the attendant said, "but if you don't go to the rear of the plane and find another seat I am going to call security and have you removed from the plane!"

"Well, you just bring them on," he replied and that was all he got out before he grabbed the crotch of his khakis and started yelling at the top of his lungs. "Let go! Damn, that hurts! Let go! I'm going! I'm going!" and he started stumbling back toward the rear of the plane while continuing to yell and moan.

"That was certainly strange," the attendant said to Lilith and me. "I apologize for such rude behavior."

"Why should you apologize?" I asked her. "It isn't your fault that rowdy drunks sometimes get on the plane.

"What do you think just happened to him?" she asked us.

"Who knows," Lilith said. "Maybe his conscience got hold of his balls and gave a big squeeze."

I looked at Lilith in astonishment at her remark and the attendant and several people sitting around us started laughing. "Well, I don't think you will have to worry about him anymore," the attendant said and walked away.

Communicating silently, I said, *"I can't believe my ears, Lilith!"*

"It was pretty funny, wasn't it?" Lilith said and I heard Harmonie giggling.

"Thanks for your help, Harmonie." I said. *"This was one situation that would have been hard to explain if Lilith or I had done something to that guy."*

"It was my pleasure, James, to help out," Harmonie said. *"I know that you cannot use your powers when so many people are around."*

"Well, we could," said Lilith, *"but it is best that we don't. Thank you for helping. Did you really grab him by the balls?"*

"I did and I would do it again to help my friends," Harmonie said. *"I held on to them while pushing him to the rear of the plane."*

"That's why he was stumbling along," I said. *"Could you really rip off his penis like you threatened to do?"*

"I could and I would have if necessary," Harmonie said.

"Remind me not to ever make you mad," I said and both Lilith and Harmonie started quietly giggling.

CHAPTER THIRTY-TWO

The rest of the flight home was uneventful and we slept most of the time anyway. There was hardly a peep at all out of Harmonie and we certainly weren't bothered by the obnoxious "ugly American" anymore. We learned from the attendant who had been involved in the little scene before takeoff that he had been asked to take a later flight, thus the quiet flight back to the states. Hopefully he would forget about the incident in Munich and not come looking for us, especially for his own good. Harmonie chimed up when she caught a glimpse of the coast line of the United States coming into view and kept saying over and over, *"Oh my God! Oh my God! Oh my God!"* Lilith and I didn't say anything to her, because we didn't want to put a damper on her excitement. We only wished that we could have actually seen her excitement about arriving in a new country.

After the plane from Miami to Sarasota had landed and we had gotten off, I said silently to both ladies, *"Well, it's certainly great to be back home ladies! As much as I enjoyed most of our trip to Europe this time, it just feels good to be home again."*

"That's an understatement!" Lilith said. *"As you may have guessed, Harmonie, James and I do not like flying. Besides, each time that we have been to Europe we have encountered ghosts, so-called mythological creatures, and not-so-nice people."*

"I did get that feeling from you about flying when you let me have the window seat," Harmonie said. "I am so sorry that you had to deal with me and those other evil things on your second honeymoon, Lilith.

"Well, Harmonie, Lilith said, "James and I are just glad that you have changed your ways and if you hadn't tried to take James away from me, we would never have become friends in the first place. I guess what they say about everything happening for a reason is true."

" Thank you for your kind words, Lilith," Harmonie replied. "Another question for you, where do you suggest I stay tonight? I hope that we can meet tomorrow and talk about where I should go and what I should see."

"Well, Harmonie," Lilith said, "we assumed you would stay at our house for a few days until we could come up with a plan for your adventures in the United States."

"Is that ok with you, James?" Harmonie asked.

"Absolutely, Harmonie," I replied. "After all, we couldn't ask any friend who has come to visit us to stay anywhere else when we have plenty of room."

"Thank you both so very, very much," Harmonie said. "I could not ask for better friends even if I were alive."

"That's very sweet of you, Harmonie," Lilith said. "Ah, here's our taxi to take us home. We should be there in just a few minutes. Sarasota is nowhere near as big as Paris."

When we were back at our house and inside we showed Harmonie our guest bedroom. We told her she could roam anywhere in the house she wanted to go, but she could not under any circumstances come into our bedroom if the door was closed. She said she understood that and knew that we needed our privacy at times. It was just starting to get dark when we got home and Lilith and I were very tired from our flight back, so we told Harmonie that we were going to bed early. Lilith told Harmonie that it would be best if she didn't go outside at night as that would certainly scare the living if they bumped into her. Harmonie agreed and we didn't hear anything from her until the next morning.

When Lilith and I were dressed and ready for breakfast, we signaled Harmonie that we were waiting for her in the kitchen where we usually ate our meals when home. We had contacted Evelyn at our gallery before leaving Venice to tell her when we would be home, but that we wouldn't come by the gallery until the next day. Our plan was to keep Harmonie close and take her to the gallery with us that morning and introduce her to Evelyn and her parents. We asked Harmonie to let us know that she was always present when she was with us by simply touching us on the shoulder every once in a while. When we arrived at the gallery a little later that morning, we went through the traditional hugging and greeting expected with Evelyn, and, quite frankly, it was great to see Evelyn and be back in the environment that we so treasured. We didn't see Evelyn's parents around anywhere and she told us that they had gone back to New Mexico two days earlier, because they felt they would be in the way when we got back.

When all the greeting was done, I said, "Evelyn, Lilith and I have someone with us that we would like for you to meet. Now, considering what you went through back home in New Mexico, we don't want you to be frightened when you meet our new friend."

"That kind of frightens me some already," Evelyn said, "but if this person is your friend, I will try not to be scared. Who is it that you want me to meet?"

"Well," Lilith said, "when we were in Paris we made a new friend and she is here with us right now. However, you can't see her and you will have to communicate with her telepathically."

"What?" Evelyn said with a little bit of a tremor in her voice. "Is . . . is she some kind of . . . some kind of a ghost or something?"

"That is correct my dear, Evelyn," Harmonie communicated silently and Evelyn took a couple of steps back from where she thought the voice had come from. *"I am a ghost and you do not need to be scared. I am now a good ghost, as Lilith and James will tell you. However, I was not a good ghost when we first met, but Lilith and James have taught me to change my ways, so now I am a good ghost."*

"Ok, guys," Evelyn said, "this is a joke, right? One of you learned ventriloquism on your trip, right? Please tell me that's right."

"No, Evelyn," Lilith said, "this is not a joke and we are not ventriloquists. There are such things as ghosts, even if you never believed our story about the one we encountered in Venice many years ago."

"Oh yeh, that one," Evelyn said. "I really wanted to believe that, but I did think you were pulling my leg."

"Did Lilith and James hurt you when they pulled your leg?" asked Harmonie and all three of us started laughing.

"Did I make joke?" Harmonie asked.

"I'm sorry for laughing at you," Evelyn said. *"That wasn't meant literally, it's just a saying meaning I thought Lilith and James were teasing me."*

"Oh, I get it now," Harmonie said. *"I understand the humor in it now."*

"Evelyn, the voice you just heard is a young lady named Harmonie and she is a ghost. We first encountered Harmonie in Paris and she came back with us on the flight from Venice where she had traveled there looking for us.

You see, Harmonie wanted to leave her life in Paris and Europe and explore other parts of the world. So, she thought it would be interesting to find James and me and come back to the states with us."

"*Ok,*" Evelyn said silently, "*I guess I'm glad to meet you Harmonie, wherever you are.*"

"*I am going to touch you on the shoulder, Evelyn,*" Harmonie said and lightly laid her hand on Evelyn's shoulder.

Evelyn jumped just a little when she saw that neither Lilith or I had touched her in any way. "*I'm sorry, Harmonie, but I'm still having a hard time believing in something I can't see.*"

"*You do not need to apologize, Evelyn,*" Harmonie said. "*I know how frightening the idea of ghosts can be to the living. I will try not to frighten you when I am near, but will let you know so that you are not afraid.*"

"*That would be great,*" Evelyn said.

"*Evelyn,*" Lilith said, "*the main thing you will have to remember is that you must communicate with Harmonie silently. Otherwise, people will think you are talking to yourself.*"

"*Is that the only way you can communicate, Harmonie?*" Evelyn asked. "*I mean, in the movies ghosts go around screeching and howling all the time.*"

"*How you say, James, something else to blame on the movies?*" Harmonie answered,

"*That is what we said, Harmonie,*" I replied. *Unfortunately, movie producers can make more money by introducing ideas that have no base in reality, not that they actually believe in ghosts, and especially ideas that will scare the pants off you. Harmonie can only communicate silently,* which *Lilith and I found interesting since being Voreshan means that we also often communicate silently.*

"Gotcha!" Evelyn said. *"Welcome to the United States and Sarasota, Harmonie. I do hope that we can be friends as well and that your stay in this country is enjoyable."*

"It is already very enjoyable just to be around living friends," Harmonie said.

"Back to speaking out loud, so that others won't think we are ignoring them if they happen to come in, how has business been while we were gone, Evelyn?"

"Can Harmonie hear us if we are talking out loud?" Evelyn asked before answering my question.

"Yes, Evelyn, I can," Harmonie replied.

"Ok, then," Evelyn said. "Business has been great! As a matter of fact, we only have six paintings left in stock and they are hanging on the walls right now. So, you two need to get down to business and start cranking out some paintings!"

"Are these your paintings?" Harmonie asked. *"They are so beautiful! Your are very talented artists."*

Looking around to make sure no one had slipped into the gallery, I said, "Thank you, Harmonie. Painting is what Lilith and I live for and we have been fortunate enough to be successful doing what we love."

"I do not doubt that," Harmonie said. *"You should exhibit your work in Paris, my friends. People there would love your work."*

"Thank you, Harmonie," I said. "That is an idea we might have to pursue at a later date."

"Well, James," Lilith said, "I guess we had better get our photographs developed and get started on doing some painting."

"You are absolutely right, dear," I said. "Harmonie, you are welcome to join us in the back in our studio if you like, or if you want to roam around the area some that is ok, too."

"I will stay here for now and watch you create your beautiful work," Harmonie said. *"Maybe we can go out together later until I become familiar with your city and people."*

"That is a very good idea," Lilith said. "It will still be daylight when we close and all four of us can go to our favorite restaurant nearby for dinner."

"I don't mean to sound stupid or rude, Harmonie," Evelyn said, "but do ghosts eat?"

"No, Evelyn," Harmonie replied, *"we do not eat, but I will still enjoy being in your company and observing how other Americans consume their food."*

"This is really strange you guys," Evelyn said. "I mean, knowing that someone that I can't see, but who is sitting at the same table as me, is simply observing how I feed my face."

"That is very funny saying," Harmonie said. *"I have many American sayings to learn about."*

"Well, Harmonie," I put in, The three of us don't even know all of those sayings, so don't get disappointed if you can't learn thcm all."

"I will do my best to learn as many as I can," Harmonie replied.

"Well, we do have some photographs developed and lots of sketches to work from," I said. "Lilith, my love, shall we get into the studio and start catching up on our painting?"

"Absolutely, James," Lilith said and the four of us went back into the studio where Evelyn had already set up our easels and prepared our palettes and necessary accessories.

"Wow, Evelyn," Lilith said, "it looks like you were anticipating our return and getting back to work immediately."

"Well, you two," Evelyn said, "I can't sell what's not on the walls out front."

"You have certainly done a marvelous job of running the gallery, Evelyn," I said. "I only hope that you will stay on for the remainder of your time at art school."

"That will not be a problem!" Evelyn exclaimed. "Who knows, maybe I'll want a permanent job here after I graduate."

"I certainly think that could be arranged, Evelyn," Lilith said, "but wouldn't you rather go back to New Mexico where your parents live? Santa Fe is such a great artists' Mecca."

"It is that, but I have already talked this over with my parents and they just want me to be a successful artist like you and James. Besides, I have come to really love living here in Sarasota and my parents are even talking about retiring here in the not too distant future. Can I ask you another question?"

"Absolutely, Evelyn," Lilith said.

"Do you think my art work will ever be good enough to sell in a gallery like yours?"

"Are you kidding me?" Lilith said. "James and I have already talked about your art work and were going to ask you if you would be interested in exhibiting here in our gallery."

"No way!" Evelyn exclaimed and started almost dancing around the studio. "Do you really mean it? You would want me to exhibit here some day?"

"No, not some day, Evelyn," I said. "We were considering showing your work now, that is, if you are really interested," I said as teasingly as I could manage.

"Oh my God!" Evelyn almost shouted loud enough for the ghosts of Venice to hear. Throwing her arms around Lilith's neck and then my neck and hugging us nearly to death and with tears in her eyes, Evelyn said, "I love you both so much! I promise to be the best gallery salesperson ever!"

"It seems that you have already achieved that goal, Evelyn," I said. "Before Lilith and I left Venice we made a decision to ask you to be the gallery manager," and I thought Evelyn was going to pass out as she steadied herself against the wall. Still not saying anything, but as wide-eyed as I have ever seen anyone in any situation, I said, "Of course, it would mean a substantial raise in your salary."

"I . . . I . . . I'm sorry, . . . I don't know what to say," Evelyn stammered. "This . . . this is . . . this is a dream come true for me," and the tears actually started flowing down her cheeks.

"Lilith and James," Harmonie put in with a shaky voice, *"you two are the best people in all the world to make Evelyn so happy. I knew you were good when you befriended me back in Paris, but this is unbelievable."*

"Harmonie, are you crying to?" I asked.

"Yes, but they are tears of happiness," Harmonie answered and it sounded like she was sniveling.

"Ms. New Gallery Manager," I said, "why don't you take Harmonie back out front in the gallery and tell her what it is that you do here. In the meantime, Lilith and I will try to get down to work," and the two of them went back out into the gallery sniveling in two part harmony. "Oh, by the way," I called after them, "don't forget that if customers come in you will have to communicate with each other silently. Otherwise, Evelyn, they will think you are talking to yourself."

"Will do," Evelyn called back.

"Well, James," Lilith said, "that was certainly interesting."

"How do you mean?" I asked.

"I wasn't sure that Evelyn would want to take on that much responsibility," Lilith said, "and I never expected that she would want to stay here in Sarasota."

"That was kind of surprising," I said, "but maybe she was encouraged by her parents since they are considering retiring to Sarasota."

"That's probably part of it, I guess," Lilith said, "but the thing that amazed me the most was to hear a ghost crying because she was happy. Just doesn't seen natural."

"Has to be because of the movies' influence," I suggested. "Once again, people, including us, almost always believe what they are told instead of the truth, even though the truth in this case is not known by very many."

"Has to be," Lilith said. "Who would have ever thought that the next chapter in our adventure together would include another Voreshan managing our gallery and exhibiting with us, not to mention having Harmonie the Friendly Ghost as a friend and ally?"

"Certainly not me back in high school," I said.

THE END (maybe)

Other works by Jim Meaders

*****

The Summer of My Fourteenth Summer

*****

Hitchhikers in Each Other's Minds

*****

Signals from Passionate Minds

*****

Minds Against Wicked Things

available ebooks: W & B Publishers
available print: A-Argus Books

Proof

Made in the USA
Charleston, SC
10 October 2013

pg. 17, line 19: ... have weaponry far ✱
superior ...

19- 1st sentence, last para: "... ~~over~~ that during the ~~past~~ last
century ...."

94- ~~7~~ lines from the bottom: ...on guard
and know that ~~there~~ their new....

110- line 12: All of this simply ~~meat~~ meant
that....

110- line 24: ... supposed to be about ~~26~~ 29
years old.

164- line 13: ... skip on by where ~~your~~
you're hiding ....

182- line 2: ..., but then ~~decide~~ decided to
call....

204- line 1: ... that would result in
~~combing~~ combining the ydping....

~~251 - last line ... you only search out~~

261 - line 2: ..., so we slipped ~~in~~ an open
back door ....

263 - 3rd line from bottom: ... I got a large
garbage bag ~~from the~~....

278- 1st and 2nd paragraph are one paragraph

AncestryDNA.com   over

294 - 5th line from the bottom: We decide(d)
   to go back....

300 - line 12: period (.) after cabernets